I0680801

K. L. HAWKER

WHEN WORLDS COLLIDE

A DREAM KEEPER NOVEL

WHEN WORLDS COLLIDE

Copyright © 2019 by K.L. Hawker

All rights reserved.

No part of this publication may be reproduced, scanned or distributed

in any printed or electronic form without permission by the author.

Please do not participate in or encourage piracy of copyrighted materials

in violation of the author's rights. Purchase only authorized editions.

This is a work of fiction. The characters and events portrayed in this novel are fictitious. Any

similarities to real people, living or dead, business establishments, events or locales is en-

tirely coincidental and not intended by the author.

When Worlds Collide / K.L. Hawker

ISBN: 978-1-7753011-5-8

Written by K.L. Hawker

www.klhawker.com

Cover Design by Design for Writers

www.designforwriters.com

Published by Pages & Stages Publishing

www.pagesandstages.com

For all you dream warriors out there . . .

Whether you know it yet or not, you have a purpose.
You are a warrior for something. Find your passion
and you'll find your purpose.

Thanks for being a light in a sometimes darkish world.

~ K.L. Hawker

"Every great dream begins with a dreamer.
Always remember, you have within you the strength,
the patience, and the passion to reach for the stars to
change the world."
~ Harriet Tubman

K. L. HAWKER

WHEN WORLDS COLLIDE

A DREAM KEEPER NOVEL

War of the Worlds

~ RILEY ~

DANA PUSHED THROUGH the double doors, and we entered the meeting place. She was holding onto my arm as if she expected me to change my mind. But even if I were to change my mind, where would I go? I was in her world now, without a key to get back to my own. I was at her mercy.

But I trusted her. We had the same agenda. We both wanted nothing more than to see my brother dead. With Luke gone, that meant I would become Etak's keeper. But for Dana, she stood to gain nothing but the satisfaction that the man who was responsible for her lover's death would exist no more.

Keagan, Dana's new second-in-command, was already seated at the round table when we arrived. He had poured us each a drink, which I hesitated to take. There were few people in the seven worlds that I trusted, and Keagan was not one of them. Maybe it was because I knew he had a soft spot for Sarah. Although we did have one thing in common—he hated Luke almost as much as I did.

I took a seat across from Keagan. Dana sat down next to me, and there was still one unattended seat where a drink was placed.

"Riley," Keagan said, nodding his greeting.

I lifted my head with a short nod. "Who are we waiting for?"

Dana smiled. "Victor," she said, and there was a mixture of excitement and jealousy in her eye.

"Of Leviathan?" I said, although it was clear that this was who she meant. What other Victor was there? The only Victor that mattered was Leviathan's keeper. The darkest lord of all of the seven worlds. Suddenly I realized that whatever plan Dana had in mind was going to include more than just getting rid of my brother. If Victor was involved, there would be much more to it.

The door opened, and Victor walked in. At least I assumed it was Victor, having never met him face to face before. He was tall and thicker than I had pictured. His hair was kept short and his eyes were the darkest black I had ever seen. He wore dark clothing with big black boots and walked with an air of defiance and importance. I felt myself stand as he approached the table, but realized I wasn't alone as Dana and Keagan were both standing now too.

Victor pulled the chair and sat down. He pushed the drink away and folded his hands in its place. "So you want to start a war." His deep, commanding voice seemingly echoed off the walls.

"It's time we take Earth," Dana said, keeping her eyes on Victor as she spoke. "They're weak. They turn on each other every chance they get."

Victor nodded, thoughtfully, but kept silent.

"And how do you propose we do that?" I asked, causing Keagan to grin and Dana to break her stare with Victor. "I mean, I thought we were just here to discuss how to get rid of my brother."

"We'll get to that part," Dana said. "Right now we make a plan to take over and rule Earth."

"Who will rule Earth?" Victor asked.

"Both of us, of course," Dana answered. "We'll share it."

"Share it," Victor repeated with a grin. I could tell sharing wasn't something he was used to doing.

"We'll set fire to every inch of that planet," Dana started, "and then when it's burned to the ground, we'll—"

"I have a better plan," Victor said, ignoring what he clearly thought was a juvenile, ill-thought-out plan. "And in the end, *I* will rule Earth, and *you* will benefit from my generosity for sparing your life right now."

Dana opened her mouth to refute, but the fire at the ends of Victor's fingertips made her close it.

Victor leaned forward, pressing his forearms into the table. "There is only one way to take Earth," he began, "and you're going to need a lot more firepower than you currently have." Flames erupted from his shoulders as if proving his point. "But as dark world allies, I think we all stand to gain from this . . . merger."

Dana visibly relaxed, and a smile formed at her lips. "Yes," she agreed. "I like the sound of that."

"Okay, so you take Earth," I interrupted. "Then what? How does Luke die? How do I become keeper of my world?"

"No one wants Luke dead more than me," Keagan said, "so don't worry—it will happen."

"I'm pretty sure your anger toward him because he embarrassed you in front of Sarah isn't as strong as my hate for how he took away my honour and threw me into prison," I said.

"Keagan is my second-in-command, Riley," Dana said. "He shares my hate for Luke as well. Your brother is the reason Ella is dead. We loved each other, but somehow your brother snaked his way into her mind and made her believe her purpose was to die for Sarah." She spat the last words.

"Sounds like you all have reason," Victor said. "So I assume by killing Etak's keeper, you plan to turn Etak back into the dark world it was intended to be?" His question was for me, but I still couldn't make my eyes meet his.

"That's the plan," I said. "And because Yelram and Etak are united now, it won't be long before Yelram's mine, too."

"You're not to touch Sarah," Keagan said under his breath but loud enough for all of us to hear.

"Got a soft spot for her, do you?" Victor asked.

"She's never done anything to any of us," Keagan said.

"Sarah's not our target," Dana clarified, "but if she gets in the way, or dies trying to save Luke, that's not on me."

Keagan frowned but didn't dare backtalk his new master.

"Seems like she has you all under a spell," Victor noted. "I look forward to meeting this temptress and seeing what she's capable of once she loses Luke."

"Speaking of which," Dana said, "how about we go take a walk and I'll show you just how we plan to make his death happen."

"Is it ready?" I asked eagerly.

"Just about," Dana said. "All we need is a key." She turned to Victor. "I was hoping that once you saw our weapon, you would be willing to loan us your second-in-command key."

Victor narrowed his eyes on her. "You're asking a lot."

"Wait 'till you see what it's for."

And with her eyes alight with excitement, we all followed her out of the room, through the passageways, down a long narrow staircase, and into the solid steel wing of the castle where she kept the beast tethered.

CHAPTER 1

Happily Ever After

~ SARAH ~

THE SUN HAD been up for hours, but Luke was still sound asleep, his arms wrapped tightly around me. I hadn't minded watching the sun crest over the windowsill and spill onto the wide planked flooring. I hadn't minded watching the dust dance through the beam of light as they prepared to settle for the day. I hadn't minded watching the hands of the grandfather clock move slowly around and around. Luke's arms were around me, and we were warm and together and safe. I wondered if this feeling would ever get old.

I brought his hand to my lips and kissed his fingers softly, then tucked them under my chin.

"You awake?" he asked in his broken morning voice.

"Mmmm," I answered.

"Go back to sleep. I'm not ready for morning." He kissed my head and I smiled.

"That's good because it's almost noon."

He squeezed harder and groaned. "I don't care what time it is. I'm not getting up yet and neither are you."

I rolled over and nuzzled my face into his neck and let his warm arms bring me back to a resting state.

"Have I told you lately how much I love you?" he said as his lips brushed my forehead.

I smiled. "Tell me again."

He held his lips to my forehead. "My love for you is taller than a kitten and softer than a mountain, deeper than a lion and fiercer than a canyon."

I snickered. I loved hearing his mixed up reasons for how much he loved me. It was a game he played with me every morning.

"Because my love for you is mixed up and daisy, with a pocket full of crazy," I said, finishing his line for him.

He laughed and rolled over, taking me with him until he was my bed. I wrapped my legs around his and kissed his neck softly as my fingers trailed his chest.

We were interrupted by a light knock on the door. I slid off as Luke groaned his disapproval. "Really?"

"It's Elizabeth," I said. "If she doesn't hear from me by ten o'clock, she comes to find me."

"Why?"

"Because it's her job." I sat up and pulled my top down over my head. "I'm awake, Elizabeth. I'll be down soon."

"Why do you need a maidservant?" Luke complained.

"For when you're away," I said. "She keeps me company."

"But I'm never away for long," he countered, and I smiled because it sounded like a whine.

"I saved her life once, and she wanted to repay the favour. She has a little girl, Rachel, and I like having them around."

"You like having the little girl around?" he asked. There was skepticism in his voice as if he found it hard to believe.

"She's sweet," I said. "You'd like her."

"I doubt it," he said flatly.

"Luke," I said, shooting him a look of disapproval. "You'll meet her someday and you'd better be nice."

"Of course I will," he said. "I'm just not a huge fan of kids. They don't really seem to have a *purpose*."

I laughed as I pulled on a pair of pants. "They're not supposed to have a *purpose*. They're just kids."

He grunted.

"Don't you want to have kids someday?" I pretended to fuss with the button on my pants. We hadn't discussed children, but I never imagined it being an issue. I wasn't even sure how I felt about it either, but it was something probably important enough to discuss.

"I don't know," he said. "But definitely not anytime soon." He was out of bed now, too, and pulling on his own clothes.

I watched him get dressed, but we didn't speak about it again. I was okay with his ambivalence to the subject as I didn't know the first thing about being a mother since I couldn't remember my own childhood, but his coldness was mildly unsettling. There was a lonely resentment to his words that I didn't like. Was he afraid of having a child that resembled him?

"Will you come to Etak with me today?" he asked, pulling me from my thoughts.

I looked back at the door, where I was sure Elizabeth was standing on the other side, waiting for me to emerge so she could come tidy my room and make my bed.

"Why don't you stay for breakfast?" I suggested. "You always leave as soon as you get up."

"But I'm always back before lunch. Do you miss me that much that you can't wait a couple of hours?"

"I do," I admitted.

"Babe, I have things to take care of in Etak," he said. "Riley's up to something and I need to make sure he's not convincing everyone that my allegiance is to Yelram now."

"I'll come with you then," I decided. "Your people seem to like me."

"Our people," he said. "Etak is just as much your world now as it is mine."

I smiled. "And Yelram is yours," I reminded him. "So don't be afraid to get to know your people here."

He frowned. "Yelram's people love you, Sarah."

"And they love you," I argued.

"No. They obey me. There's a difference."

"Well maybe if they saw us together more," I offered. "We should take a tour of the world together. Visit all the towns and show them how amazing you are."

He smiled. "Why are you so cute?"

I smiled, although I knew he was avoiding the suggestion.

"I'll make you a deal," I said. "If you stay and have breakfast with me here, then I'll go to Etak with you for the whole day."

"Deal," he said. "But for the record, I would've stayed for breakfast, anyway."

THE KITCHEN WAS empty except for Omar, who had his back to us and was busying himself with our breakfast.

"You slept in again, Miss," Omar said as he flipped an egg in the frying pan.

Luke tickled me and I giggled as we took a seat at the long wooden table behind Omar.

"Yes, sorry about that, Omar. I hope I didn't spoil anything for you." Omar had schedules he liked to adhere to, and he didn't like when I missed a meal.

"Well, it's not healthy to be eating irregularly, you know," he scolded. He pushed the eggs off onto a plate and turned around with a steaming plate of bacon, eggs, and toast in his hands. He stopped when he saw Luke. "Oh, I, uh . . ." he stumbled. He did a sort of bow and stammered, "I didn't know you would be joining Miss Sarah, Master Luke."

Luke gave me a quick look, one that suggested he was right earlier when he said Yelram's people obey him but don't care for him.

"Yes, Omar," I said. "I finally convinced him to try your food." I winked so that Omar would know I was kidding, but he didn't relax.

"Well, I will make more right away. I'm sorry that I didn't assume, Miss Sarah."

"It's okay, Omar," I assured him. "This is plenty for both of us." I nudged Luke under the table. "It's almost lunch time anyway."

"Of course," Omar said, nodding quickly. "And what would the Master and you like for lunch today, Miss?"

"Omar," Luke said. "Please, just call me Luke."

Omar's eyes widened with what looked like fear. "Of course, Maste—Luke."

Luke was frustrated, and I suddenly realized why he

16

didn't enjoy spending time amongst Yelram's people.

"We'll actually be in Etak for lunch," I said, noticing the horror pass over Omar's face. He was old school when it came to the division of the worlds. In his eyes, the light worlds and dark worlds should never mix, much less marry.

"Are you . . . are you sure, My Lady?" Omar stuttered.

"I'm sure," I said with a smile. "Etak is my responsibility now, too. I need to get to know my people there." I glanced at Luke. "Just as Luke will do here."

Omar's eyes flickered to Luke's and they smiled at each other, both nervous at what this meant.

We finished our breakfast in silence as Omar busied himself with cleaning the kitchen. I slid my hand onto Luke's lap and squeezed gently, letting him know that we were in this together. He was not alone. This was *our* world.

ETAK WAS COLD and dark when we arrived an hour later. Luke's demeanor always completely changed whenever we came here. He shot out orders at everyone as if they were machines, but he did this, I knew, because this was how they responded best. This was what they were used to and what they respected. I, on the other hand, was no good with them. Yes, they respected me, but that was because I was powerful. The story of how I threw Devon, Luke's second-in-command and greatest warrior, off his wolf using just my mind, had quickly circulated. Devon was powerful and no one, other than Luke, had ever been able to hurt him. And even Luke, according to the rumors, wasn't even that strong. This was why Etak's people respected me, but why they liked me was for a completely different reason. I helped them. Even with the darkness that always surrounded them, they each carried a small flicker of hope. A spark of light. And I loved to foster that by helping them with their jobs—whether big or small. They weren't used to kindness, so at first they were resistant and skeptical. They were afraid. They thought that Yelram's keeper— the one who had captured their own dark lord's heart— was there to torture them. They had heard the story about Devon and assumed I was dangerous. It took some time, but eventually they began to trust me, and I saw their walls of defence breaking down. And lately, whenever they saw me, the young ones especially, they would run to me, arms opened wide. It warmed my heart, although Luke was uneasy about it. He always scowled and shooed them away from me. We just laughed at him, but I was always careful to obey him in front of his people.

"Where is everybody?" I asked as we walked through the empty corridors of his castle.

He shrugged, a frown at his brow.

"What's wrong?" I slid my hand into his. His pace was much too fast for mine, and I had to skip every few steps in order to keep up.

Luke took his key and squeezed it, then muttered, "Devon." The key glowed for a second, then he dropped it onto his chest again. He had summoned Devon, something I had seen him do a few times before. I hadn't yet tried calling for Maddy that way because I always felt it seemed a little cruel—to force someone away from whatever they were doing just so you could talk to them then and there.

A few seconds later Devon appeared in the hallway behind us. Luke didn't slow down, and once Devon had a hold of his bearings, he jogged to catch up.

"What is it?" he asked as he took to Luke's left side.

Luke didn't answer, and the sound of their heavy boots slamming against the stone floor was all that was heard. Devon leaned back so that our eyes met. He raised his eyebrows, asking if I knew what was going on. I shrugged.

Then we came to a large wooden door and Luke pushed it open and walked through, dropping my hand as he did. I hesitated in the hallway and watched as Devon followed him in.

The room was empty, save for a globe suspended in the middle of the room. Luke went straight to the sphere and circled it. Devon followed quietly behind, his hands behind his back, waiting for his instructions.

"Sarah, get in and shut the door," Luke ordered, and

I didn't hesitate, but before I could grab the handle, the door slammed shut, startling me. Luke had done it, and the fear that it instilled in me made me angry for a split second. I inhaled deeply and slowly turned around, ignoring the urge to yell at him.

"Where's Riley?" Luke barked, directing this at Devon.

"I . . . I don't know," Devon said as he began to study the globe, too. Now that he knew what he was looking for, his fingers moved swiftly across the globe while his eyes followed.

"He's not here," Luke growled. "I put a marker on him so that I could always know where he is. The moment I got here, I knew he wasn't here. I could *feel* it."

"You put a marker on him?" I asked, keeping my distance near the door.

He just glanced at me, but ignored my question. "Devon, I told you to watch him."

"I did," Devon said. "I mean, I have been. Where could he have gone? He doesn't have a key."

"This is on *you*, Devon!" Luke yelled, jabbing a finger toward him. Devon lowered his eyes.

"Luke," I tried, "it's not Devon's fault—"

"Stay out of it, Sarah!" Luke snapped, and my mouth closed in response. I wished it had fallen open in surprise, but I couldn't be surprised that he was this angry about his brother escaping Etak.

"How did he get out?" Luke said, returning his accusations to Devon.

Devon shook his head as he studied the globe some more. "I . . . I have no idea."

"Someone came to get him," I said, wondering why this hadn't been obvious. "It's the only way out. Someone with a key must have come for him."

Both were looking at me now. "But who?" Devon asked. "Ella's dead. Dana would have no use for him. Where would he go?"

Luke swept his hands through his hair. "Find him," he growled.

Devon watched Luke's back as Luke stormed away, grabbed my arm, and pulled me from the room.

When we were finally alone in his bedroom, he let go of my arm and slammed the door behind us. I rubbed my wrist and healed the burn at the same time.

"Sorry," he mumbled when he saw what I was doing.

"You should be."

"Let me guess," he said. "You think I overreacted."

"Like always," I said. "Yes."

"Why don't you see the danger in Riley? Do you not remember how he tried to kill you before? How he tried to kill me?"

I nodded. "But you take your anger out on everyone else, Luke. Devon didn't have anything to do with Riley's escape."

"I left him with one job—to watch my brother."

"Well, then I can't blame him for screwing up."

"What?" Luke snapped as he poured himself a drink.

I went to him, took the glass from his hand, and set it down. I wrapped his arms around my body and then draped mine around his.

"Devon is your second-in-command, Luke. He's above babysitting duties. You need to give him some real responsibility."

"Watching Riley was the *biggest* responsibility there is!" he shouted. He tried to pull away, but I wouldn't let him.

"It was babysitting," I reiterated. "It wasn't a duty fit for a second-in-command."

"Then who should I have babysit him? You want me to get Elizabeth to come over here and do it? She seems good at babysitting."

This time I let him pull away, because if he hadn't, I might have pushed him. He picked up his glass again and took a drink of the amber liquid, then hissed as it burned his throat. I sat down in the chair by the fire and watched him.

"Forget Riley," I said. "You're letting your hate for him consume you."

He took another drink and then set the empty glass on the table.

"Give Devon a real job," I continued. "Give him

22

authority over the army. Let him train them and build their morale. He needs to feel a sense of purpose."

He frowned and sat down in the chair across from me. "Do you believe him?"

"I do," I said, knowing he was referring to Devon. "He was just as surprised as you were that Riley was gone."

"The only way in and out of this world is with a key," Luke said. "I have one and Devon has the other. And I sure as hell didn't take Riley out of here."

"Yeah, but the other worlds have keys too, babe," I reminded him. "It could've been Dana or Victor."

He didn't respond, but I knew he was thinking it through. He wanted to believe Devon didn't have anything to do with Riley's disappearance, but he also didn't know what to make of Riley aligning with the rulers of the darkest worlds—Leviathan and Nitsua.

"There's nothing we can do about it right now, anyway," I said, "so you might as well assign Devon to something useful."

His brow furrowed as he struggled with his resistance to this.

I went to him and knelt down in front of him. I took his hands and brought them to my lips. "You are stronger than this." My voice was almost a whisper. "Please don't let it consume you."

"I just . . . I just have a bad feeling about it."

"Dwelling on the unknown will only make you sick."

He considered this and then let his face relax. "I'm sorry for being . . . and saying . . ."

I nodded. "I know. Maybe you should come back to Yelram with me."

A smile played at the corner of his mouth as he studied my eyes. "Are you trying to lure me back to your bed, Miss Sarah?"

I grinned. "Maybe."

He leaned forward and took my face in his hands as he planted his lips on mine. Then he pulled me up so that I was sitting on his lap. "What's wrong with my bed?"

"Absolutely nothing," I breathed as he kissed my neck.

He lifted me up and carried me blindly to his bed while our lips mated and my fingers pulled his head closer to mine. Then I was on my back and his restless body was pinning me to the mattress, our breaths heavy with anticipation for what the next few minutes promised.

CHAPTER 2

Tricked & Treason

~ SARAH ~

"WHERE'VE YOU BEEN?" Maddy was waiting for me in my bedroom when I returned from Etak. After Luke had relaxed, he agreed to talk to Devon and give him more responsibilities, so I left them to it and came home.

"Etak," I told her. "Riley's missing."

"Oh yeah?" Maddy stood up and set down the book she had been reading. "Where is he?"

I laughed. "I don't know, Mad. If I knew, he probably wouldn't be *missing*."

She laughed too. "True."

"Luke put a marker on him so he could always find him, but he can't find him, which I guess means he's not in Etak anymore."

Maddy nodded. "Do you think it means something?"

I shrugged. "Luke does. He's quite upset about it. I don't like seeing him like this. He just jumps to conclusions and gets so worked up. It's not good for him."

"You calmed him down, though? Before you left him?"

I grinned and winked. "Of course I did."

Maddy rolled her eyes and let out an exaggerated sigh. "You two! You act like newlyweds or something."

"We are newlyweds," I reminded her.

"It's been three months, Sarah. The honeymoon's over." She was teasing, I knew, but part of her wondered when we would get over the newness of it all and carry on with life.

"How are your parents?" I asked, trying to change the subject. Maddy had just spent the last three days on Earth visiting her parents. They didn't know about the dream worlds, or that Maddy had taken up a position as my second-in-command and now lived in another world. They assumed she was taking a year to do some travelling. It wasn't completely untrue. She and Drew had been spending more time together, and he took her to places around the world she had never been before.

"They're good," Maddy said, a shadow of guilt on her face.

My mindbending had become quite natural and strong and she wasn't even aware that I could see inside her mind better than even she could. She tried to hide it, but I knew her guilt came from her sympathy toward me for not having parents to visit or love.

"You need to get better at closing your mind," I said, reminding her that she hadn't practiced at all since receiving the craft when I made her my second.

She shrugged. "I have nothing to hide." She was smiling, smugly.

"How's Drew been? I haven't seen him for a few days." I watched as she shifted her weight and leaned against the window.

"He's good," she said. What she really meant was, *"He's great. He's perfect. I love him. . . . But he keeps his distance sometimes and I'm not sure what that means."*

"Did you see him while you were visiting your parents?"

"I may have spent some time with him." She tried to hide her pleasure, but I saw right through the facade. I heard it in her voice. "Don't you ever get sick of being locked up in here?" she said, pushing against the window.

I joined her at the window and looked out over the town to the mountains in the distance. "Sometimes," I admitted.

"Let's get out of here, then." She took her key from

her shirt. "Let's go to the mountains. Let's do something."

"You want to ride?" I said, and there was a spark of excitement in her eye. "Let's go get the cats."

WE FOUND LUCIA, my beautiful rainbow-striped tiger, and Raven, Maddy's gorgeous striped companion, in the tiger fields next to the palace. As soon as we mounted them, we held hands and I ported the four of us to a forgotten forest in the Northeast. One we had been to only a few months prior in search of the Garden of Hope.

The valleys were quiet and green again, no longer covered in blood shed by the battle that took place not long enough ago. But the caves were now empty. The people had been rescued, and their towns and homes restored. They were safe once again.

Lucia and Raven raced through the valleys while Maddy and I held tight to their manes. But suddenly they stopped, nearly throwing us both forward. Lucia pawed at the ground while Raven lowered her head, swinging it back and forth and growling.

There was someone in the field ahead, at the edge of the forest. He was tall and handsome and wearing a pair of faded blue jeans that I loved, and his hair was gently tousled by the wind.

"Luke." I left Maddy and the cats and appeared next to Luke at the edge of the forest. "You scared Lucia," I told him.

"Sorry," he said as he glanced toward Maddy and the tigers.

"Is everything okay? What are you doing out here?"

"Where should I be?" He grinned.

Confused, I let out a small laugh. "Home? With Devon?"

He looked disappointed. "Right."

"Not that I mind having you here." I was beginning to sense that something was wrong. Something was off.

His eyes were full of lust and as I reached for him, he took me into his arms and pressed his mouth to mine. But it was rough and void of love and I didn't like it. I pushed him away and as I did, I saw a flicker in his eye that was familiar, but yet not familiar enough. My mind raced to make sense of it. He reached for me again, and I fumbled for his mind. He was quick and slipped right through. Why was he avoiding me? What had gotten into him?

Before I knew it, he pulled me into him again and kissed me hard. I tried to get away, but he kept a firm grip. I searched my waist for my sword, but it wasn't there. I hadn't brought it. So I bit his lip and he pulled away, but kept his body pressed into mine. There was a desire-filled look about him that didn't sit right with me.

I heard a loud roar and Luke pulled away to find Lucia only a few feet away, her teeth bared and eyes narrowed on him. Luke pulled his sword on her.

"Put that away!" I warned him, but he was fixated on Lucia, and they circled each other menacingly. Raven caught up and joined Lucia, and then Maddy slid off Raven and took her place next to me.

"What the hell is going on?" she said, breathless. She had her sword, thankfully, and I pulled it from her holster.

"It's not Luke," I realized.

Maddy faltered, showing her surprise. "You don't think?"

I shook my head. "I know it isn't."

"Show yourself!" I demanded, shoving the sword into his back.

Our eyes met, and for a second, a look of confusion slipped over his face. He shook his head and pinched his eyes closed. "I . . . I'm . . ."

I glanced at Maddy who was concentrating hard, her eyes boring into Luke. She was trying to get into his head.

Luke shook his head again, and I distracted him from Maddy by asking another question. "Why are you here?"

He let out a growl and drove his sword into the ground. Then he fell to his knees and gripped his head. "Get out of my head!" he yelled.

I dug the tip of my sword into his throat as my mind raced for an explanation. Dana was the only shapebender I knew, but for her to come here and risk her life like this seemed uncalculated and unlike her.

Maddy pressed harder into the shapebender's mind, and Luke's image flickered. The next second, Keagan was kneeling on the ground in front of me.

"Keagan," I gasped. "How did you do that?" My eyes searched his as I helped him up from the ground. "Did Dana put you up to this?"

"I can do things now," he answered, cryptically.

"How did you find me?"

"Your maid girl told me you were riding in the Northeast." He grinned. "You really should have better security."

I frowned. "What are you doing here?"

"I loved you, Sarah," he said.

"You *thought* you loved me," I corrected.

"If it weren't for Luke, you and I would be together right now. He took you from me!" he shouted as he pulled his sword from the ground.

"Keagan, I cared about you, but I was always Luke's."

He scowled. "We could've been happy together."

"Why are you here, Keagan?" I asked calmly as I tried to piece together how he was here in the flesh, bending like an expert. "You didn't come here to kiss me. Why did you come back?"

Keagan's brow was furrowed in frustration. He did come here to tell me something, but the talk about Luke got him riled up. Finally, he said, "I came to warn you. *You*, not *Luke*."

I nodded, ignoring his hatred for my husband. "Warn me about what?"

"Victor and Dana are going to storm Earth with their armies, slaughtering anyone who doesn't submit."

Maddy's eyes widened, but I tried to keep my composure. "How do you know that?"

Keagan shook his head and turned away. I looked at Maddy and nodded, urging her to take hold of his mind again and open it so that he would answer my questions truthfully. He grabbed at his head, trying to shake her out, but he couldn't.

"I'm . . . I'm . . ."

"You're what, Keagan?"

"I'm Dana's . . . second-in-command," Keagan finally admitted. He was breathing heavy, frustrated that Maddy was inside his mind.

"I'm sorry, Keagan," I said, "but I need more. When are they planning this invasion?"

"No," Keagan answered. "I've already said too much."

Maddy's eyes narrowed as she fervently focused all of her power to bending Keagan's mind wide open.

"When, Keagan?"

"As soon as their armies are strong enough!" he shouted, and then he threw his sword toward Maddy, which narrowly missed, but broke her hold on his mind. Lucia leaped at Keagan and he bent into a tiger to match her strength. Lucia knocked Keagan to the ground next to me, and I dove out of the way, hitting my head against a rock. The fight was blurry, but I could see them rolling around on the ground, their teeth and claws ripping at each other.

"Keagan, get out of here!" I yelled as Raven let out a ferocious roar and waited for an opportunity to help Lucia. A second later he was gone, and Lucia was left panting angrily and bleeding from more than one wound.

I stood to go to her, but as I took a step, I stumbled from the dizziness in my head. Finding a seat again on the ground, I grasped for my bearings. Lucia was too angry to heal now anyway.

Maddy slid to the ground until she was resting with her head in her hands against a tree. Raven stood protectively beside her, watching the place that Keagan had just been.

"Are you okay?" I managed to ask.

"I hate doing that."

"You'll get used to it."

"I don't want to get used to it," she snapped. "It's not natural getting inside someone's head like that."

"Did you see anything he wasn't telling me?"

"He was fighting it pretty good," she admitted. "But I think we got the truth."

"Yeah, I couldn't get in," I told her, unnerved by this.

33

"I see why it's so important for no one to know about my craft. They can learn to defend themselves against it. But you got in, Maddy. That's awesome."

"Only because he wasn't expecting it from me." She picked up her sword and sheathed it. "So Keagan works for Dana now, which means she must know about your craft."

I shook my head. "I don't know."

"Why do you think he came?"

I shook my head again and noticed my vision took longer to correct itself.

"We should tell Luke," she said.

I shook my head harder. "Not right now. He has enough to think about with Riley."

"But maybe Keagan and Riley are connected somehow," she considered.

"Maybe," I said. "But if I tell him about Keagan now, I'll have to tell him that he kissed me, and I know he can't handle that right now."

"We have to tell Drew and Luke what Keagan said."

I nodded at the same time that Lucia nudged me, signaling her desire to get back to the palace. It was only a light nudge, but somehow I lost my balance and tripped, landing on the ground next to Maddy's feet.

"Are you okay?" she asked.

I touched my head where it hurt. "I'm just a bit dizzy," I admitted, but the words made me nauseous and the next second I was leaning over and hurling over the moss covered ground.

"Sarah," Maddy said, scrambling to her feet. "We need to get you to the hospital."

I tried to stand, but the edges of my vision were turning black and a strange numbness in my body took over as I slowly lost consciousness.

CHAPTER 3

Earth's Creation

~ SARAH ~

WHEN I OPENED my eyes again, I was staring at a white ceiling, and there was a constant, rhythmic beeping in my right ear. I turned to the sound and found a machine monitoring my heartbeat. There were wires taped to my chest, a tube connected to my arm, and a bandage wrapped around my head. A quick survey of the room told me that I was in a hospital.

I tried to sit up but was held in place by the wires. This, I thought, was ridiculous. I was the world's keeper. I didn't need modern technology to heal me. I was capable of doing that all on my own.

"Maddy?" I called as I picked at the tape on my arm.

Maddy quickly came through the door. "I'm right here," Maddy replied. "She's awake," she called into the hallway. A doctor and a nurse followed her through the door and soon my bed was surrounded by the three of them.

"What the hell is going on?" I demanded. "I fainted. That's it. What's with all the gear?"

The doctor and Maddy exchanged a look that said nothing. "You bumped your head," the doctor said. "And normally you'd be able to heal yourself, but currently you aren't in a position to be able to do so, and you may not be for . . . quite some time."

"What are you talking about?" I said.

"Well, we ran some tests while you were . . . resting"—he cleared his throat, uncomfortable with the news he was about to deliver—"and it appears that—"

"You're pregnant, Sarah," Maddy finished.

My eyes slowly found Maddy's. "What did you say?"

"You're pregnant."

"Your healing abilities are being used up on the baby right now," the doctor added.

I shook my head. "Stop saying that. I'm not pregnant!"

The nurse turned her clipboard around and showed me a piece of paper with numbers and words and checkmarks. "See, My Lady, we have your results right here. You are most definitely pregnant."

"No," I said, interrupting her. "That's impossible."

"It's not," Maddy said with a grin.

"But I . . . I don't want to be pregnant," I stammered.

Maddy was shocked by this, but she turned to the doctor and nurse and said, "Can you give us a minute?"

They both nodded and took their leave.

"And," Maddy added before they were out the door, "I don't need to remind you that this is strictly confidential. No one is to hear a word about this before Sarah and Luke announce it for themselves."

"Of course," they both said in unison.

"You two are the only ones who know, so if this gets out, I'll know who to blame," she added darkly.

They both nodded again and hurried out of the room. When the door closed behind them, I pulled off the wires attached to my chest.

"Maddy, this is ridiculous!" I said. "This can't be right."

"Sarah, you just need to relax for a minute." She held me in place. "What are you afraid of right now? You should be happy, no?"

"No." I shook my head. "Luke doesn't like kids," I admitted. "And I . . . I don't know the first thing about being a mother. How can I possibly do this? And if Keagan was telling the truth, then a war is coming, Maddy, and I can't be pregnant. This is not what I need or want right now."

"Sarah." Maddy took my hand. Hers was so warm. "You don't have a choice, okay? There is a living soul inside of you. It's yours to protect and love. You can do this. I know you can."

My chest heaved with the panic inside. "I can't tell him," I said. "Not yet. He's not in a good place right now. He won't want to keep it, and I . . . I'm not strong enough to argue with that right now."

"Okay," Maddy said as she brushed the hair from my face. "But you'll tell him soon, right?"

"Yes," I promised. "Soon. When I'm ready."

She smiled weakly, but I could tell she was uneasy with this.

The doctor returned a minute later as I was unravelling my head dressing. The wires hung over the bar on my bed.

"Are you leaving, My Lady?" he asked.

"I am."

"But you're not healed yet," he said.

"Luke will be back soon. He will heal me. I'll be fine until then."

The doctor looked to Maddy for direction. She nodded, assuring him that we would be fine.

"Okay, you can go," he reluctantly allowed. "But get some rest." He called after us as we left the room, "And I will need to follow up with you tomorrow."

WE WENT STRAIGHT back to the palace. I hadn't planned to speak to anyone until I had time to process everything and decide on the best way to tell Luke. Would I just come right out and say it? Should I arrange for him to spend time with Rachel first so he could see how sweet and lovely a child could be? What if he didn't want to keep it? What if he couldn't look at me the same? My eyes watered with these thoughts.

Maddy slid her hand into mine as we approached the palace steps. The gesture brought tears to my eyes. I was lucky to have her in my life. Lucky to call her my best friend.

"There they are," Luke said, his voice calm and beautiful and oh so perfect.

We both looked up the steps and found Drew and Luke sitting at the top. We climbed the steps toward them as I mentally prepared myself.

"What are you doing here?" Maddy asked, her question meant for Drew.

"I wanted to talk to you guys about what's happening on Earth."

"What's going on?" I nervously asked, sensing the concern in Drew's thoughts.

"There have been fires," Drew explained. "A lot of them."

"Orphanages and schools," Luke added. "All within the last several hours."

"Some sort of terrorist attack?" Maddy asked.

Drew shook his head. "They're too far apart and there doesn't seem to be a human link between them." Drew frowned.

My head started to spin so I took Luke's hand and sat down next to him.

"It has Leviathan written all over it," Drew said. "I just can't prove it."

Maddy's torment piqued before she blurted, "It's Victor. He and Dana plan to storm Earth with their armies and slaughter innocent people if they don't submit to them."

Luke and Drew turned their full attention to Maddy, mouths agape, and waited for her full explanation. I closed my eyes and inhaled. She would tell; Luke would lose it.

Maddy turned away from us and descended a few steps. "I ran into Keagan when I was on Earth. He's working for Dana now. He told me this was their plan."

I exhaled. She didn't tell.

"And you just thought to tell us this now?" Drew barked. "When did you see him?"

"Just today," she covered quickly.

"Wait," Luke said, "Keagan's working for Dana?" His face hardened as his jaw clenched.

Maddy glanced at me and then lowered her eyes as she nodded. "He's her second-in-command."

"What a coward," Luke hissed. "I should've killed him when I had the chance."

"Maddy, did Keagan give any indication *when* this would happen?" Drew asked.

Maddy shook her head. "He just said when their armies were strong enough."

Drew and Luke exchanged a look. "The fires," Luke said.

Drew nodded. "Makes sense now."

"What does?" I pressed.

"The dark worlds get power from fear and hate," Luke explained. "By killing innocent people, especially children, they cause mass hysteria, fear, and outrage, and they can use that energy to grow their armies."

"But why would they want to start a war?" I asked.

"If they control the heart, they control all of the worlds," Luke explained.

"And it's not the first time they've tried something like this," Drew continued. "The dark worlds were once almost successful in capturing Earth. Nevaeh had to flood the whole world, and we started over."

"The Great Flood," Maddy wondered aloud.

Drew nodded. "The world was plagued with fear and hatred."

A cold chill swept up my spine. Could that be Earth's fate again?

"And then in 1347 an air-borne virus was released on

Earth by a dark world," Drew continued. "It took more than fifty million lives, and caused mass hysteria, before the light worlds were able to stop it."

An *air*-borne virus. That would've been from . . . Etak's world? I glanced at Luke, but his eyes, full of shame, never met mine.

"And again in 1933, Nitsua unleashed a monster that was responsible for killing millions of innocent people and instilling fear and hate in millions more," Drew finished. His eyes were moist with sadness.

My mouth was dry and my stomach squeezed with unease. "What do we do now?"

"We get ready. If this is true, then it means war." Drew turned to Luke. "We need to let Trinity and Eli know right away."

Luke nodded. "I'll have Devon start readying my army."

"And when they bring their armies through, we'll meet them with full force."

Luke pulled me into him and I felt his desperate need to win this war. "We just need to make sure our armies are bigger and stronger than theirs. That those who are with us are more than those who are with them."

"Yelram needs an army too," Maddy declared, a new determination to her voice.

Luke and Drew just looked at her.

"I can put one together," she continued. "I've already

had people come forward and ask if we planned on building an army again."

Drew nodded. "I'll go to Nevaeh and Lorendale to warn Trinity and Eli to get their armies ready." He reached for Maddy's hand. "Come with me?"

She smiled, her unease melting, as she took his hand, and they left for Nevaeh together.

As soon as they were gone, Luke turned to me and took my hands. "You okay?"

I nodded, and he lowered his head so that I couldn't avoid his eyes anymore. "Just processing everything," I said.

Processing the news that Keagan was working for Dana.

That the dark worlds were planning on destroying Earth.

That I was pregnant.

His fingers laced with mine. "This is the beginning of the end, Sarah." His voice was so strong but guarded. "Earth will never be the same after this. No matter who wins this war."

"*We'll* win this war," I said, definitively.

Luke nodded and smiled, but I saw his uncertainty. "Victor wouldn't start something he couldn't finish."

CHAPTER 4

Rallying the Troops

~ MADDY ~

NEVAEH'S GARDEN WAS quiet and peaceful. There were no clouds in the sky to show the movement of the atmosphere—the trees were still, the lake was void of ducks, and the flowers were bright and perfect. The only thing that made it real was a soft ripple that spread across the lake from a rogue leaf.

Drew was sitting on a bench nearby, his arms across his knees as he waited, but my eyes were restless, searching for more evidence that my surroundings were more than just a lovely painting.

A loud clanging noise interrupted my thoughts, and the large golden gates slowly swung open, revealing

Trinity in a long white dress that hugged her shape perfectly, then cascaded down around her legs. Her blonde hair hung in neat curls around her shoulders.

Drew stood up immediately when he saw her and went to greet her. She extended her arms and they embraced. Hannah, Trinity's second-in-command, stepped out from behind. She, too, was dressed in white, although a little less formal in tight white pants, tall white boots, and a smart white blazer.

Hannah and Drew shook hands and when she smiled, I noticed that he blushed. A tightness in my chest prevented me from extending my own hand for greeting.

"Hello, Maddy," Trinity said, a look of warmth on her face. Drew took my hand and pulled me toward him so that I was practically leaning on him.

"Trinity," Drew began, "As I'm sure you know by now, Victor has been setting fires on Earth, murdering hundreds of innocent children."

Trinity's eyes welled up as she lifted her chin. "I'm well aware. We've been quiet busy welcoming them to our world."

"We think this is a power play to strengthen his army before they storm Earth with their armies."

Trinity's eyes wandered as she considered what this meant. "Okay," she nodded. "We will get our army ready and wait for your command."

Drew and Hannah nodded at each other and then she

turned to leave, presumably to inform the army.

"Maddy," Trinity said before we left, "please tell Sarah that I look forward to fighting alongside her in this war and seeing her skills in action."

My heartbeat quickened as I pictured Sarah and Trinity riding alongside each other—Sarah on Lucia's back, and Trinity on the back of one of her beautiful white-winged unicorns. It was a stunning vision, yes, but it wouldn't be an easy mission. There would be death all around, and Sarah . . . well, Sarah, had a life inside her now. The middle of a war was not where pregnant Sarah belonged.

"Thank you," I finally allowed myself to say. "I'll let her know."

Trinity left us, and I slid my hand into Drew's, waiting for him to port us to Lorendale to relay the news of the war to Eli. But Drew didn't move.

"What is it?" I asked.

"You let go of my hand right before you told Trinity you would let Sarah know."

"Sorry?"

"It's one of your tells," he said. "When you lie, you don't touch or look at anyone."

"What are you talking about?"

"It's like you don't want to taint anyone else with the lie, but it's what you do. You did it earlier, too, when you told us about what Keagan said."

I hadn't consciously dropped his hand, but was he right? Was this something I did when I lied?

"What's going on, Maddy?"

I let his hand slip again, but this time I was more aware of it. I tried to reverse it, but it was too late, he noticed.

"Please don't lie to me."

I considered telling him the truth. *Keagan came to Yelram, bent into Luke's figure, kissed Sarah, and then tried to kill me. Oh yeah, and Sarah's pregnant but doesn't want Luke to know.*

But how could I? He would definitely tell Luke. And Luke would want revenge. What if he convinced Drew to go after Keagan with him? What if Sarah was right and it *was* a trap? I couldn't risk it. Besides, I promised Sarah.

"I'm not lying," I said. "I just . . . I just don't think she needs to know that Trinity's eager to fight alongside her. She has a lot going on."

"Like what?"

"Well, for one," I said, "she's worried about Luke. Apparently Riley has escaped Etak, so he's been pretty angry about that."

Drew nodded, studying me for a minute. I was hoping he would ask more about Riley, but he didn't. He was still trying to figure out my secret.

"I know you're worried about Sarah," Drew began, "but she'll be safe with us. She's more powerful than any of us. You know that, right?"

I didn't respond because if I had to be honest, I didn't plan on letting her join the war. Not in her condition.

"Maddy?" he pressed.

I fought the urge to turn away from him, knowing this would give me away. "I don't think there's any need for her to go to Earth," I said.

Drew watched me for a second, a look of surprise on his face. "And why not?"

"I'm her protector now. Naturally, I have a duty to keep her safe."

"And do you expect her to listen to you?"

I shrugged. "I don't know."

"There's more," he said. "You're not telling me everything."

"I don't need to tell you everything," I said. "Just trust me when I tell you I know what's best for her, okay?"

I sat down on the bench and put my head in my hands, praying he wouldn't ask any more questions. I didn't want to have to lie to him, and I couldn't betray Sarah and tell Drew her secret.

"Okay," he said, and a wave of guilt washed over me.

"Thank you." I stood up hastily, but avoided making eye contact.

After a minute when I realized he was still in no rush to get us to Lorendale, I sat back down.

"Maddy," he said carefully, "I don't want you to fight

in the war, either."

"What? Why?"

"If something happens to you, I . . . I'd never forgive myself." Drew took my hands and seemed to summon strength as he caressed my fingers with his. "You're really important to me, Maddy. I can't . . . I can't lose you."

A sob built up in my chest, but I held it down while I promised, "You won't. We're a team. Okay?" I ran my hands through his hair and reached for his lips. "We're a team." He wrapped his arms around me while our lips stayed together, mating perfectly and slowly.

Eventually, though, our moment ended when he pulled away. "We have to go," he said.

As much as I didn't want it to be true, I knew he was right. I took his hand and without another word, he ported us to Lorendale.

WITH HIS SECOND-IN-COMMAND at his right side, Eli appeared at the river's edge only seconds after we arrived. We met on the bridge where Eli and Drew shook hands, and then Eli stretched his arms out for me and we embraced.

"This is Paul, my second," Eli announced. "Paul, this is Drew, Earth's keeper, and Maddy, Yelram's second."

"Pleasure," Paul said as he shook our hands.

"We don't come with great news, Eli," Drew

continued. "The dark energy on Earth has been getting stronger, and Dana's second-in-command told Maddy that they plan to destroy Earth."

I tried to control it, but my hand perspired with my lie that was now on Drew's lips. Drew's hand tightened around mine, confirming he felt my unease.

Eli nodded slowly. "Never thought I'd see this day."

"None of us did," Drew replied. "Which is why we've come for your help. Can we count on your army to fight with us?"

Eli looked at Paul, who quickly nodded his commitment. "Of course."

Paul spoke up, "I will leave now and prepare the army. Send word, Drew, when you're ready for us."

"Thank you," Drew said.

Paul left immediately, and Eli thanked us for the warning before saying goodbye.

This was it. The worlds were getting ready. Whenever Victor and Dana started their invasion, we would be ready, and the war would begin.

CHAPTER 5

Secrets

~ SARAH ~

LUKE PORTED US into the hallway just outside the room with the suspended globe. He held his key and muttered Devon's name, and then led me into the room. I kept watching over my shoulder for Devon to arrive, and within a few seconds he appeared, confused and eager to get his bearings, but once he did, he followed us into the room and closed the door behind him. I wondered how it didn't annoy the hell out of him to be plucked from whatever he was doing without any warning.

"What's going on?" he asked, his eyes pinballing between mine and Luke's.

"Victor and Dana want a war," Luke answered.

Devon's eyes lit up. He liked what this meant. It was the promise of a challenge. A chance to feel alive again.

"How do you know?" Devon asked.

"Orphanages are burning on Earth," I said, "and Keagan told me . . . told *Maddy*."

Luke's eyes flashed to mine, and I knew he caught my slip. I kept my eyes on Devon's and pretended not to notice.

"Keagan," Devon said, trying the name out himself. "That's the guy that—"

"Yeah, that's him," Luke growled.

"How would he know anything about this?"

"Apparently he couldn't handle rejection," Luke scoffed. "He turned to the dark side. He's working for Dana now."

Devon smirked at me, and although I tried to ignore it, I felt my cheeks turning pink.

"We need you to start preparing the army," Luke told him.

"Already on it."

"How many do we have?"

"We lost almost half to the monsters in Yelram, but after the merger of the worlds, another five hundred came forward, eager to enlist." He smirked at me again. "Apparently, Sarah has a way with people. Seems they're all quite taken with her."

I blushed and Luke narrowed his eyes on me. "Isn't

everyone." There was an accusation there that I chose to ignore.

"We should recruit the giants," I said. "They'll be happy to get their revenge for what the beast did to them."

Devon nodded and pointed to me. "Good idea."

"Sounds like you've got your work cut out for you then," I said.

"We'll be ready when you give the order."

"Thanks, Devon," Luke said. "You can go. I'll let you know when something happens."

Devon nodded to Luke, winked and smirked at me, and left the room.

"You okay?" I asked when Devon was gone.

"Yeah." He pulled me into him. "Sometimes I still get a little jealous, you know?"

"Jealous," I laughed. "About what?"

"All these guys who can't seem to get enough of you."

"No one does, Luke. It's all in your head."

"Keagan," he said, and I silenced. He had his arms around me, but I still felt the distance. "When I think about him bending your mind into wanting him, and when I think about his hands on you, I just want to . . . kill him."

I laid my head on his chest, not only because I wanted our closeness to erase his jealousy, but because I knew that if he saw my face, he would know I had a secret. And

I couldn't tell him that Keagan showed up in Yelram and kissed me. This would break him. It would send him into a jealous rage that would be ill-timed with the impending war. But . . . but maybe that's what Dana wanted. Maybe that was their plan. They probably knew that once Luke found out that Keagan kissed me, he would go after him. It was probably a trap. Yes, that was more likely. I couldn't tell Luke. I definitely could not tell Luke.

Now that I didn't feel guilty for my secret, but instead felt a sense of duty and protection, I was able to raise my face to his.

"You know I love you and only you, right?"

"I do," he said, his smile only half.

"Do I need to prove it to you?" My fingers trailed the rim of his t-shirt and then found his skin above his belt.

His smile broadened. "That might not be a bad idea."

I reached for his lips and massaged them with mine. "You look like you need a rest," I said. "Let's go to your room."

"I WANT TO show you something," Luke said a little while later as we shared a drink by the fire with me in his lap.

"Do I have to get up?"

He laughed. "Nope." Then he stood, easily taking me with him and carried me over to the far corner of his room where a large wooden wardrobe stood. He set me down next to it and said, "It's my father's battle sword. He passed it down to me before he died." He opened the wardrobe, and I nearly fell over with surprise. The sword's hilt was pitch black and, for some reason, scared the hell out of me.

"It's . . . big," I managed to say.

"Yeah, isn't it great? I think I'll use it in the battle." He took the sword from the stand and held it out in front of him. "How does it look?"

I smiled, but looked away too quickly, suddenly feeling disoriented.

"Hey," he said, lifting my chin. "You okay?"

"I'm fine," I lied.

"You're not fine." He replaced the sword and came to me. "Are you scared?"

I scoffed, but he didn't buy it.

"Babe," he said softly, then led me to his bed where we sat down together. "Have you lost faith in me?"

I shook my head. "I'm just tired of fighting." My voice was weak.

"If this war happens," he said, "it'll be the last one we'll ever have to fight."

"What if we don't all make it out alive?" I said, almost under my breath.

There was a pause. "You don't have to go," he said.

"I want to," I said before he could come up with reasons why I shouldn't.

He smiled. "I knew you would." He went back to the wardrobe and closed the doors. "But I'll be keeping you next to me the whole time."

"I knew you would." There was a flutter deep in my belly, and I immediately gripped it tightly, ignoring the reason for it.

"What's wrong?" he asked, watching me suspiciously as he tightened the vest.

I couldn't tell him. I still hoped that it was a mistake, and I wasn't pregnant. I still hoped that the doctor was wrong, or that the pregnancy wouldn't last. If I told him, he would never let me fight in the war, and how could I watch him go without me, not knowing what would happen to him while I was sitting at home growing something inside of me that scared me more than the beast ever did?

"It's been a long day," he said, pulling me into him. "Let's stay here tonight."

"Here?" I said, looking around his room. It wasn't often we stayed in Etak.

"Please?"

The truth was, I didn't want to go home. I didn't want to deal with the reality of Yelram—I was their keeper. I was their *pregnant* keeper. So I agreed, and we laid together and slept in each other's arms where I was able to ignore the reality of my life and, instead, replace it with the simplicity and comfort of Luke's love.

WHEN WE RETURNED to Yelram the next morning, Maddy was proudly standing in the entry, pacing the floors, evidently waiting for our return.

I smiled when I saw her. "What's got you in such a good mood?"

"We've been spreading the word about the army and guess what? People are just up and leaving their homes to come fight for you. And not just men. Women, too! Almost a thousand already! It's incredible! Ridiculous, really. We are going to have the biggest army ever!"

"No," I reacted, the same time Luke said, "That's great!"

"No?" Maddy said. "What do you mean *no*?"

"They don't know what they're getting into. Most of these people will die."

Maddy nodded. "I told them that. I explained that this was the war of all wars and we were fighting for Earth's freedom, but that it would cost greatly. I told them most would die."

"And they still signed up?" Luke asked.

"Not one even hesitated."

My heart was beating wildly, trying to escape my chest. How could people just throw down their lives like that? Didn't they see the danger in it? Or did they have so much faith in me and my powers that they assumed I could protect them? I would have to go to Earth with him.

Without me there, they wouldn't have a fighting chance.

Luke's hand was on my back. "Babe?"

"We take four hundred," I decided. "That's it."

"Sarah, we'll need all we can get," Luke tried.

"I said four hundred."

I left the two standing there, but heard Luke mutter to Maddy, "I'll talk to her."

"SARAH," ELIZABETH SAID when I entered my room, "the doctor was by to see you last night and again this morning."

Her full attention was on me, so she noticed when I turned quickly to ensure Luke wasn't right behind me, then I closed the door and locked it.

"Sarah?" she said as I crossed the room to the window. "Do you have something you want to tell me?"

"No," I said.

"Okay, that's fair. Do you have something you *should* tell me?"

How could the doctor be so careless? What if Luke had been here when he came? I gave them orders to keep this a private matter.

"What did he tell you?"

Elizabeth sighed. "Nothing, unfortunately. I didn't press him, though, because I knew . . . well, I *thought* you would tell me everything when you got back. I thought you trusted me."

59

"It's not that I don't trust you, Elizabeth," I sighed. "It's that I haven't even processed it myself yet."

She was next to me now, her hand on my back. "You're pregnant," she guessed, and I pinched my eyes closed. One more person that knew made it that much more real.

"That's what they say, anyway."

"Well, this is great news, no?"

"No. No, it's not." I covered my face with my hands and tried not to cry.

"I don't understand."

"You wouldn't."

"What's that supposed to mean?"

I sighed. "You have a daughter, and you love each other. That's special. Of course you would think having a child is a good thing."

"Sarah," Elizabeth said, her tone full of sympathy. "Does this have anything to do with your relationship with your mother?"

"What relationship?" I muttered.

She recoiled as if this personally hurt her. "Your mother loved you more than any mother ever loved their child. You were her world. She sacrificed so much for you."

Now it was my turn to recoil. The mention of my mother's *sacrifice* brought flashbacks of beasts, and clues, and near death experiences.

"I'm sorry, My Lady," Elizabeth said softly.

I wanted to tell her that it was okay. But none of this was okay. I hoped that if I ignored the fact that I was pregnant, that it just would go away. The doctors would be wrong, Maddy would forget, and I would continue my life without ever having to learn how to be a mother.

"So I guess this means you won't be fighting in the war," she said, and I immediately started plotting ways to fire the doctor.

"I have no plans to sit out," I said. "Yelram's people need me, and they'll be stronger if—"

"My Lady," she interrupted, her eyes wide. "With all due respect—"

"If you want to give me respect, Elizabeth, you won't finish that sentence." I headed for the exit and had my hand on the doorknob when she said, "Luke doesn't know, does he?"

I froze, the punch to my stomach feeling worse than if it were real. "No," I said. "I will tell him when the time is right. Is that clear?"

Her look of disappointment passed right through me. I pulled the door open to leave, and Luke and I nearly ran into each other.

"Hey," he said. "You okay?"

I glanced over my shoulder at Elizabeth who was now averting her eyes to the floor. "I'm fine."

We turned to leave, but Elizabeth said, "My Lady, I

wish to remind you of your visitor earlier who would like to see you as soon as possible."

I fought the urge to scream at her and, instead, turned slowly so that she caught my burning stare. "No need for the reminder, Elizabeth."

"What's that about?" Luke asked as he followed me down the hallway.

"I have some errands to run," I said. "Why don't you go help Maddy get the army together, and I'll meet up with you guys when I'm done?"

"Did you want me to come with you?"

I shook my head. "No, it's fine. I'll be quick."

"Okay." His eyes were on me, but I kept mine forward. "Meet us at the training centre?"

"I'll be there as soon as I can," I finished.

He leaned over to kiss me, which I gladly received, the guilt of my secret washing over me. The kiss from Keagan was a secret I needed to keep, but was this one? If I told him, would he make me stay out of the war? And if he didn't, would it be proof that he didn't want a child? And what if we both didn't want the baby—then what?

"Something's wrong with you," Luke noticed.

"I just have a lot on my mind."

"Don't worry about your people," he said, assuming this was the reason for my distance. "They're in good hands. We'll train them well."

"Then you better get started." I smiled weakly, then

departed, leaving him to go in one direction while I went to the hospital to fire someone.

"**WHAT THE HELL** did I tell you?" I demanded when I found the doctor in the staff room. Two others were with him, but when they realized they weren't my intended target, they quickly gathered their things and left.

"I'm sorry, My Lady, I'm afraid I don't understand," Dr. Carver stumbled.

"I asked you to keep this a private matter."

"I assure you, My Lady," he began, his voice lowering to a near whisper, "that we have not told a single soul."

"And what about your visit to my home earlier today?" I demanded. "What was that all about?"

"I . . . well, I just wanted to check on you. I hadn't received word if Master Luke was able to heal you, and I was concerned about you, My Lady."

"Of course he was able to heal me," I said, irritated. "It was a freaking bump on the head."

"I'm sorry, My Lady, I didn't mean to upset you."

"It's fine," I said, trying to settle myself. It wasn't a big deal. Elizabeth knew, but that was fine. She wouldn't tell anyone.

"I assure you I was only there to check on your head. That is all." He slowly gathered his lunch items and added carefully, "Would you like me to listen for the baby's heartbeat while you're here, My Lady?"

"The heartbeat?"

"Yes." He smiled, cautiously. "It's really a beautiful experience—"

"No," I said. "We're getting an army ready for the war. Have you heard?"

"Yes, of course." He looked down at the table.

"I'm sorry," I said. "I've just been under a lot of stress lately. I'm sorry for my outburst."

"It's not trouble at all, My Lady. I should be the one apologizing. As your doctor, I was just concerned about your health."

I hated that he was walking on egg shells around me. What had I become? The last thing I wanted to be was someone that my people feared.

"I appreciate your concern," I said. "I will be in touch."

CHAPTER 6

Building Yelram's Army

~ SARAH ~

THE TRAINING CENTRE had been built long before my parents' reign, so although it was made of concrete, stone, and brick, it had seen better days. However, with two enormous training stadiums—one inside and one outside—it was the perfect place to train hundreds of to-be-warriors.

When I arrived thirty minutes later, there was a long line-up into the building and leading to the outdoor stadium, which was near full. I found Luke, Maddy, and Drew set up inside the stadium at the front of the line, interrogating each of the new recruits.

Maddy would start by taking the sheet of paper from

the recruit then asking a question. She would nod, scribble something on the paper, and hand it to Drew as the recruit moved on to him for the next part of the test. Drew would size the recruit up and ask another question or two. And then the recruit moved on from him, and it was Luke's turn. Luke always started with a surprise attack—whether it was a hit to the head, kick to the leg, or a shove to the chest. It wasn't hard, but it was quick and meant to check their reflexes. He'd ask another question, then make some notes on the paper and move them on into the next room, where they presumably waited for the outcome.

They did this for twenty minutes while I watched. No one was turned away—not even the very young or very old. They were all just sent to the indoor stadium to await their next instructions.

I joined Luke at the end of the line and collected the pile of applications on the table next to him.

"Hey, babe," he said.

"How's it going here?"

"Great. We'll probably be here all day, but we're getting through them."

Two men were waiting for their tests, so he returned his attention back to his job.

I flipped through the papers and then pulled up a chair to the table and sat down. Each paper had a handwritten number circled in the top right corner, which looked to be a sum of the three scores that Maddy, Drew, and Luke had given each recruit, the highest possible score being thirty.

"You can divide those into piles, if you want," Maddy called over her shoulder. "We have to cut six hundred, apparently." She added this as testament that she didn't like how I capped our army at four hundred when more were willing and able.

As the papers kept coming, I divided them into three piles—lowest, medium, and highest scores, and when I had the opportunity, I read the notes that were being made on each of them.

On one form, Maddy had written: "No kids / construction worker—10," while Drew had scribbled: "Fit, strong, likeable—10," and Luke scrawled: "Took a punch without flinching—10." His name was Daniel. Daniel would be in my army. Daniel would be fighting for Yelram. There was a good chance that Daniel would die.

The more forms I scanned, the louder my heart pounded, and the more sweat my palms produced. There were hundreds of applications. Hundreds of names. Hundreds of life stories and hundreds of calculations.

It took most of the day, but eventually the crowd was in the indoor stadium and we were alone to deliberate on the three stacks of paper in front of us.

Maddy tapped one of the piles. "I think we've got

some good prospects," she said.

"Yeah, I have a good feeling about this army," Luke added. "Especially if we can teach them to channel even a fraction of Sarah's energy."

"What do you mean?" Maddy asked.

"Sarah's their keeper. They should be able to channel her strength, especially with her being in battle with them."

"Sarah won't be going," Maddy said quickly.

Drew turned to study her. "We talked about this, Maddy," he said. "Of course she's going." Then he turned to me. "Sarah?"

"Yeah." I nodded, dismissing Maddy's reaction. "Of course I'm going."

"Maddy," Drew began, "Sarah is more powerful than any of us. She'll be fine. And we'll need her."

Maddy held my glare for a few seconds, then lowered her eyes.

"Okay, back to business" Luke said. He picked up the pile of highest scores. "I think we should divide them all into four groups, and we each take a group and train them. It'll be faster and easier that way."

Drew nodded. "Good idea. We'll put a mix of experienced and inexperienced together in each group so they can learn from each other."

Maddy was silent. She was trying to read me. She didn't like that I hadn't yet told Luke.

"And then we should pick one leader from each of our groups," I said, trying to draw Maddy back into the conversation, "and that person can be responsible for the group when we go into battle. It'll free us up in case we're needed elsewhere."

Luke put his hand on my shoulder. "Great idea."

"But first," Maddy said, "we need to narrow this pile down to four hundred."

"What are you talking about?" Drew asked, confused.

"Sarah only wants four hundred going into battle. We have one thousand people willing—"

"Sarah, you can't be serious," Drew said.

"Look at these," I said as I picked up the stack with the lowest numbers. I read from the first one, "Her name's Tina. She's married with one child. Her husband is also applying." I looked up at Maddy. "I'm not sure why she wasn't cut at this point." I brought my eyes back to the paper. "According to Luke, she was too fragile-looking to punch, and all Drew could say about her was that she is 'a hard-core Sarah supporter.'" I dropped the paper. "Really, guys? Why would you even consider her?"

"Sarah," Maddy tried, "these people aren't doing this because they think they have to. We didn't *make* them come here. They're here because they *want* to be here. They believe in saving Earth, and they want to be a part of that."

K.L. HAWKER

I sighed. "Then she'll be part of the reserve. Four hundred go to Earth, and the other six hundred can stay here and protect Yelram."

Maddy opened her mouth to argue, but Luke shook his head. "Okay," he said, "but they still train with the rest of them. We'll each train two hundred and fifty recruits, with the goal of taking the top one hundred from each group into battle with us."

WE DIVIDED UP the piles until we each held a stack of two hundred and fifty names of people we would train for battle. My stomach churned as I followed Luke into the stadium and stood next to him on the platform as he silenced the crowd with his presence.

He took the microphone and said, "Listen up. We're dividing you up into four groups. When your name is called, you will make your way to wherever I tell you to go. You will be given weapons when you get to your group, and we will train you in these groups. Sarah and I would like to personally thank you for your loyalty and commitment to Yelram and Earth.

"I'll be leading the first group, and we'll be starting today with combat skills. The second group is with Sarah, and you'll begin with archery skills. The third group will go with Maddy to the tiger fields where you'll practice riding. The tigers will be going into battle with us." He glanced at me when he said this. He knew it was news to

70

me, and I wouldn't like it. He was right. "And the fourth group will be with Drew and starting with sword skills. Each day, you'll rotate into another training activity. If I call your name, you're with me this evening in the outdoor stadium, left side."

Luke proceeded to read through the names in his pile, and I watched until they were all gone and the crowd in front of us was two hundred and fifty people less.

Maddy nudged me toward the microphone next. It slipped in my warm hand, but I caught it.

"And if I call your name," I started, "you will grab your weapons and head out to the right side of the outdoor stadium." I looked down at the first name, and it moved on the lines of the pages. I blinked hard and focused. "Andy Coleman . . . Jessica Rushton . . . Jason Samways . . . Brent Pottle . . . Beth Wilson." I hesitated at the sound of her name; the familiarity was enough to catch me. I looked up into the crowd and managed to find her pushing her way through the hundreds to get to the far door leading to the outdoor stadium. It *was* Beth. Beth from the mountains. Beth who helped us navigate through the dangerous, dragon-infested mountains to find the Garden of Hope. She was a true warrior and someone I felt so happy in knowing she would be with us.

I continued through the list, and when I was finished, I handed the microphone to Maddy and followed my group to the outdoor stadium.

Luke had assembled his group into ten lines of twenty-five each. They were turned in toward each other and already practicing basic blocks and punches.

On our end of the stadium, ten wooden targets stood erected at one end.

"Line up, please," I instructed, but the group was already forming lines, playing with their bows, trying out how the arrows felt between their fingers. It made me uneasy at how unnatural these people seemed with their weapons.

Once my group was organized, I stood between them and their targets, and then called on Beth to help me demonstrate how to hold a bow, aim, and release an arrow. She had the respect of many in the group already, and it was easy to see she had earned it.

Beth made her way through the lines until she was standing in front of me, and I couldn't help myself—I took her in my arms as all of the memories and emotions from our journey through the Northeast Quadrant came rushing back.

"Thank you for being here," I choked.

"It's my honour," she said. "Your Highness, I would fight next to you any day, in any war. You delivered us from hell. I would gladly lay down my life for you."

"Beth," I said, a tear spilling from my eye, "I am definitely not worthy of your sacrifice, so please don't get any crazy ideas in your head." We both smiled and embraced again. "And please, call me Sarah."

The first person in each line took a turn shooting their arrows, and as they went to fetch them, we taught the next ten how to hold, aim, and release their arrows. It worked well, and when we found more people that were already skilled with archery, we had them help teach the others, and soon, more and more arrows were hitting the targets.

"OKAY, THAT'S IT for tonight, everyone," Luke hollered over the noise of splitting targets and plucking strings. He was standing behind me and startled me.

"We're all done?" I asked, turning to see that his group was now gone.

"Everyone's done. We have cots set up inside. The recruits will sleep there." He turned his attention back to the crowd. "Head inside and grab a bed and a hot meal. You'll be in the tiger fields tomorrow, and you'll be starting early so get some rest."

It felt so strange seeing all of these new warriors trading in their comforts of home life for a cold cot and a so-called hot meal. But no one hesitated or seemed to have regrets. I followed them inside and watched as they talked excitedly to one another over their plates of food, proudly got their beds ready, pulling them together with their spouses or friends, and shined their swords before they lied their heads down.

"So that went well," Maddy said as we walked back to the palace with Drew and Luke.

"I think so," Drew agreed.

"A lot of them have some real natural talent," Luke noticed.

"That's probably because they've spent the last sixteen years fighting for their lives every day," I reminded them.

No one said anything, and I felt bad for mentioning it.

"We don't know how much time we have until Victor and Dana bring their armies to Earth," Drew pointed out, "so I think we need to keep on the recruits. Train them hard."

"What about the tigers?" I asked. "How do we choose which ones will go to Earth?"

Maddy's voice was quieter now. "Well, we only have half as many tigers as we have fighters, Sarah, so . . . we'll need them all."

Luke took my hand as we walked, knowing there wasn't anything he could say to comfort me in that moment. The tigers would die first. The enemy would target them first, knowing the fighters weren't half as fast or fierce without them.

"We'll keep a handful to breed," Luke said quietly. He

was trying to comfort me, but the thought of losing even one of these beautiful creatures was tearing me up inside.

Then Drew's key began to glow against his chest. He gripped it as his eyes widened. "It's my father," he said. "And another fire. I have to go."

Maddy reached for him, but the wind pushed her back and he was gone. "Where'd he go? What's happening?"

"His father summoned him," Luke explained. "He must need his help."

"We have to go too!" Maddy insisted.

I nodded then took my key. "Drew's house," I said, and we left Yelram.

CHAPTER 7

The Fire at St. Joseph's

~ MADDY ~

WE APPEARED IN Drew's living room, but the house was eerily quiet with no sign of Drew or his father. Luke hurried outside and checked Mr. Spencer's workshop, while Sarah checked the backyard, and I searched the bedrooms.

"Where else would he be?" I asked, desperate to know Drew was okay.

"His father summoned him," Sarah started, "and he said something about another fire. Maybe his father went to a fire to try to help, and he called Drew for backup."

"The stove was still on," Luke said as he entered the room. "Looks like Mr. Spencer left in a hurry."

Sarah picked up the TV remote from the coffee table. "Maybe it's on the news." She took a seat on the sofa, much to my frustration. Why was no one taking this seriously? Didn't anyone else see that this could be a trap? If the fire was set by Victor, and Drew's dad was in trouble, we needed to be there, too!

"We can't just *sit* here!" I protested.

"Maddy, if we knew where they were, trust me, we'd be there to help," Luke said as he joined Sarah on the sofa.

Sarah flicked through the stations until she found what she was looking for—a news anchor reporting on a burning building.

"According to our sources," the young male reporter was saying, "St. Joseph's Home for the Lost is now the sixth orphanage to catch fire in just two days, leaving us with the question: who or *what* is doing this?"

I slowly took a seat next to Sarah, and the three of us watched as the horrific scene unfolded on the television. The old two-story building was fully engulfed in flames as firefighters rushed in and out, dousing the fire with water.

"Although the number of casualties have not yet been confirmed," The reporter continued, "we are hearing that St. Joseph's was home to forty-six children ranging from three months to thirteen years of age. At this point, I am told that an unidentified man has been responsible for rescuing at least a few children from the blaze. Those children are now being attended to by emergency personnel." The reporter paused before adding sadly, "There have been no reported survivors from the previous fires."

Before the reporter could string together another sentence, a loud rumbling and creaking noise covered the air waves, and then the building collapsed from the cruelty of the flames.

Luke's hands were balled into fists on his lap. Sarah reached over and ran her hand over top of his until his opened, accepting her fingers.

"We'll get him," she promised.

Suddenly the air whipped around us, and Drew appeared in the living room, carrying his father in his arms.

"Drew!" I rushed to his side and helped lay his father on the floor. Mr. Spencer's body was scorched and almost unrecognizable. I tried not to, but I had to turn away, nearly vomiting at the sight and smell.

"Sarah!" Drew cried. "Heal him!"

Sarah hurried to Mr. Spencer's side and laid her hands on his charred body, but I knew as well as the rest of them that there was no point. Drew wasn't able to heal his father because he was already gone.

After several minutes of Drew silently crying and shaking his head back and forth as he watched Sarah fail at bringing his father back to life, Luke closed his hand over Sarah's shoulder, signaling that enough time had passed.

"I'm sorry, Drew." Sarah wrapped her arms around his waist.

A cloud of anger covered Drew's face. "I'll kill him," he growled. "I'll kill him now." He reached for his key, but Luke intercepted.

"No, man, that's not a good idea. Think about it—this is definitely what Victor wants. If you go to him, he has an army waiting for you. Waiting for *us*. Because you're not going alone, and if I'm being honest, I'd rather not die today."

Drew's eyes fixed on Luke's as he breathed heavily.

"I promise you, Drew," Luke continued, "we will kill this son of a bitch. Just not today. Not right now."

Drew's lip quivered and he turned away so that we wouldn't see his weakness. "If Victor wants a war, I'll give him one."

AFTER SOME DISCUSSION, it was decided that Mr. Spencer would be buried at Earth's portal, under the old apple tree. Having keeper blood, he wouldn't get a second life in another world, but instead, his body would become one with Earth, transferring his energy, strength, and wisdom to Earth's core for all future keepers to draw from. This was how Luke explained it, although the knowledge of this didn't seem to make Drew any less vengeful.

Drew sat for a long time under the apple tree next to the mound of fresh earth that concealed his father's fate. Sarah thought it best if she and Luke returned to Drew's house and help tidy up any painful memories of Mr. Spencer. But I stayed with Drew. Not too close, as he was distant and quiet and I wasn't entirely sure he wanted me there, but close enough for when or if he needed a hand to hold.

I tried to keep a barrier around Drew's thoughts, but they were strong, consumed with thoughts of anger, sadness, resentment, guilt, and hatred. I gently pushed positive thoughts in his direction, thinking about how much I loved him, and how proud his father was of him. I thought of the way our bodies fitted together so neatly and perfectly, and how my skin felt against his.

Eventually, Drew inhaled a long, deep breath and then exhaled.

"Are you okay?" I asked as I moved closer.

"Oh, hi. I didn't realize you were still here."

Ouch.

"You should go," he said, rather coldly.

I took a few seconds to swallow my pride, and the response that I wanted to spit out, and instead I said, "I want to be with you."

He snickered as if I was naïve or childish. "Maddy, just do yourself a favour and get out of here."

"Drew, I—"

"*Please.*"

I picked at the string on the end of my sweater, hoping and waiting for him to change his mind. He was hurting, I knew that, but why was he pushing me away? Did I not bring him comfort?

"I just want to be alone," he added when I didn't move.

"Are you staying here? Drew, I'm worried about you."

He turned his cold eyes toward mine. "Don't be," he said dismissively.

"Don't do anything stupid, okay?" I pleaded.

Drew pursed his lips in a grin, then nodded his head toward the forest, signaling his request for my departure.

I watched him through the water in my eyes as I took my key and whispered, "Drew's house."

"WHERE IS HE?" Sarah asked when I landed in the living room. She had been tidying up the blankets and pillows on the sofa.

"He didn't want me," I said, and the lump in my throat multiplied in size, prohibiting me to elaborate.

Sarah carefully set down the pillow and came to me. "Oh, Maddy, I'm sure that's not true. What did he say?"

I couldn't keep the tears from coming, so I just let them fall as I sobbed, allowing Sarah to take me in her arms. "He wanted to be alone. He was so . . . cold, Sarah."

I heard Luke enter the room and Sarah gestured to him. "Go check on Drew," she told him. Then, to me, she added, "He's hurting."

"I know." I pulled away and dried my tears on the back of my hand. "I just wish he'd let me be there with him."

"He just needs some time alone. He has pride, and he won't want anyone to see him like this. Luke will go check on him, but I'm sure he's okay. He just wants to be alone."

I nodded, telling myself that she was right. His father had died, and he just needed time to process it.

AN HOUR PASSED before Luke returned alone. There was no sign of concern or care on his brow as he strode into the room and sat down next to Sarah on the sofa.

Sarah and I both watched him, waiting for an explanation for his time away.

"He's fine," Luke assured us. "He'll be here soon."

"He's *fine*," I repeated. "Were you *with* him that whole time?"

He chuckled and nodded. "Where did you think I went?"

The familiar lump in my throat started to grow again. "I just . . . I thought . . . he wanted to be alone."

Sarah widened her eyes at Luke, something that did

not go unnoticed by me.

"Oh yeah, I mean he did," Luke covered, "but I just stayed. We talked a bit. Plotted our revenge on Victor."

"No plans were made, I hope," Sarah warned.

"Just dreams and schemes," Luke replied lightheartedly.

The air turned, and Drew appeared at the edge of the living room. Relieved that he was okay, I threw myself into his arms.

His body relaxed as his arms folded around me. We stayed like this for a long time, but still not long enough. Then he pulled away and said, "I'm okay now. You can all go home. I'll see you tomorrow for training."

The hug was nice, and his words seemed sincere—he was better after his talk with Luke. But he didn't invite me to stay the night with him. Something had changed in him, and his distance was tearing me apart.

CHAPTER 8

The Core Four

~ SARAH ~

WE TRAINED THE recruits hard for the next three days. My group had no issue connecting with the tigers and learning to trust them. We even added targets to the field so they could master shooting while riding. Then the next day we moved on to sword fighting. I enjoyed watching the recruits train as it reminded me of when Luke taught me how to use a sword.

After swordplay, we spent a day training in hand-to-hand combat. I was exhausted by this time, and Luke had to come help the group as I didn't seem to have it in me to do it myself.

After leading the recruits through yet another

offensive attack drill, Luke instructed them to continue practicing, then took a seat next to me on a bench where I watched with exhaustion. "What's going on with you?" he asked.

"I'm just tired."

He considered this, then said, "You're sleeping well, though."

I smiled and nudged my shoulder into him. He watched me for a minute, and then stood up and addressed the group, "Okay, keep working on those drills. We'll be back in a bit." He took my hand. "Let's go."

"Where are we going?"

"I think it's time we pick our leaders."

Relieved, I followed him, more than ready to hand over the fatiguing task.

Maddy was in the same stadium working on archery with her group, but Drew was working with his team in the tiger fields. Luke left to fetch Drew, and they met us in the indoor stadium where we gathered on the balcony above and watched the recruits clash swords with each other.

"They're doing great," Drew said.

"Yeah," Luke agreed. "I haven't even been with them all morning. David's leading them." He pointed to an average-build guy in black pants and a white t-shirt. "He's a quick learner, really smart, and a natural leader."

"He's your pick?" I asked.

"He's my pick."

"I like him," I said. "Okay, let's move on to my group." I led them back to the outdoor stadium where my group was still working on the drill Luke had left them with.

"Beth," I said, pointing her out as we walked by. "There's a lot of great leaders in this group, but I trust Beth the most."

"The girl from the mountains," Maddy remembered.

Luke nodded. "Yup, good pick."

Beth looked up as we walked by. She smiled nervously, knowing she was the topic of our conversation.

As we moved on to Maddy's group, she said, "Another fighter from the mountains. I pick Simon."

Simon was at the front of the line showing another how to hold his bow.

"Simon?" I asked. "I mean, sure, he's talented and brave, maybe sometimes a little stupid, but didn't he also get on your nerves?"

"Yeah, but he's different now. He's a good leader."

"Why, 'cause he's good looking?" Drew said.

"Do you think so?" Maddy teased. "I didn't think he was your type."

"Is there not anyone else in your group that you think would make a better leader?" Drew challenged. "Simon's an idiot."

"Drew," Maddy scolded. "Simon's a good fighter, and you know it. I've got a good feeling about him. I like him."

"Okay then," I said. "Settled. Simon is Maddy's pick." I knew this didn't sit well with Drew, but there wasn't much I could do about it, and dwelling on it would only upset Maddy. Personality differences aside, Simon had skill and would be a good leader.

When we reached Drew's group in the tiger fields, he was still flustered about Maddy's decision to choose Simon.

"Drew?" I prodded. "Have you decided?"

"Jenna," he said, keeping his eyes straight ahead.

"Jenna," I repeated. "She's your pick?"

"Yeah." Drew nodded toward a cluster of tigers about thirty yards from us.

"Which one is she?" I asked, searching the riders.

"Oh, let me guess," Maddy said as she pointed to a tall, pretty girl with her blonde hair in a high ponytail, swaying back and forth as she flirted with some others in the group. "Is that Jenna by chance?"

"It is." Drew smirked.

I had no doubt that Drew's decision to pick Jenna was at least in part due to the fact that he wanted to make Maddy jealous, or show her how he felt when she picked Simon. Maddy knew it, too.

"Drew, you're only picking her because she's pretty."

"Isn't that why you chose Simon?"

"Grow up, Drew," Maddy snapped. "This is serious. Pick someone else."

He narrowed his eyes on her. "No," he said. "She has skill and the others look up to her."

"I'm sure they do," Maddy hissed, "but not for the right reasons."

It was quiet for a minute while Drew and Maddy glared at each other, and when it was clear that Drew wasn't changing his mind, Luke said, "So it looks like we have our core four. Let's call them in and let them know what they're in for."

Luke and Maddy left to go collect their groups' leaders, but before Drew could leave, I held his hand and waited for Maddy to disappear around the corner.

"What?" Drew said, annoyed.

"What are you doing?"

"Jenna's got talent and skill, Sarah."

"No, I'm sure she does, Drew. I know you wouldn't intentionally screw this up. But I'm talking about Maddy. You've been so distant and cold with her. Why?"

Drew frowned but didn't answer.

"I know you love her, Drew—"

"I *don't* love her," he hissed, "and don't *ever* let anyone hear you say that!"

Completely taken aback, I shook my head and

gripped his hand harder. "You're lying. Why are you lying?"

The muscles in his jaw tensed and then he pulled his hand from mine and turned away. "I don't love anyone, Sarah."

"Drew," I tried to touch his arm, but he moved aside.

When he brought his eyes back to mine, they were glistening and full of pain. "Victor killed my father to get to me. No one I love is safe."

"Drew," I said softly, "don't be afraid to love something just because you might one day lose it."

"I'm not afraid," he said, his eyes large and cold. "I don't love her." He blinked and a tear fell down his cheek, but then he turned quickly and hurried off into the fields after Jenna.

CHAPTER 9

Techniques & Tension

~ MADDY ~

"YOU'RE HERE BECAUSE you were chosen to lead your group into battle," Luke began as David, Beth, Simon, and Jenna stood in front of us.

Simon turned to me and smiled. He knew I had chosen him. They all knew who had chosen them—Jenna included. She gave Drew a smile that wasn't just appreciative, it was suggestive, too, and I wanted to throat punch her.

"You will help train your group from now on, until the war begins," Sarah began. "At that point, you will help us select the top one hundred in your group, who you will lead to Earth for battle, and the remaining hundred and fifty will stay here as the reserve force."

"Wait," Simon interrupted, "why are we leaving a hundred and fifty behind?"

"We're not," I clarified. "We're leaving six hundred behind. A hundred and fifty from each group."

"Nice math," Drew snickered, which was directed at Simon.

"Six hundred," Simon said, ignoring Drew's dig. "Why the hell would we leave six hundred behind?"

"Watch your step," Luke warned.

"If we need them, we'll come back for them," Sarah explained. "But Yelram will need protecting too, and I'd rather not slaughter everyone if I don't have to."

Simon closed his mouth and found his place back in line, obviously as bothered by Sarah's decision as I was.

"You have your orders," Luke said. "Now go make it your personal mission to ensure the success and safety of your team."

David and Beth nodded, respectfully. Simon raised his eyebrows, seemingly having more to say, but thought better of it. Jenna kept her eyes on Drew, and when he finally noticed her, she tilted her head down so that she saw him through her long lashes, and then smiled again.

"You can go now," I said to Jenna. And she did leave, following Drew as he led her back to the mess hall where the others were gathering for lunch. Sarah, Luke, Beth, and David left next, leaving Simon and me alone.

"Thank you, Maddy," he said when we were alone. "For choosing me."

"You're welcome," I said. "You deserve it."

He smirked. "Too bad Drew didn't share the same opinion."

"I know Drew is hard on you, but he doesn't see you like I do."

"Oh? And how is that?" He stepped closer, and I wondered if this was just because our voices were low and it was hard to hear our murmurs, or if there was something else to it.

"I just mean that you're a strong fighter, and you're dependable. The others look up to you, and I think you'll make a good leader." He was watching my lips move. "Please don't let me down."

"You don't have to worry about that, Maddy. This war is going to be epic."

"Epic?" I laughed. "Strange choice of words."

"What? You're not excited?"

"I wouldn't say I'm *excited*," I said, "but between you and me, I'm not exactly dreading it, either."

"I've heard a lot about Leviathan, but never seen their powers in motion. I just think it'll be awesome to see what such dark powers are capable of."

I pulled him closer to me, shushing him with my finger. "Don't let anyone else ever hear you say that, you got it? I know you don't mean anything by it, but it does make you sound a little too untrustworthy."

We were too close now, but at least I knew no one would hear me scold him. Footsteps crossed the floor, and we separated quickly.

"Oh, listen," Drew said, "don't break it up on my account." He picked up his sword from the table and left the room before I could explain. I wished I had an easy explanation. How could I explain that I was trying to keep Simon in line already? Had I made a mistake in choosing him?

WHEN THE SUN was beginning to set, and my head was starting to pound like the arrows striking the targets, we sent the recruits in for dinner and some downtime before bed. Luke called a meeting with the core four, and the eight of us met in a private room, this being the first time I saw Drew since lunch. He kept a cold distance, and it bothered me more than I thought it would to see Jenna standing so closely to him, even if Drew didn't seem to notice. It wouldn't take her long to sink her perfectly manicured nails into him.

Luke addressed the core four. "From here on out, you four will be in charge of training. We'll be there to help, but it'll be up to you to lead them and earn their trust." The four nodded. "We'll spend an hour with you every morning and every evening, showing you all that we know, so that you can teach your groups."

I liked this idea. It would mean Drew wouldn't have to spend all day, every day next to Jenna. We would all train the core four together, and then Jenna could go off and lead her own group, if she was even able to. I still wasn't convinced that Drew knew what he was doing.

"I think our biggest weakness is in hand-to-hand combat," Luke said. "We have a lot of smaller fighters and we need to spend more time teaching them to be smarter fighters."

"But did you notice how those smaller fighters are sharp shooters with the bows?" Simon asked.

"I did," Luke said.

"And they're great with their swords," Simon continued.

Drew rolled his eyes and leaned against the wall, happy to let Luke teach Simon a lesson.

"I'm not sure what you're getting at, Simon," Luke said.

"I just mean that we don't really need to focus on the one thing they're *not* good at, when they're great at everything else."

I cringed because I knew this wasn't the position he should've taken. Beth leaned forward and gave Simon a warning look, which he seemed to ignore.

"Simon," Luke began, "I know you don't have much experience with dark lords, so I'm going to give you a break on this one. But consider this—we're going to storm Earth with four hundred warriors and about half that many tigers. We'll probably put the smaller fighters on the tigers so they have a better chance, and they'll use their bows from a distance, but soon they'll be too close for arrows. At this point, the tigers will be fighting the other dark world creatures—fire-breathing dragons, ferocious oversized panthers, and enormous black stallions—and so our warriors will be on the ground fighting. And what happens if they lose their sword? If that's the only thing keeping them alive, then they're as good as dead."

Sarah gripped her head and sat down. She hated hearing the ugly truth about the war—at least some of her people were going to be slaughtered.

"I get that," Simon began, "but—"

"And the other thing you should know about dark lords," Luke said, cutting him off, "is that whether you agree with them or not, you should learn when to shut the hell up."

Drew snickered as Simon stepped back into line.

"I agree with Simon," I said, "in that the warriors are making great progress in the other areas, but I also agree with Luke that they need more combat experience." I hoped this would smooth things over and show Simon that I still backed him. I didn't want him to get discouraged. He meant well, he just had a tendency to want to rise to the top too quickly.

Luke took Sarah's hand and led her into the centre of the room. "To demonstrate how a small fighter can use their size against a larger, stronger opponent, watch Sarah and me."

Sarah squared off in front of Luke. She raised her fists and began her light bounce on the balls of her feet.

"Stop!" I shouted, immediately enraged at Sarah's lack of consideration for the fact that she was carrying a child. "Sarah," I prompted, giving her the opportunity to back out of the fight, but she didn't. She only looked at me briefly, shook her head, and brought her eyes back to Luke's.

"Okay, well obviously," I said, "it'll be easier for the core four to learn if they're part of the fight."

"Fair," Luke said, then nodded to David. "You're up." David stepped forward, taking Luke's place in front of Sarah. Luke leaned in and muttered, "Hurt her and I'll hurt you."

"Okay, that's a little ridiculous," I said, desperate to stop anyone from hurting Sarah, or worse, Yelram's future heir. "Simon and I are obviously a better match. Simon, come here. Sarah, sit down."

Sarah scowled at me but didn't argue as she took her place next to Luke. Drew folded his arms, annoyed at my suggestion to fight Simon, but there wasn't anything I could do about it. It was more important to protect Sarah from a miscarriage than it was to protect Drew's feelings.

"Okay, Simon," Luke said with a chuckle, "let's see what you got."

Simon took the first swing. He was fast, but it wasn't as hard as it could've been. I blocked it, and as I was preparing for my counter-punch, his right hand came out of nowhere and smashed into the side of my face. I fell to the floor, but got up quickly, thankful I hadn't let Sarah take the fight. I shook off the dizziness and ignored whatever Drew was shouting. Simon came at me again, this time with a kick. I jumped up at the same time, leveraged myself off of his leg, and kicked him in the chest. He stumbled back, but not enough for me to continue an attack. I was a smaller fighter, so I had to be smarter. I had to use his moves against him, so unless he was in a vulnerable position, I had to wait until his next move.

We circled each other for a few seconds, then he made a move toward me. I stepped back in response as if it were a dance and our movements were the same. Then our eyes met, and I suddenly remembered Luke's instruction back at the cabin in the woods when Drew and Luke first decided to take Sarah and me on our dream worlds mission. Luke had told Sarah to stop watching Drew's arms and legs, but instead look in his eyes and predict his next move. He would've known then that Sarah was Yelram's missing keeper, so he probably suspected she was gifted with mindbending, which meant that the technique he was teaching her was most likely to see if she was able to use it. Regardless, I was no match for Simon. He was stronger, faster, and a smarter fighter than me, which meant if I wanted to win this fight, I had to predict his next moves.

His almond-shaped eyes were dark and mysterious, but handsome all at the same time. There was a depth to them that I didn't understand, but was curious to learn. Suddenly I was on the ground and my ribs burned. I jumped back up and hissed at the pain that seared through my side where his foot must've just hit. How did I miss that?

He was smiling, but I saw a flicker of his concern as Drew was next to me now, trying to help me up. I pushed his hand away. "Leave me. I'm fine," I hissed.

My eyes were locked with Simon's. I slowly stood, favouring my left side, and this time I saw his eyes flash to my left leg. I prepared for it, and as his leg came sweeping around, I timed my jump so that I leveraged myself off of his knee and drove my own knee into his chin, sending him to the ground. I hooked my arm around his neck and squeezed until he tapped out, then I dropped him to the ground to catch his breath as Sarah came to me and put her hands on my ribs, touched my split lip, and ran her fingers over my chin.

"See?" Luke said as he helped Simon up from the ground. "It's not all about the attack. Sometimes strategic defence can be more helpful than aggressive offense."

Simon extended his hand to shake mine, and as I reached for his, a pain shot through my side. I tried to recover quickly, but my injuries were noticeable. Hadn't Sarah healed me? She was watching me with curious concern, but in an effort to not draw attention, I returned to my place against the wall next to Simon. It didn't overly hurt, anyway. Nothing was broken. Just Sarah.

We trained with the new leaders for over an hour, with Luke showing us new ways to trick the opponent and use their strengths against them. We mostly watched Beth and Jenna take turns against David and Simon, while Luke healed the injured (Sarah feigned exhaustion as her reason for not healing). I wanted to join in and train too, but I knew if I did, it gave reason for Sarah to, so I sat out with her and just watched the other fights, giving pointers when I could.

Finally, energy levels dwindled and Jenna announced she was going to take a shower. I was pleased to see Drew ignore her. David and Beth followed her from the room, and as Simon was about to leave, Drew grabbed him by the arm and pulled him aside.

"Listen," he said, his voice low and steady enough that Luke, Sarah, and I pretended not to notice, "I just want you to know that I think you're a good fighter."

"Thank you," Simon said, and I smiled to myself as I picked up my bag of arrows from the ground.

"But," Drew continued, "if you ever hurt Maddy like that again, I will kill you."

I froze. Sarah did, too, but Luke was grinning, still pretending not to listen.

"No offence, man, but I know Maddy better than you think. I know what she can handle."

I dropped my satchel and hurried to step between them. "I got it from here, Simon, thank you." I dismissed him, and he left with a nod to me and a smirk to Drew. Luke and Sarah followed his leave, Sarah giving me a sympathetic look as they passed.

"What the hell was that?" Drew shouted the minute we were alone.

"What?"

"*I know Maddy better than you think.*"

"He meant nothing by it, Drew."

"*Simon and I are obviously a better match,*" he mimicked in a high-pitched voice that was presumably supposed to be mine when I was trying to stop Sarah from having to fight.

"You're insane," I said, because I couldn't tell him why I had to fight Simon.

"*I'm* insane?" he laughed sardonically. "So I'm reading this all wrong, then? You didn't just want to spar with Simon for no reason? And he didn't just tell me that you two are close."

I shook my head. "I don't know what you heard,

Drew, but that's not what he meant."

"Then tell me why that just happened?"

"I can't!" I blurted, and then my eyes went wide and I hoped he wouldn't press me further.

"You can't," he said slowly.

"Just leave it alone, Drew! It's no big deal!"

His eyes were wide and his mouth was slack. "It's no big deal."

Then I lost my cool. "What right do you have to talk to me like this right now? You haven't touched me in days, and I know you just lost your father and we're getting ready for a war, but you're not the same. So you tell *me*, Drew—what the hell is going on here?"

"You're changing the subject," he said, his anger matching mine.

"I'm not at all, Drew. You're sitting here accusing me of having feelings for someone else when all I want is for *you* to hold me. All I want is to be *your* girl." I surprised myself with my boldness. "All I want is for you to—"

"If that's what you want, then what are you keeping from me?"

I shook my head. "No," I said. "You don't get to do that. You don't get to bribe me with your affection."

He threw his fist into the table. "Why won't you tell me what you're keeping from me? Is it Simon? Do you like him? Just tell me, Maddy! I can take it!"

Before I could respond, his hand went straight to his

key. He pulled it from his shirt—it was glowing red. His jaw clenched, and he pulled me out of the room where we ran into Luke and Sarah in the hallway.

"Do you think it's started?" Sarah asked, studying the key in Drew's hand.

"It doesn't feel like it," Drew said, "but there's only one way to find out."

"Come on," Sarah said. "Let's go check it out and come back for the armies if it's time."

"No, Sarah," I said. "We'll go. You stay here."

"Don't, Maddy," Sarah warned.

"Yeah, Maddy," Drew said. "It's *no big deal*."

If only he knew the reason for my elusiveness. If only I hadn't been forbidden to tell him Sarah's secret.

Luke took Sarah's hand. "We're wasting time. Let's meet at the portal." He grabbed his key. "Take us to Earth."

Drew took my hand. "Take us home."

I loved how he sometimes forgot that I had my own key and could transport myself.

CHAPTER 10

To Earth

~ SARAH ~

VICTOR, DANA, KEAGAN, and Riley stood less than thirty feet away, expecting our arrival. A blaze of fire encircled the portal, trapping us inside with them. Luke and Drew stepped forward, putting Maddy and I behind them.

"It's about time," Dana said. "You kept us waiting." There was an eager smile to her otherwise stoic face.

"What do you want?" Drew said, his eyes narrowed on Victor. Like me, he wondered where their armies were, and why the four of them were waiting for our arrival. But his thirst for revenge was challenging his ability to remain calm.

"We'd like Earth," Dana said simply. "As you know, Earth has been on a path of self-destruction for a long time now. We just want to speed things up, and we'd like to make an offer."

"You want to make an offer for *Earth*. Not happening."

"Drew, you know as well as anyone, Earth has no future. There is too much negative energy here now. If you fight us, you won't just lose Earth, but you'll lose every single warrior you send in to protect it."

My heart quickened. Was this a dead-end mission? Were we needlessly slaughtering hundreds of innocent people?

"Alternatively," Dana continued, "you can just hand over Earth's key now, and step away while you still can."

"And why would we do that?" I said. "When you destroy Earth, our worlds will crumble, too."

Dana's eyes found mine and Luke's hand tightened around his sword as he moved closer to my side.

"So, no deal?" Dana said. "That's disappointing. I guess we'll have to carry on as planned."

"And what exactly does that mean?" Maddy asked.

Dana sneered. "It's a surprise."

Riley stepped forward, glaring at Maddy. "I see blondie's wearing a key. She must be your second-in-command now, is she, Sarah?"

I lifted my chin, proudly. "She is."

"Don't talk to her," Luke spat at his brother.

"No, I just think it's interesting, is all," Riley said. "I mean, all these humans becoming second-in-commands."

My eyes flickered to Keagan's.

"That's right," Riley said, an arrogance to his tone that I didn't like. "First Maddy, then Keagan. I mean, what are the worlds coming to?"

Luke's arm flexed under my grip, but I held him there, knowing Riley was just trying to goad him.

Riley went on, "Yeah, and I hear Keagan's a pretty good shapebender now, too. Kind of got that whole craft down pat, don't ya, Keag?"

Keagan found my eyes, and I felt my face redden, fearing that he was about to divulge our kiss.

"So, Maddy," Dana began, "now that you're Sarah's second, why don't you tell us what your new craft is? What is Yelram's oh-so-secretive power?"

Maddy glanced at me, and I tried to keep the confusion from my face since she was having a harder time masking it from hers. Keagan knew about my mindbending. He knew that it was Yelram's craft, which would then become Maddy's. If he was Dana's second, he would've told her. Why was she pretending he hadn't?

Keagan was watching me, but his cold stare was now a little softer. He hadn't told her! Was there a part of him that was still trying to protect me?

"Oh, come on," Dana said, mocking impatience. "We told you our secret weapon—Keagan's a shapebender. Why won't you tell us yours?"

"We didn't ask you to tell us," Maddy said, trying to avoid the question.

"I suppose it wasn't really a secret anymore, though, was it?" She turned her eyes to mine. "You knew, didn't you, Sarah?" She blinked, and her eyes were now on Luke. She was baiting me. She blinked again and brought her eyes back to mine. "Or did you think when Keagan kissed you the other day that it was actually Luke?"

Luke's arm slipped from my grip and he threw Dana aside with a blast of wind, took a few fast strides forward, and hurled his fist into Keagan's face. Keagan fell back but recovered quickly. He changed into a dragon and blew fire at Luke who dived out of the way as I hurled a stream of water toward the fire with one hand, and a fireball toward the dragon with the other.

"A firebender," Victor spoke, breaking the ominous silence that encircled him. His voice was much darker and stronger than I had imagined.

"I'm not like you," I hissed as a sea of anger churned inside of me. "I don't murder innocent people!"

"Then what are you, Sarah?" he asked.

"She's none of your business!" Luke shouted.

"I'm half keeper and half human," I told Victor.

Victor held out his hand and fire licked his fingers as he moved them, seductively caressing the air. "Yes, a hybrid," he chuckled. "I heard the rumours that your mother was a human spirit. I guess this means you have dreamer powers, too. Let's see what you can do."

"I don't have to prove anything to you."

Luke was between us now, expecting Victor to throw the fire at me, but I knew that he wouldn't. He was testing me. Testing my strength and my restraint. And there was a small part of him that was wary of me. Not quite afraid, and not just curious. He was wary.

"What other powers do you have?" he asked again, and his eyes lit up, showing me his curiosity, although he tried to mask it with indifference.

"Don't answer that," Luke said over his shoulder to me.

"All of them," I answered.

Victor's hand squeezed the fireball slightly, enough to tell me that this answer was one he had both suspected and feared.

"So you think you'll be able to stop us?" His greed for knowledge was overpowering his self-control.

"I never said that." I let my mouth curl up slightly but my eyes stayed locked on his. I had his mind, but he didn't yet know it. "What is your plan?" I asked calmly, imploring his mind to answer me immediately.

"To kill you all, then take Earth," he said too quickly.

Dana glanced at Victor, unnerved by his boldness.

"Why?" I prodded.

"Because it's the heart of the worlds," Victor answered. "With Earth's power, I could conquer any world. Any universe."

"How do you plan to take it?" I knew I was pushing it, but there was more he wasn't telling me.

"With the elements—"

"Victor!" Dana hissed.

If I didn't let his mind go a little, she would know what I was doing. He was telling me too much. But I pushed just a little further so that he would elaborate on their plan.

"I will go after each stone until I own every human being on the planet, then I will find Earth's stone and no one will be able to stop me with an army of human warriors—"

"VICTOR!" Dana shouted, and I let go of his mind.

"I won't let you do that," I said, and Victor believed me. He knew I was powerful enough to stop him. I made him believe this.

"You have a weakness," he said, and his eyes flashed to Luke.

I clenched my jaw. "He's not a weakness. He's my strength."

Dana pulled her sword and held it out at Luke, who counteracted with his own sword. "And what if I kill him right now?" she said.

"You can't," I said darkly, then flicked my wrist and she flew through the air. Keagan caught her, and with the tensions running as high as they were, the fight finally broke out.

Dana roared as she ran toward me with her sword blazing. Luke threw her away again with a gust of wind, but Keagan was coming at him now, and he turned his attention to Keagan while Dana came back at me.

Drew advanced on Victor, flying through the air toward him and kicked him in the chest as he came down. Victor threw a ball of fire at him, which was the last thing I saw before I was engaged in a sword fight with Dana.

I tried to grip her mind, but my thoughts were everywhere—on Luke fighting Keagan, and Drew fighting Victor, and now Maddy doing everything she could to defend herself against Riley. She was holding her own, from what I could see from my quick glances in her direction as I clashed swords with Dana. Keagan and Luke had dropped their swords and were now fighting with fists. Luke kicked him hard, and Keagan soared through the air at least ten feet, hitting Riley, which gave Maddy a small advantage. But my eyes lingered on them for too long, and the next thing I knew, Dana had me pinned to the ground with her sword at my throat.

"Any last words?" she said as she dug her foot into my chest and pulled the sword high.

This was it. I could see my friends fighting, but knew that if I called for their help, the distraction could kill them. Keagan had an advantage over Luke in that he could change shape, but it took strength from him and Luke was stronger. Drew was able to fly out of the way of Victor's fire, but he was distracted by Maddy who wasn't beating Riley.

Riley kicked Maddy hard, and she fell to the ground, and when she looked up, our eyes locked. She saw Dana's sword in the air above my head. I closed my eyes as I didn't want to see the horror in hers as Dana's sword came closer, and there was nothing I could do.

Maddy screamed, "STOP! SHE'S PREGNANT!"

Dana's sword halted. Everyone froze.

Keagan and Luke were bloody from beating each other, but they now stood side-by-side, breathing heavy, both stunned by what they had just heard. Riley's jaw had fallen slack and there was a struggle in his stare that confused me. And Victor . . . Victor was smiling.

"Ahhh, her weakness," Victor said. "Let the war begin."

Luke and Riley both threw their hands in my direction, then Dana lost her grip on her sword as we flew through the air together, the trunk of the apple tree coming too fast.

And then there was darkness.

CHAPTER 11

Change of Plans

~ MADDY ~

SARAH'S BODY HIT the tree and folded to the ground. Without concern for anything else, I raced toward Sarah and dove to the ground next to her. With my key in one hand, and Sarah's arm in my other, I ported us back to Yelram.

My whole body trembled with adrenalin as we landed in the palace foyer. I scooped Sarah up in my arms and began screaming for help.

Elizabeth burst through a doorway down a corridor. "Maddy? Maddy! What is it?" She met us at the bottom of the staircase and frantically ran her hands over Sarah's body searching for the story of her condition.

A few others, including Oma, the cook, had hurried to the scene of the commotion.

"Get the doctor!" Elizabeth shouted to a man that guarded the doors. "Now!"

The man left, hastily, while others joined us in carrying Sarah's body up the staircase and into her bedroom where we laid her softly on her bed.

I pushed my hands through my air, still processing everything that had transpired within the last ten minutes. As I slowly backed up toward the door, I heard Drew and Luke's arrival. Luke's voice boomed throughout the corridors: "Where is she?!"

A smaller voice directed him to the bedroom and when he entered, I couldn't bring my eyes to his. He pushed past me, then Elizabeth, while Omar and two other men backed away, their eyes full of concern and fear.

Luke knelt next to Sarah's bed and pressed both hands into the sides of her head. "Come on, Sarah," he muttered.

Drew joined me and just stood next to me, afraid to go any closer.

After a minute, Luke stood and yelled, "Where the hell is the doctor?"

"He's coming, Luke," I said, and I noticed the waiver in my voice. Drew noticed it, too, and put his arm around me.

Another minute later, a team of doctors rushed into the room as another team of staff pushed in equipment — monitors, tubes, medicine, bandages. Unsure of what they were going to find, it appeared they brought everything.

Dr. Carver searched the room for me and when our eyes met, he gave me his concern: was the baby still a secret?

"She's pregnant," I announced to the room. "Make sure the baby is okay, too."

A few gasped, Elizabeth's shoulders fell in relief, and the doctor nodded his thanks before continuing his care and assessment of Sarah and her baby.

"Don't worry about *that*," Luke shouted. "Fix *her*!"

I noticed Elizabeth's horror at Luke's insensitive response.

"Okay, everyone out of the room," I said. "The doctors need their space."

I said thank you and goodbye to the men who helped carry Sarah upstairs, and nodded our thanks to the extra hospital staff who helped bring in the equipment. Soon it was just three doctors, Luke, Elizabeth, Drew, and me. I slid my hand into Drew's and led him out into the empty hallway.

Drew dropped my hand and took a step away. He was quiet for a few minutes before asking, "Are you okay?"

I nodded, my eyes stinging with the threat of tears. "It was so scary, Drew. I thought she was dead."

He swallowed and nodded, too. "You did well against Riley. I'm sorry I couldn't help more."

"Don't be. You fought *Victor*. How did *that* feel?"

Drew shook his head. "He's stronger than I ever thought possible. I'm glad it ended when it did."

There was another pause of ominous silence, and I tried not to read his thoughts, but he wasn't guarding them, and if I wasn't mistaken, he wanted me to hear them. He was upset with me. He was hurt.

"Now you know my secret," I said quietly.

"Which one? Sarah being pregnant? Or her kissing Keagan?"

I winced. "Both."

"Maddy, you never should've kept those things from me. Or Luke."

"I know, but what could I—"

Luke entered the hallway, silencing my response. He pounded his fists into the wall and stayed there with his head pressed against the hard wood.

"How is she?" Drew asked.

"Alive."

"And the baby?" I asked.

Luke turned and glared at me so darkly that I regretted asking.

"How long's it been?" he asked, a hard coldness to his

words.

"I don't know. She's maybe two or three months along. We only found out when—"

"I'm not talking about that! I don't care about that! How long has she been keeping the secret about Keagan? When did he kiss her?!"

My mouth closed in response to his coldness and anger. "Same day we found out she was pregnant," I said defiantly.

"WHEN?!"

"Well, if you had let me finish the first time, you'd know!" I shouted back.

Luke stepped forward. "Don't toy with me, Maddy!"

Drew stepped between us and turned his eyes to mine, silently urging me to play nice. He probably knew there was a better chance of calming me down than Luke.

"He came to Yelram the same day the fires started on Earth. He appeared as you, but when he kissed her, she pushed him away. She knew it wasn't you. Lucia tried to tear him apart, but he bent into a tiger and they fought. Keagan left and Sarah fainted, so I took her to the hospital, and that's when we found out she was pregnant."

"At least Lucia had some common sense. You should've killed him."

"And that's why Sarah didn't tell you. She figured it was part of their plan to get you to go after Keagan. She thought it was a trap."

Luke laughed mockingly. "So she lied. Nice."

"She did it to protect you, Luke."

He looked away, took in a deep breath, and narrowed his eyes. Once he exhaled, he said, "I can't heal her. It'll end up killing her if she doesn't learn how to block it."

"What do you mean?" Drew pressed.

"How do you think it's still alive in there? It should've died after a hit like that." He clenched his jaw. "But it's practically invincible because it takes all of her healing abilities."

I knew the "it" to which he was referring was "the baby," which made me wonder if Sarah's fear was right — that Luke never wanted a baby.

"So how does she get better?" I asked, my voice shaking with concern.

Luke just stared into the distance. He didn't have an answer, and his guilt for being the one to put Sarah in that situation was tearing him up inside.

"You saved her life," I gently reminded him.

His face hardened. "Our plans have changed," he said darkly. "Victor and Dana don't want to destroy Earth. They're going to take it over using the elements."

"What are the elements?" I asked.

"They're gemstones embedded in pieces of armour," Drew said. "All infused with a power so great that whoever wears it will be stronger and more deadly than anything you can imagine."

"Every world has an element on Earth that stores and controls its power," Luke explained.

I just stared at them, so many questions on my tongue, but not knowing where to start.

Seeing my confusion, Drew began, "When Earth was formed, it was just a sphere of authority that kept the worlds connected with its powerful energy. Its heartbeat. The worlds knew how important the heart was for survival, so they worked together to create an indestructible protective barrier. Leviathan covered the Heart in a liquid fire so hot that it would melt anything that came too close. Lorendale then covered the fire in rock, iron, and nickel, creating a firm foundation for the rest of the worlds to leave their coat of protection. Nevaeh sent a brilliant blue waterfall that covered the new world in the powerful oceans we see today. Etak brought twisters of air that covered the water and moved at its own will—sometimes gently, other times violent, but always moving and ready. And Nitsua brought living things that could morph and evolve into powerful, magnificent creatures that could protect the Heart."

"What about Yelram?" I asked hesitantly. "How did Yelram help protect Earth?"

Drew grinned and his eyes softened. "Yelram brought free will and independence to every living being, by fortifying their minds so that they could access the energy from all of the worlds—they could bend air, ground, water, fire, shapes, and even gravity."

"Which is why the elements were placed," Luke added, almost as if he were disgusted. "Manmade wars began destroying Earth, and humans became too strong. It was either the elements were placed, or we risked losing the Heart."

"What do the elements do?" I asked.

Drew answered, "The elements were created with the purest form of energy from each world, and then placed on Earth to store and control each world's powers. Eventually, as the worlds separated and became more independent from each other, so did the elements. They broke off from each other, creating the seven continents we know today."

"So there's an element on each of the seven continents?" I wondered aloud. "And now Victor wants to take the elements for himself? What will that prove?"

"If the elements are removed, the powers of the worlds can't be contained. There will be earthquakes, mass fires, floods, tornadoes, hurricanes, you name it," Luke said. "If Victor possesses the elements, he will have their powers. And if he manages to find Earth's element, he can control every single human alive."

"He *won't* get Earth's element," Drew said, almost before Luke was finished.

There was an uncomfortable silence before Luke

continued, "Victor and Dana know where their elements are, and once they retrieve those, their elements will lead them to Lorendale's and Nevaeh's elements."

"Why will they lead them to Lorendale's and Nevaeh's?" I asked.

"Because the dark and light worlds are paired, for balance. Back when Earth was created, the word 'dark' meant something different. The dark worlds weren't *bad*, they were just different. Balanced."

"So they'll be able to find four of the seven elements," I said, trying to keep it all straight. "And what can they do with them?"

Drew glanced uneasily at Luke. "If Victor wears the elements, every single human destined for those worlds will belong to him and share his thoughts and desires."

"Which are . . .?"

"Get rid of us so his job will be easier," Luke added darkly.

Drew nodded. "With each element they possess, they'll have more and more humans on their side, believing and thinking the same way they do."

Suddenly the heaviness of the situation was weighing down on me as I realized the severity of our dilemma. "Can Victor make them fight us? There are literally billions of humans, Drew. How will we win this?"

"Without Earth's element, Victor and Dana can't *make* the humans join their armies," Drew explained.

"But," Luke interjected, "humans have free will so if they want to join, they can. And if Victor gets his hands on Earth's element, he can take away their free will, turning them into super warriors, hell bent on one purpose."

"To kill us."

Drew and Luke exchanged a look before Drew answered, "Their first purpose will be to get rid of us. We're the ones standing in their way."

"How do we ensure they don't get Earth's element?" I asked.

"None of the other elements can lead them to Earth's element," Drew explained. "It's hidden and I intend to keep it that way."

What were we getting ourselves into? This all was beginning to sound a little more impossible. Were we setting ourselves up for certain failure? What was our alternative? Did we even have one?

"Before you say it," Drew began, "the keepers have to go to Earth. Their armies aren't nearly as strong without them."

"But Sarah," I said.

There was a long pause before Luke said, "Obviously Sarah can't go now."

"Etak and Yelram have merged," Drew said, "so maybe Luke's presence will bring some strength to Yelram's army." He didn't believe his own words.

Neither did Luke.

Luke's hands balled into fists before he turned and went back into Sarah's room, leaving Drew and me alone in the hallway.

"He's upset," I said.

"Can you blame him?" There was a hardness to Drew's face that suggested he was angry, too. But not at the dark lords; at me.

"Drew," I started, "I'm sorry."

His face softened, but the hardness was replaced with hurt. "I thought we were a team," he said.

"We were. We *are*." I reached for him, but he backed away and took his key.

"I have to go back to Earth," he said.

"What? Why? You can't go back there, Drew. It's not safe."

"I have to warn the world leaders about what's coming. They'll need to get their armies ready in case we need them."

"Please don't go," I begged.

"I'll be back in the morning to help you with Yelram's army." He hesitated as if he were going to reach for me, but then thought better of it. The air whipped around my body as he departed, leaving me cold, lonely, and full of regret.

THE CHAOS OF scurrying doctors continued throughout

the evening. Sarah's room was full of contraptions that monitored her breathing and heartrate, and machines that scanned her body for internal bleeding and swelling. The most important device was one that surrounded her head and was responsible for monitoring her brain activity.

I hated seeing her in that condition. Luke did, too, evidenced by his constant pacing and violent outbursts that would lead to him leaving the room, only to return several minutes later with red puffy eyes and swollen fists.

After a difficult goodbye, Elizabeth left for the night. Her apartment, which she shared with her daughter, was in the palace, and she promised she was only a holler away if we needed anything.

Luke visibly relaxed when she was gone, and I allowed myself to read his thoughts long enough to learn that he was irritated by her constant presence. Taking care of Sarah was his job, and he didn't like sharing it with Elizabeth.

It was near midnight when I finally allowed myself to curl up in the window seat and close my eyes for only a moment. Soft footsteps crossed the floor and Dr. Carver covered me with a warm blanket.

"Get some sleep, Miss. You'll need your strength."

I smiled, but it was weak with exhaustion. Luke was leaning against an armoire, his eyes glued to Sarah. I wondered if he would sleep tonight, or if he . . .

And then I was asleep.

"ARE YOU SURE?" It was Luke's voice, and although it was hushed, it still startled me out of sleep.

"She's been stable all night. No internal bleeding or swelling, and her brain activity is improving. She'll be fine," Dr. Carver finished.

I pushed the blanket off and slowly stood. "She's going to be okay?"

Dr. Carver was mildly optimistic. "According to all of the data we're receiving, yes, she will be fine. The rest is up to her. Once she wakes, plenty of rest and time is all she'll need."

"Thank you," I said.

"Maddy, go wake the army and get them training," Luke ordered.

I looked outside at the pitch black sky, then down at my watch. It was 3:33am. "Luke—"

"You heard the doctor, Maddy. Sarah will be fine, and we have a war to prepare for."

I closed my mouth and bit my tongue. My guess was that he had spent the night pacing the floors instead of sleeping.

I pushed past him and went to Sarah. I stroked her face, then bent down to kiss her forehead. "I'll be back," I promised.

THE SKY WAS still dark and the streets were quiet and still. Even as I approached the training centre, all lights were out, and the only sound that could be heard was an occasional snoring of one or two sleeping warriors.

I slipped through the front doors and quietly walked through the building toward the sleeping quarters, dreading having to wake one thousand physically exhausted people. But, I told myself, it would be better to be woken by me than Luke.

Outside the sleeping quarters, I noticed someone sitting in the hallway, his silhouette lit only by a soft light above him. He was sharpening the blade on his knife, and when I got closer, I realized it was Simon.

"What are you doing?" I questioned as I approached.

"Can't sleep," he said. "You alone?" he looked passed me down the dark hallway.

I nodded and swallowed the emotions that floated too near the surface.

"How's Sarah?" He lowered his knife and watched me carefully.

"Doctor said she'll be okay."

"Pregnant, huh?" He gave me a half-smile. "News travels fast." When I didn't answer, he said, "Where's Drew and Luke?"

"Luke's with Sarah; Drew went back to Earth."

"Earth," Simon repeated. "Doesn't sound like the

safest place to be on your own right now."

"That's what I tried to tell him."

He watched me, and I pretended not to notice. "He should listen to you more often."

I smirked. "Wouldn't that be nice."

"You deserve to be happy, Maddy."

"Sorry, Simon, I know you mean well, but it's probably best if you don't worry about me. Thank you, though."

He nodded and returned his attention to sharpening his knife. "I'm here if you ever want to talk."

"Appreciate it."

I turned toward the door and took a deep breath.

"Why are you here?" Simon asked, noticing my hesitation.

"Luke wants me to get everyone back into the training ring."

Simon jumped to his feet. "Couldn't agree more." He pushed open the doors and clapped his hands together. "Rise and shine, everyone! Break time's over! A war's coming! Get up!"

I stood in the doorway, thankful for not having to be the one to carry out the cruel task. Simon continued walking up and down the aisles, clapping his hands and shouting. I couldn't help but laugh to myself. Yeah, he was a good leader.

CHAPTER 12

Bed Rest

~ SARAH ~

MY HEAD THROBBED as if it were caught in a vice grip. I tried to touch it, but my arms were stiff and unwilling. I tried to speak, but it came out as an unintelligible groan.

"Did you hear that?" a gentle voice said, and then I felt something soft touch my face, followed by footsteps crossing the floor, and then a loud thud as if a heavy book had been dropped on the floor. Or a door suddenly slamming shut from the wind. I wished I could see, but my head was plagued with pain and my thoughts were covered with cloud.

A female voice muttered something. Something sarcastic maybe. I sensed frustration. I focused harder and tried to move, but I was pinned to my place.

As the fog in my head began to clear, my eyelids slowly lifted, filling my vision with light. I quickly closed them again and groaned. We weren't on Earth anymore, and my bedroom was filled with early afternoon sun, so time had passed. My body was warm and cocooned in a thick white blanket, and Elizabeth was positioning a hot water bottle on my abdomen.

"There you are, Sarah," she said softly. "How are you feeling, love?"

"Where's Luke?" My throat was dry and sore.

"He was just here," she answered as she replaced the cloth on my forehead with a cold one. "He needs some time alone."

Had those been his footsteps walking away and the door slamming as he left?

"My head," I whimpered.

"Yes, you had another nasty fall," Elizabeth said, and then added more quietly, "which is why the idea of you fighting in a war is a bit ridiculous if you ask me."

"Does the doctor know?"

"Oh yes, he's been here since yesterday. He left an hour ago for some rest. He was the one who insisted we set up your care here and not at the hospital. He said this is what you'd want—privacy."

I tried to nod, but it hurt.

"We've given him the west wing to set up. He's

moved in and will be here frequently to check on you and the baby." She said it as if it didn't matter what my thoughts were on the matter, it had already been decided upon.

The door opened and Maddy came in, her sword swinging at her side.

"How is she?" Maddy asked.

"She just woke up," Elizabeth answered as she busied herself with taking my temperature. "And she's looking for Luke."

Maddy waited for her to read the thermometer and then she motioned for her to take her leave. "I need a minute with her," she said.

"What's going on?" I asked when Elizabeth was gone. "Where is Luke?"

"He's fine. He's here."

"Where?"

Maddy clenched her jaw. "I just passed him in the hallway. He's been with you, but I guess now that you're awake . . . he just needs some time, Sarah."

"Why? What happened?"

"Oh, I don't know," she started sarcastically, "first he finds out you kissed Keagan and didn't tell him, and then he finds out you were pregnant and he was the last one to know about it."

"*Were* pregnant?" I asked, an odd mixture of relief and sadness mingling with each other as I considered the real possibility that I might have lost the baby in the fight.

"*Are* pregnant," she clarified. "You're still pregnant."

"What happened?" I shook my head, trying to remember the details of our encounter with the dark lords.

"I told everyone. I had to. Dana was about to kill you. It was the only thing I could think of." She turned away from me. "And I'm not sorry, either. You should never have been there. You should never have kept that from everyone."

"She didn't kill me," I realized, ignoring Maddy's lecture and focusing instead on the fact that I was still alive.

"Only because she was caught off guard and Luke blew her off of you." Maddy looked down. "The force knocked you out." A grin covered her lips.

"Why is that funny?"

"It's not funny. It's just, I'm kind of glad he screwed up, too. Makes him realize he's not so perfect, either."

I remembered spiraling through the air and seeing the roughness of the bark on the apple tree before everything went dark. It wasn't like Luke to miscalculate an airbend like that. He could've easily just bent the air around Dana. What went wrong?

A flashback entered my mind of Riley raising his hand at the same time as Luke. Maybe Riley's bender was meant for me. Or maybe he tried to bend Dana's sword to finish me off.

"Why are you thinking about Riley?" Maddy wondered aloud.

"Riley was airbending, too. The same time Luke was."

Maddy's eyebrows popped up. "You think he sent you flying?"

"Or their winds collided and created something no one intended."

Maddy frowned. "Come on, Sarah, it's Riley. He's been trying to kill you since he discovered your existence."

A laugh slipped out. "So nice of you to point that out."

"I mean, I think it's cute that you're still living by the old mantra: 'You can't heal hurt with hate,' but I think we can all agree that Riley has proven himself to be an enemy."

I wasn't sure why it still hurt, after all this time and evidence, to think of Riley as a traitor and murderer. Was it because he was Luke's brother, and it seemed like his actions were driven by jealousy more than hate?

To change the subject, I asked, "What happened to Dana after I hit the tree?"

"I wasn't around to see it, but Luke said she disappeared after I ported you back to Yelram. Then Victor left with this smug look on his face."

"And Riley?"

"He got away, too. With Keagan."

"Did anyone say anything?"

"Just Victor announcing the war had begun."

"He wants to take Earth," I remembered.

Maddy looked down. "You don't need to worry about that right now."

"I won't let them."

Maddy snickered. "And how do you plan on stopping them, huh? Have you forgotten you're pregnant?"

I ignored her because something else was pushing at the edges of my memory, eager to be recalled. "Victor's afraid of me," I heard myself say.

Maddy nodded. "He seemed intrigued by you."

I sat up, ignoring the pounding in my head. "He doesn't like how I don't conform. He doesn't know what I can do, and it scares him."

"You think so?"

"I do," I said. "I think we can use this." My mind began to recall more details of our encounter with the dark lords. "Victor said they'll use the elements to take Earth. What does that mean?"

"Apparently each of the seven worlds has an element hidden on Earth that stores their power. If Victor finds any of these elements, he'll gain that world's power, and also be able to influence every single human destined for that world."

"What is Drew saying? How likely is it they'll be able to find these elements?"

"Drew said Victor and Dana know where their own elements are, and those elements will lead them to their pairs—Lorendale's and Nevaeh's."

This wasn't good news. "We need to stop him before he gets started, then." I tried to stand up.

"Easy, warrior." She easily held me down. "You're not going anywhere for a while."

"Why not?"

"Luke's orders." She looked away at this and didn't return her eyes to mine. She kept her mind blocked, too. She was a fortress.

"So he's mad at me for not telling him?"

"And at me for not telling him."

"I'm sorry," I said.

She shook her head. She was frustrated, but not because of Luke. It was Drew's anger that bothered her most.

"Does Drew know I told you not to tell anyone?"

She nodded and a tear slipped down her cheek, which she quickly wiped away and replaced with a frown.

"He'll come around," I assured her.

"Eventually," she agreed. "I'm sure they both will, but Sarah, I've never seen Luke this upset before."

"I need to see him," I said, pushing the blankets away. She held me down.

"You need to rest," she said. "You took a hard hit yesterday, and you're pregnant."

"Will you send him in to see me?" I asked. My head was spinning, so I laid it on my pillow, squeezing my eyes closed. "I want to see him."

"Sarah," Maddy said, her voice delicate, "he just needs some time. Darkness runs deep in his veins. The only way he knows how to process what's going on is by working through his anger. We need to give him time."

My stomach churned with nausea. What had I done? Luke had never been mad at me before. It was unlike him to avoid me when I was in such a vulnerable position. And suddenly I was angry at myself for letting my guard down with Dana. I could've taken her. I could've finished her off, but I was too concerned with the fights going on around me.

I closed my eyes and inhaled deeply. "This is a mess."

"It's not a mess," she said. "It's a bump in the road." She glanced down at my stomach. "No pun intended."

Elizabeth returned with a glass of water in one hand and a facecloth in the other.

"I should go," Maddy said. "I'll be back later." She leaned over and kissed my forehead. "Get some rest."

I watched her leave. She was clear at first, but then became a watery blur as it occurred to me that I had screwed everything up.

CHAPTER 13

Luke's Anger

~ MADDY ~

I HATED SEEING Sarah like that. She was a complete mess without Luke. She couldn't have the one person she wanted most, but was stuck with a baby she didn't want at all. And it frustrated me that Luke was so angry with her. Yes, she should've told him, but in her defence, she was struggling with her own feelings on the baby; she didn't need Luke's thrown into the mix, especially if his weren't supportive and positive. But all that aside, she needed him now, and he was being selfish, in my opinion, to be avoiding her.

The training centre was a ten minute walk away, and it allowed me the time to clear my head before I had to see him again.

Luke's second-in-command was coming toward me as I made my way down the hallway to the gym. I liked Devon. He was honest, almost to a fault, but you always knew what you were getting with him.

"You're wasting your time," he said as we walked toward each other. "He won't give it to you."

"What makes you think I want something?"

"No one in their right mind would want to be around him right now unless they needed something from him." He smirked, but there was frustration behind it.

"What do you need from him?" I asked. We were standing in front of each other now, both with arms crossed—he was discouraged; I was apprehensive.

"Just looking for some direction." He narrowed his eyes and looked away.

"Sarah's awake. Why don't you go see her," I suggested. "She'd gladly help you if *he* won't." I wasn't trying to hide the fact that Luke was annoying me.

Devon laughed and jerked his head toward the gym. "Somehow I don't think that would go over well."

"Listen, Sarah told me something, but I'm not sure I should tell Luke."

"What is it?"

"When we went to Earth, right before Luke threw Dana off of Sarah, Sarah saw Riley bend air, too. It might explain why Sarah was thrown."

Devon nodded, his brow tightening with both anger and confusion.

"And I kind of want to tell Luke so that he knows it wasn't his fault because I think he blames himself for Sarah's condition, but I also don't want to tell him because—"

"He'll kill his brother."

"Exactly. But maybe we want him to kill Riley. He clearly wanted to kill Sarah."

Devon's eyes narrowed. "You're probably right. But you're also right about not telling Luke. Maybe it's good for him to shoulder some guilt. Might soften him a little."

I looked toward the gym door where you could hear the grunts and poundings of an angry Luke. "If that's softened, I'd hate to see what he'd be like otherwise."

"Let's not find out." Devon winked. "You still going in there?"

I nodded. "I have to try to talk some sense into him. Sarah needs him."

He sniggered. "Good luck with that." Then he left me standing in the hallway, staring at the gym door, and wondering if this was a death wish.

Luke was pounding on the heavy black punching bag when I slowly opened the door. Each time he threw his fist into the bag, he let out a loud guttural grunt. This went on for several minutes, and I wondered if he would ever wear himself out. His shirt was soaked with sweat, and his arms glistened and bulged as he hammered on the bag. Finally, I got the nerve to speak.

"She's awake and talking," I said, expecting to see some element of relief. His swing was uninterrupted as his fist pounded into the bag, sending a spray of sweat into the air.

I went farther into the room and circled the bag so that I could see his face. His eyes were red—tired but determined.

"She wants to see you," I said.

His eyebrows pulled down, and he nailed the bag even harder.

I took a few steps closer so that we were only five feet apart. "I told her that she needs rest right now."

He gripped the top of the bag and pushed his forehead against the black leather.

"And that you need some space," I added.

"Maddy," he said, and his voice surprised me. It was dark and deep and angry. "Why aren't you training the army?"

"I was," I said. "I will. I just went to check on Sarah."

He pushed himself away from the bag and started punching it again. "You shouldn't be wasting your time. We are about to go to war."

"I know that," I defended. "But she needs you, Luke."

He clenched his jaw. "She should've thought about that before lying to me." He nailed the bag again, which startled me.

I sighed heavily, showing him my frustration. "She would heal faster if you were with her, Luke."

"Again, she should've thought about that before she lied."

"Luke."

He seemed to rethink his answer. "No one can help her now, Maddy. That fetus will suck the life right out of her unless she learns how to stop it."

"And how does she learn how to do that?"

He pounded the bag again. "If I knew, don't you think I would've made it happen already?"

"Can't you just forgive her, Luke? She made a mistake. She's *human*, if you haven't forgotten."

"Go train your army, Maddy."

"And what about you?" I snapped.

"I'll be there when I'm ready!"

"Any idea when that'll be, Luke? Because—"

"GO!" he yelled.

I shook my head. Sarah's dishonesty had damaged a nerve in him that I didn't know how to fix.

"She needs you," I said as I crossed the room to the door. He didn't return his aggression to the bag, so I closed my eyes and added, "And if you ask me, you're being extremely selfish right now." I pushed the door open as Luke roared, and a combination of crashes and bangs culminated from his anger.

Once the door was closed tightly behind me, I slammed my fist into the wall and let out a cry of frustration.

"You okay?" It was Simon, and he was coming quickly down the hall.

"You probably don't want to go in there right now," I said, nodding toward the gym and massaging my hand.

"Why not? What happened?"

"Luke's in there," I said. "He just wants the gym to himself for a little while."

Simon nodded slowly, his eyes lingering on the door for a few seconds. "Anything I can do to help?"

"We have to get the recruits back in the training centre."

"I'm not sure what good that'll do. They're exhausted." He was as displaced by this as I was.

"There's a war coming," I said.

"I know, Maddy, but—"

"End of story." I tried to walk away, but he grabbed my arm.

"Maddy," he said, bringing my hand up to inspect the swollen knuckles. "You need a rest, too. Look at you." He lifted my chin so that our eyes met. "You look exhausted."

"You know that's just a polite way of telling someone they look like shit, right?"

He grinned shyly. "Well, that's far from the truth in

this case." His smile faded quickly. "You're still beautiful."

I felt my cheeks warm. It had been a while since anyone had complimented me. Drew had been too distant to get any amount of affection from.

I took Simon's hand from my chin and brought it down by my side. "I think I am tired," I said, letting my eyes fall from his. I stepped back and when I did, I saw Drew standing at the end of the hall, watching us. I dropped Simon's hand, causing him to turn, too.

"What's going on?" Drew asked, although it wasn't a question.

"Simon was just telling me how I look like shit," I said with a smirk, hoping the joke would distract him from the truth.

"Is that right?" Drew bridged the gap between us. Simon backed up.

"Something was bothering Maddy," Simon said. "I was just trying to figure out what it was."

"That's not your job," Drew said.

Simon nodded as if he was going to accept this and leave, but then his eyes narrowed and he challenged, "Is it yours?"

Drew clenched his jaw and then turned his eyes to mine. "You're damn right it is," he growled through gritted teeth.

My heart smiled with his threat, and I suddenly

wanted Simon to disappear so I could taste the passion in Drew's jealousy.

"I guess I should get back to work then," Simon said. "Break time's over, apparently."

Drew let him go while he kept his eyes on mine. We watched each other until the hallway was empty, and then when I thought he would kiss me, he didn't.

"What's bothering you?" he asked.

"Oh, I don't know, maybe it's Luke and how he won't go see Sarah, or maybe it's you and how you seem to hate me right now."

"So, what? You just thought you'd go in and try talking to him? You thought you could reason with a dark lord?" He ignored the part about him hating me, which felt like a slap in the face.

"It's Luke."

"Exactly. And I told you to leave him alone."

"I know you did, but Sarah's awake and wanted to see him, and —"

"And he needs time, Maddy. Don't you get that? Maybe guys are different than girls, but we have a harder time letting things go. Especially things like *this*—when the girl you love is off kissing someone else and keeping secrets from you." He said it with such distaste that I wondered if we were still talking about Luke and Sarah.

"So we just sit back and wait for him to come around? Sarah needs him *now!*"

"Sarah should've thought about that before she lied to him."

There was a moment of silence between us. Drew and Luke obviously shared the same position, and it was clear that I did not have Drew's support on the matter. He understood where Luke was coming from, which frustrated me. To an extent, I understood it too, but Sarah was recovering and she needed Luke for strength. Just being there with her would help her heal.

"If he would just stop to listen for a minute, I think I could make him see—"

"Leave him alone, Maddy," Drew said, shaking his head. "I know him better than you do."

"No." I crossed my arms in defiance. "He's being an asshole and he needs to know that." I tried to pull away, realizing that I had decided to go back to have words with Luke, but Drew grabbed my hand.

"Maddy," he warned, "don't."

The gym door swung open, slamming against the wall. Luke emerged, wiping sweat from his neck with a towel. I smirked at Drew, but before I could open my mouth to challenge Luke, Drew pinned me against the wall, and his mouth was closing in on mine. I knew it was a ploy to shut me up, but as hard as I tried, I couldn't fight it—my body yearned for the taste of his lips and the softness of his tongue.

Luke's steps grew louder, then quieter, and when it

was clear he was gone, Drew's kiss faded and his lips lingered on mine for only a second. I kept my eyes closed, hoping for more, but he was finished.

"Drew?" I said when he stepped back, putting distance between us. "Where are we?" It was brave and I felt stupid for asking, but I had good reason for asking. Ever since we started training the army, he had become someone different. As if he loved me one minute, but then couldn't stand to touch me the next.

"You lied to me, Maddy."

"I didn't lie to you, Drew," I said. "Sarah *forbade* me from telling anyone."

"And I'm just anyone?" His eyes were softer, but there was hurt hiding in there.

"No," I said, reaching for his hand, but he pulled away, "you're not just anyone. I . . . you've just been different lately, and I haven't felt connected to you."

"You haven't felt connected to me because we haven't been connected, Maddy. I knew you were keeping something from me. You were lying to me. And then you and Simon—"

"What about me and Simon? Drew, there's nothing there."

"Tell that to *him*." He shook his head and backed up. "It doesn't matter," he said, and when I couldn't find the words or energy to continue the fight, he left.

CHAPTER 14

Combined Forces

~ SARAH ~

I WOKE EARLY the next day, and even though I hadn't seen Luke all day, and I had fallen asleep hugging his pillow, I was still surprised and disappointed when I woke up alone. It was the first night since we were married that he hadn't stayed with me. A tear slipped over the bridge of my nose and onto my pillow.

It was early; I could tell from the way the sun shone high on the wall. No longer tired, I rolled out of bed and slowly made my way to the bathroom where I showered and dressed for the day. My room wasn't spinning like it had been the day before, but by the time I came out of the washroom, my head was pounding and I had to close the curtains to keep it from screaming. I lied back down and closed my eyes, willing the pain to subside.

There was a small click that came from my bedroom door, and I froze as the handle slowly turned. My heart lifted for a minute as the door creaked open, but then Elizabeth quietly slipped into the room, and I closed my eyes again and let my heart fall.

She tiptoed across the floor and when she reached me, she gently laid her hand on my forehead, then ran it through my hair, stopping when she felt the wetness.

"Oh," she said softly, "are you awake, Sarah?"

"I am," I answered, my eyes still closed. "I can't sleep, but my head hurts. I had to lie back down."

"The doctor said you have a concussion, love. You need all the rest you can get to keep you and that baby of yours healthy."

I must have recoiled because she quickly corrected herself. "Your full recovery is the most important thing right now."

"Do you know where Luke slept last night?" I asked.

She sat on the edge of my bed and stroked my hair again. "Oh, sweet Sarah," she said softly. "I'm sorry, but I don't know the answer to that."

Another tear escaped, but I kept my eyes closed.

"Here," Elizabeth said as she cupped my neck with her hand. "Why don't you sit up and drink this. It'll help with the headache."

I followed her lead and put the metal straw to my mouth. The thick liquid was sour and bitter, and I made a face and pushed it away.

"That's probably enough for now, anyway." She set the cup down on my bedside table.

"Why haven't I been able to heal myself?" I asked, frustrated by the screaming pain in my head.

"The doctor says you are slower to heal while the baby needs so much from you," she said, but I sensed she was holding something back.

"And Luke? Why hasn't he healed me yet?" How could he let me endure this pain when he knew how to heal me?

She lowered her eyes and busied herself with smoothing the blankets. "He's tried, My Lady."

"What do you mean *he's tried*? It didn't work?"

She shook her head.

"Why not?"

"Master Luke has a theory of his own." She paused to take time to stand. She didn't want to tell me his theory.

"And?" I pressed.

"He thinks the baby is *absorbing* all of your powers."

"Why? Why would he think that?"

She shook her head. "He didn't elaborate. The subject seems to upset him."

Could Luke be right? Could this baby be taking my powers? I carefully raised my hand and willed for energy to flow down my arm, through my fingers, out my fingertips, so that it would capture the air and manipulate it, so that it would grab the curtain and move it aside.

Nothing happened.

The curtains were frozen in place.

"Well, this is a setback," I finally said. "How am I supposed to protect my army without any powers?"

"You . . . you still plan on fighting in the war?" Her eyes were on the cup of tea in her hands as she waited for my response.

"I don't have a choice, Elizabeth."

"You do have a choice, Sarah." She sat down next to me and leaned in. "You always have a choice."

"If I don't go, there is a greater chance our people will die. They are stronger when I'm with them. They can draw on my strengths."

"What strengths?" Elizabeth snapped. "I'm sorry."

But she was right. What strengths did I have now? I was powerless. Useless.

Elizabeth closed her eyes, realizing my dilemma. "It's too dangerous for you. Especially now that the dark lords know you're with child. They know your weakness."

I fell back down onto my pillow, my head spinning with dizziness. "I guess it doesn't matter right now anyway. I can't even stand up." My eyes stung, pierced by the tears.

"You need to rest, Sarah." She touched my forehead.

"If you were all better, I could see your dilemma—you're a very strong warrior, and our people could use your strength on the battlefield, but not in your current state. You wouldn't survive a day. You're in no condition to fight."

"I never wanted this," I cried. "I never wanted a baby."

She was quiet, probably trying to understand how I felt. At best guess, Elizabeth was in her late forties or early fifties and had only one child. A child who wasn't even ten years old yet. At her age, having a child was a rare blessing. But I was still young. I had too much fight left in me.

"Sarah," she finally said, "you will make a great mother."

I scoffed. "I doubt it."

She was looking at my abdomen, probably imagining this child growing up in a loveless home.

"I don't know the first thing about how to love a child. My first mother abandoned me, and the next three only wanted me for a pay check."

"Sarah," she said softly, a quiver to her voice, "your mother loved you so very much. I'm sorry that you don't remember her the way we do."

"Me too." I rolled over to face the wall and hoped that she couldn't tell I was crying.

Another minute passed and then she stroked my hair

one last time and stood up. "I will come check on you in a little while. You get some rest, okay?"

I nodded and saved my sniffles until she was gone.

ELIZABETH DIDN'T RETURN again, and by lunch time I was too hungry to wait for someone to come feed me. I bent over to put on my shoes, but the movement made my head throb. I kicked off the shoe, drank the rest of the remedy that Elizabeth left for me, and instead pushed my feet into a pair of slippers.

There were some berries and almonds in the kitchen, so I grabbed a handful of both and snuck back out before Omar caught me skipping lunch. I wasn't sure where I was going, but my goal was to find Luke. With the impending war, he would be training. And with my betrayal, he would be training harder than he should. So the training centre would be my first stop, but I had to avoid both Elizabeth and Maddy. Neither would approve of me leaving my bedroom, much less the palace.

I slowly made my way down the hallway to the landing, keeping close to the walls and railing for fear that the dizziness would cause me to fall. It was bright outside, and I slid on the sunglasses that I had the foresight to bring with me. I pulled my hood over my messy hair and entered the sunlight.

My journey down the palace steps was interrupted by

hundreds of bouquets of flowers, teddy bears, and cards placed all over the steps from the very bottom to the top.

I slowly made my way through the maze of flowers and stuffed animals, momentarily stunned by their abundance. When I reached the bottom, I bent over and plucked a card from one of the bouquets:

Our Queen, we are praying for your full recovery.
The future prince or princess is also in our
thoughts and prayers.
The Boudreau Family

I reached for another card and read:

Sending love and prayers for you and your unborn.
Lilly and Austin Hearnshaw

How did all these people know about the pregnancy? This was all getting too real.

"Have you heard any news?" The voice startled me, and I nearly spun around, but quickly remembered that I didn't want to be seen. I knelt down and arranged some of the flowers, pretending to be busy.

"I heard she's awake. That's all," another female voice answered, then she climbed a few steps and laid a bouquet of flowers in an empty place.

"Yes, that's good news." The first woman had a teddy

bear to lay, and she sent her toddler up the steps to find a place for it. "I've seen the dark lor— . . . sorry, *the King* go in and out, but he never stays long."

"He's been busy training the armies, though."

"True. The timing could be better for all of this." The woman's toddler returned and her voice brightened. "But isn't it wonderful to have something to look forward to?"

"If it survives, yes. I heard the doctor has set up camp in the palace to keep an eye on the baby."

"Strange that the King isn't able to heal her."

"Unsettling, yes."

I stood and turned away from the women, careful not to let them catch a glimpse of the red hair peeking out from my hood.

I hurried through the town square, keeping my head low and eyes averted until someone grabbed my shoulder.

"What are you doing?" His voice excited me for a second because it was familiar enough that I believed it could be Luke's. But when I spun around, I found Drew.

"Hi," I said, trying to keep the disappointment from reaching my face.

He grabbed my arm. "You're not supposed to be out of bed," he scolded. "What are you doing?"

I pulled my arm from him and frowned. "I feel fine," I lied.

"Is that so?" He bore his eyes into mine, and I wished he didn't know me so well.

"Drew, I need to see him."

"He's busy." His tone was softer now, almost sympathetic.

"Busy with what? What could be more important than seeing his wife?" It came out sharper and meaner than I had intended.

"Sarah, it's not like he doesn't care. He was with you the whole time you were unconscious, and he sees Elizabeth and Maddy regularly for updates."

"Why won't he talk to me?" I was thankful for the sunglasses that hid my swollen and watery eyes.

Drew looked down. "He's got some things to work through."

A stab of pain shot through my abdomen, and I bent over in response.

Drew grabbed my arm and pulled me up. "Are you okay? What's wrong?"

"I'm fine," I lied again.

"Sarah, you should go back to bed."

"You know what? I *would* if Luke would come see me. I just want to see him, Drew."

He looked conflicted. "He's training the recruits right now. They're getting ready for the war. I just . . . I just don't think he'll come right now."

"Does he hate me?" My lip quivered, and he noticed.

He put his hand around the back of my neck and pulled me into his chest. "No, he doesn't hate you," he said. "Luke could never hate you, Sarah. His anger is just a mask for the hurt that he's feeling."

My chest heaved with a sob. How could I blame him for how he felt? I was angry with myself too. And my anger was a mask for the guilt and sadness that I felt. Another stab of pain entered my abdomen.

"Drew?" I wiped my face with my sleeve. "Why do you think Luke can't heal me? And why don't I have my powers?" I needed to know if he believed what Luke believed. That the baby was absorbing everything.

He tried to keep the disappointment from reaching his face, but I saw it. "You don't have your powers?" he confirmed.

I slowly shook my head, then rotated my hand as if cupping the air, willing for fire to erupt from my fingertips. They warmed, but not enough to ignite.

"Is it because of the baby? Is it taking everything from me?"

Drew made a face of concern but didn't answer.

"But I had powers on Earth," I remembered. "I bent water, fire, and air. You saw it, right?"

Drew thought for a moment, then he realized something. "You were protecting Luke," he said, thoughtfully. "You love him enough to be able to reclaim your powers to protect him." Drew was quiet for another moment while he thought this through. "Can I ask you something?"

I nodded.

"Do you want this baby?"

The question made my eyes blurry, but I held back the sobs as I shook my head. No. No, I did not want this baby. It wasn't a good time. I wasn't fit to be a mother.

Drew pressed a sympathetic smile. "And how does that make you feel?"

"What do you mean?"

"How does it make you feel?" he asked again as if it were a simple question needing only a simple answer.

"Of course I feel awful," I said, turning away so he wouldn't see me cry. "What kind of person doesn't want their own child? What kind of person wishes they could just get rid of it? Give it away for someone else to raise?"

"Or leave it on the steps of a Children's Aid Society," Drew added.

I looked up at him, realizing his intention.

"I think," he began, "your guilt is the reason you have no powers. You feel so awful for not wanting this baby, and you are so desperate for this child to not have the same upbringing you had—abandoned and unloved— that you are giving it everything you have."

I let his theory penetrate, mulling it over as I considered its validity.

"How do I . . . how do I stop it? How do I stop it from

taking everything from me?"

"You have to stop giving it." He took my hands in his. "You will love this child. So will Luke. It's not ruining your life. It's just changing it."

"What if I have to abandon it one day? Or what if it leaves me?"

"Don't be afraid to love something just because you might one day lose it." He winked, knowing I would recognize his words as the same advice that I had given him over Maddy.

I squeezed my eyes shut, realizing he was right. I was afraid to love it. I was afraid to be its mother. I was afraid I wouldn't be enough.

"You are enough, Sarah."

Was I enough, though? How could I be enough for someone when I didn't even know what *enough* was? What did a child need? Love? What experience did I have with motherly love?

"I think that when you learn to love this baby as much as you love Luke, and when your purpose is to protect this child, then you'll get control of your powers again."

"And what if I never do?"

Drew smiled sympathetically. "You will."

He had given me too much to think about. How could I ever love a child more than I loved Luke? I loved him so much that it physically hurt to not be near him.

I turned from Drew, and my feet carried me away. He

didn't call after me, which I was thankful for. I ran down the street and made a right and then a left, until I was facing the training centre. My heart was pounding. Luke would be here.

I went to the door at the side of the building that led to the balcony above the indoor stadium and pushed it open. It was darker inside, and my head was happy to be rid of the sun. I followed the rail around to the centre as I watched the recruits below. But they weren't dressed in Yelram's yellow uniforms. These recruits were wearing blue. These were Etak warriors. Luke had brought his own army here to train. I was somewhat comforted by this. At least this meant he would rather be here in Yelram with me than a world away.

The warriors were in pairs, practicing their combat skills. My eyes pinballed the crowd until I found him. He was near the middle, meandering through the fights, giving instruction when he could. He was tall and handsome, and my heart beat wildly as if it were the first time I laid eyes on him. I loved him so much, and I suffered knowing I had hurt him so badly.

Luke walked to the front of the room and yelled, "Alright, that's enough!" His voice was broken as if he had been yelling all day. It was a strange feeling to know that I would have given just about anything for him to yell at me.

"Devon," Luke said, "let's show them again. Some of

them are still not getting it."

Devon stepped out of formation and came to the front. He and Luke faced each other. Luke gave no indication that he was about to attack Devon, but still, when he threw his fist at him, Devon easily blocked it, throwing back another.

"Are you supposed to be out of bed?"

I jumped and clutched my chest. It was Simon. He was standing next to me, smiling weakly, but he acted as though I was fragile, and it immediately annoyed me.

"I'm fine," I assured him. I tried to continue watching the fight, learning from the movements that Luke and Devon were showing their army.

"Luke still mad at you?"

"Simon, please," I started, "I'm not really in the mood right now."

He raised his hands. "I'm sorry."

I nodded and returned my eyes to the session below. "What makes you think he's mad at me?"

Simon grinned but kept his face forward and hands clasped behind his back. He was enjoying this a little too much, but I needed to know. Had Luke told everyone what I had done?

"Isn't it obvious?" he gestured one hand toward Luke and Devon. "He had to bring his own army here because Maddy wouldn't let him take his anger out on hers."

I recoiled. "It doesn't mean he's mad at me."

He nodded. "Yeah, I also may have overheard him and Maddy arguing."

"What did you hear?" My heart beat heavily, and I tried to keep the curiosity and concern from my voice.

"Maddy was doing what Maddy does best—trying to fix things. She told him he should go see you, and that you'd heal faster if he were there."

"And?" I said. "What did he say?"

"You sure you want to know?"

· "Mess off, Simon," I warned.

The smile fell from his lips. "He said you should've thought about that before lying to him." Simon hung his head a little as he left a gap of silence between us. "I'm sure you had a good reason, Sarah."

I nodded and blinked away the tears as I kept my eyes forward. "I thought I did," I admitted. "But it wasn't worth it after all."

"Why don't you tell him that?"

"If he ever lets me near him, maybe I will."

As if I called his name, Luke looked up and found us on the balcony.

"I should go," Simon said, and he immediately left, afraid of Luke's wrath.

I tried to keep Luke's eyes on me. I tried to tell him I was sorry, but he looked away too quickly. Then he left the training area, closing the door hard behind him.

Even if I could find it in me to love and accept this

child inside me, could Luke?

I WASN'T READY to go home. I needed to feel free again. I needed to forget the hurt in my heart over losing Luke's trust. I needed Lucia.

I found her in the tiger fields, chasing around her best friend, Raven. I watched them for a few minutes, but then she saw me out of the corner of her eye and stopped, giving Raven the opportunity to spring on her and pin her to the ground. Lucia didn't care, she easily pushed Raven aside and raced toward me. She wanted to pounce on me, and I braced myself, but instead, she circled excitedly and only when her excitement subsided would she come close to me. She purred loudly as I nuzzled my face into her chest.

Crouching low, she let me climb onto her back, and I buried my hands in her fur and held on tight as she took me through the fields, the wind whipping through my hair. When I felt dizzy, I brought my head low to hers and held on tighter until the feeling subsided. Eventually she slowed to a canter, and then a walk, and finally she stopped, lied down in the grass, and I slid off her back so that we lied there together in the tall daisies with the sun covering us like a thick, warm blanket. Just me and Lucia. Like it used to be when she was just a dog and I was just an ordinary teenager living in a foster home. Back when we just had each other.

WHEN I RETURNED to the palace, Drew and Maddy were pacing the entry hall.

"Where have you been?" Maddy demanded. "We've been looking for you."

"With Lucia." I pushed past them and climbed the stairs toward my bedroom.

"You went *riding?*" Maddy shouted. "Sarah, what part of 'concussion' is difficult for you to grasp?"

"I'm fine," I said, ignoring the desperate desire to grab the wall for stability. "What's so urgent, anyway?" I pushed open my bedroom door and went straight for my bed.

Maddy looked at Drew before taking a deep breath and saying, "We're deploying today."

"What? You're leaving?"

Drew nodded. "Australia's burning, and Leviathan's element, the black onyx embedded in a shield, is gone."

"The dark armies are in Asia now for Nitsua's element, a ruby-encrusted breastplate," Maddy finished.

I tried to say something, but the words were hard to find. "I . . . but . . . where . . .?"

"Trinity is bringing her army to Antarctica now to protect their element—the opal sword. And Eli has brought his army to Europe to protect their amethyst lined boots."

"The elements are pieces of armour?"

Drew nodded. "Precious stones embedded in armour, which makes the armour so powerful no one can penetrate it. If Victor gets his hands on all of them, he won't just have the souls of all humans, he'll be indestructible, too."

I sat down on my bed, my head spinning. "So what does this mean?" I said. "Where are you going now?"

Maddy smiled weakly. "We think they'll go for Lorendale's element next, which is in England. Nevaeh's army is too powerful to approach with only two elements."

"Where is Luke?" My voice shook with the question.

Maddy looked at me sympathetically, which only annoyed me. "He took Etak's army through about a half hour ago."

I swallowed and nodded, my eyes filled and my breath came and went faster and heavier than it should. Luke was leaving for a war, and we hadn't even made up.

"I'll be ready soon," I said as the edges of the room moved like jelly. "I just need a bit of time to rest first, but I'll—"

"Absolutely not," Drew said. "You're staying here. We don't need you there."

I whimpered, knowing I didn't have the strength to argue with him. Why had I gone riding today? If I hadn't, I could've faked the strength to go with them.

Maddy's hand touched my shoulder. "I'll be back,

okay? I'll come back as often as I can with updates. You just stay here and rest."

She bent over and hugged me. I didn't have the strength to stand and hug her back. I knew I should have. I knew I should have given more effort to our goodbye. She was going off to war, but all I could think about was Luke.

Maddy stepped back and Drew came forward. He kissed my forehead. "I'll take care of him, Sarah."

A sob escaped my lips. "Go," I said. "Be safe."

"I'll be back," Maddy promised again. Drew slid his arm around her shoulders and they left.

When the door closed behind them, I felt nauseous. I ran to the bathroom and threw up in the toilet. Again and again.

Luke was gone.

Maddy was gone.

Drew was gone.

And I was alone.

When I had nothing left in me, I washed my face and brushed my teeth. I went back to my bed and curled up into a ball, completely defeated. I cried until there were no tears left to cry, then I wiped my face dry and rolled onto my back and counted the stars on the ceiling until a knock came to the door.

"Come in," I mumbled.

The door slowly pushed open, and a man stood in the

doorway, dressed in dark blue from head to boot. I knew right away from his posture and the way he stood that it was Luke. I sat up, ignoring the pain in my head.

"Luke?" I said, desperate to hear his voice.

"Hi," he answered. He stayed in the doorway, and my heart trembled from the distance.

"I thought you left."

He didn't answer. His eyes were resting on my body, but not my face.

"Are you okay?" I asked as I stood to go to him.

"Stay there," he said.

A sob built up in my chest as my heart ached with the distance he was keeping. I sat back down on the bed, and he stayed in the doorway.

"Maddy said you left," I said, and it came out as a whisper.

"I wouldn't leave without saying goodbye."

A whimper escaped, and I tried to hold back the rest of the sob. "Don't leave me," I begged. "Please stay."

He shook his head, and his face was distorted with emotions that I couldn't read. Anger? Sadness? Resentment?

"I have to go," he said. "Our army's already there."

I stood again, and this time he didn't order me to stay. I slowly closed the gap between us, but when I was only a few feet away, he said, "You should've told me."

I searched his face for anger, but I could only find

hurt. "I didn't want you to get angry and do something stupid. He pretended to be you, but I knew better. I pushed him away as soon as he kissed me. I promise."

His eyes stayed on mine, but he didn't say anything. I tried to get into his head, but it was a fortress and it took too much from me to try.

"And I'm sorry for not telling you about the baby. I just . . . wasn't ready to accept it myself."

I took the few steps left between us and reached for his hand, which he allowed. It was cold and unfeeling, but it was Luke. And he was letting me touch him. He was letting me near him.

His eyes were swollen and red, and even in the dark room I could see that they were glistening with emotion, too. I reached up and touched his cheek and his eyes closed. A tear slipped onto my fingers and we both wrapped our arms around each other. I buried my face into his chest and focused on his arms squeezing my body. His chest quivered with a sob that he tried to hide, and it made me cry, too.

"I love you," he said. I shifted under his weight, and he pulled back immediately. "Did I hurt you?"

"No," I said quickly. "I'm just weak right now."

He didn't pull me back into him, though; he just studied my body, his eyes resting on my abdomen.

"I don't want you to leave me."

"I know," he said, and then kissed my forehead. "But

I have to. And you have to heal." He took my hands in his. "Sarah, I need you to learn how to block this thing, okay? I need you to stop letting it take everything from you."

"Block it?"

"Yes," he said forcefully.

"How?"

"I wish I knew," but his voice trailed off as a thought entered his mind. "Can you *feel* it?" He was referring to the baby.

"Sometimes I think I can feel it move. Why?"

"No, I mean *feel* it? Can you read it?"

"I haven't tried. If I'm being honest, I'm kind of . . . trying not to think about it."

He thought about what I had said, not seeming to be hurt by it at all. "Maybe you need to make a connection with it in order to block it."

I didn't love how he kept calling the baby an "it" or a "thing." Maybe it would be easier for me to make a connection with the baby if I felt like it was something that at least one of us wanted.

"I'll try," I said. I struggled to keep the resentment from my voice. But it was true—I resented this unborn fetus. I resented the fact that I was incapable of healing myself or using my own powers, that I was being forced to stay home while the people I loved were fighting for their lives. Because now the war was more dangerous than before. Now the stakes were higher.

My heart began pounding. I couldn't sit this war out. I had to be there to bring my army more strength. More power.

"I'm sorry you can't come with me."

"Me too." My eyes stung.

"Promise me you won't do anything stupid." He touched my side, so close to my stomach, and I felt a small movement. "Promise me."

"So long as you promise to come back to me."

He smiled. "As soon as the war is over, you'll be in my arms again." But I took note that his words lacked a promise. As did mine.

There was a small knock at the door, and Elizabeth appeared, clearing her throat. We both stepped back, Luke putting his arm around my waist as we waited for the reason for her interruption.

"Sarah, the doctor is here to check on your concussion." She smiled at Luke and ushered the doctor into the room. "And the baby," she added more quietly.

Luke kissed the top of my head. "I have to go," he whispered as my hands squeezed around the fabric of his shirt. "I love you."

"I love you."

Luke turned to greet the doctor, shook his hand, thanked him, and then left, closing the door behind him.

And he was gone.

CHAPTER 15

Stonehenge

~ MADDY ~

I DIDN'T EXPECT to appear in the middle of an old English farmer's field. Drew held my hand as we watched Yelram's army pour through the portal he made.

"Is this the right place?" I asked, although I knew it had to be as Drew didn't seem displaced at all.

Drew nodded to the west. "See that circle of standing rocks over there? That's Stonehenge. Lorendale's element is buried in the centre of those rocks."

Etak's dark blue army with ferocious over-sized wolves was already there, closer to the massive stone monument, along with Lorendale's army of purple riders and gigantic gorillas. They spread out, creating a wall around Stonehenge.

When it was time to join Yelram's army, Drew said, "Maddy, please be careful." He was holding my hands and running the pads of his thumbs across my knuckles.

"You, too." I tried to sound confident, but my voice shook, and I wondered if he noticed.

Drew reached for my key and closed his fingers around it. He did the same with his, then muttered something until both keys glowed yellow. "If we get separated and you need me, just hold your key and say my name. You'll come right to me. Okay?"

"Okay." My heart smiled.

He stepped back, but kept his eyes locked with mine, until Jenna called his name. "Drew! Come on, it's time to go!"

WITH THREE FULL armies, we should've had the advantage, but as an enormous swirling black portal opened to the north of Stonehenge, and both Leviathan's and Nitsua's armies came pouring through with their dragons and armoured black panthers, I wondered if the rest of our warriors were as nervous as I was.

The dark armies wasted no time. They charged Stonehenge and were met with the full force of Lorendale's and Etak's armies.

Colours clashed. Purple and blue against red and black.

As rehearsed, the core four leaders, following Drew and me, led their units into battle. With the addition of Yelram's tigers and determined warriors, I was sure the dark side would fall fast.

Several minutes into the fight, I realized how wrong I was, and for some reason, our inflated numbers didn't seem to matter at all.

"Did you see Luke?" Drew called over his shoulder as he drove his sword into the chest of a red warrior.

"Haven't seen him," I answered, although I hadn't really had time to look for him.

Suddenly, one of the wolves let out a magnificent sound and, as if infused with supernatural energy and strength, Etak's wolves and warriors began tearing apart the enemy.

"There he is," Drew laughed as blue warriors began soaring above our heads and bending the air to destroy the Nitsuan warriors.

"Sorry I'm late," Luke said as he and Gideon suddenly appeared next to us.

"Wow," I heard myself say. "Is that what happens when you're here?"

He nodded. "Which is why it kind of sucks that Sarah can't be."

Yelram's warriors were clearly struggling more than any other army. They had skill, but they lacked the supernatural element that the others gained from merely having their leaders on the same planet.

"Etak will stay with Yelram's army," Luke decided. "My presence may help somewhat."

I hoped he was right, but if he was, the advantage to Yelram wasn't nearly as great as it was for Etak.

And then Victor and Dana arrived, with Keagan at Dana's right side. They were about a hundred feet away and surrounded by their strongest-looking fighters. Victor wore both Leviathan's element—the onyx shield, and Nitsua's element—the ruby-encrusted breastplate. He already looked near invincible, and I kept having to remind myself that he wasn't. We could beat him.

A grin crept across Drew's face—he was looking forward to avenging his father's death.

Victor extended his arms to his sides and fire erupted from the tips of his fingers up to his shoulders.

"Get ready," Drew said as he mounted his trusted tiger friend, Bella, and held out his sword with the other. "Victor's mine. Luke, you have Dana. Maddy, Keagan's all yours."

Luke nodded to me before adding, "Get a few hits in from me, would ya?"

I tried to smile, but I was too nervous. "Got it."

"Be careful, Maddy," Drew said before he leaped and soared through the air to meet his opponent.

My focus was Keagan, and he appeared to know it, too. He ran full force toward me, his sword held out and ready to slice my body apart. I looked around for Raven, hoping she would return and back me up. I had fallen off her in a previous fight and now she was off being a valiant hero while I stood shaking from fear. What had I gotten myself into?

Keagan! I thought desperately, but I didn't run to meet him, remembering my instruction—as a smaller fighter, I was better off defending and using his movements against him.

Keagan, why are you doing this? I thought again as he changed into a panther and leaped toward me. I dived to the ground, narrowly avoiding his attack. Keagan, as a panther, rolled across the ground, then turned quickly to face me again.

I tried desperately to get into his head, but he knew it was coming and he defended himself well. *Stop this, Keagan! We're friends!*

We're not friends! he thought back, and it came out as a roar.

"We *were!*" I shouted. "Until you did *this!*"

He changed back into himself and threw his blade in my direction. I blocked it, and our swords locked together above our heads. He was pushing his toward my face, and it took all my strength to hold it in place as the blades trembled with our strength.

"I don't want to kill you, Maddy," he admitted, and I saw for a minute his hesitance. "But I . . . *have* to."

"You don't *have* to do anything, Keagan," I tried.

Then a blackness took over his eyes again and the sincerity vacated. When I thought I couldn't hold his sword off any longer, an arrow flew over my head and pierced Keagan's arm. He fell back, stunned for a moment, then yanked the arrowhead from his arm.

Simon was next to me now. "Why don't you pick on someone your own size?" he growled as he punched Keagan square in the face. He glanced over his shoulder at me and said, "Go help Beth. I got this trump."

I scrambled to my feet, my heart hammering louder than the cries of the surrounding armies. "Don't kill him!" I shouted to Simon.

"Are you serious??"

"Well, not unless you have to."

Simon shook his head. "Go help Beth!"

I wasn't exactly sure where Beth was, but I headed in the general direction from where Simon had come, and soon found Raven, along with a wolf and a gorilla, attacking a dragon. I pulled an arrow and released it into the dragon's eye and when it stumbled, I gripped its mind. *Lie down!*

The dragon fell to the ground and the gorilla and wolf ripped him apart while Raven ran happily toward me.

I mounted Raven and told her we had to find Beth. She immediately took off in another direction and raced away from the monument and the raging war.

"Where are we going?"

She didn't answer, obviously, but I trusted her, and soon we were gaining on a giant that was closing in on one of Yelram's tigers and . . . Beth!

As I steadied myself on Raven's back, I loosed arrow after arrow at the giant. Finally, he turned his attention to me, but not before throwing a boulder at Beth and her animal.

As the boulder smashed into them, the tiger immediately turned to dust, completely disappearing. I heard my own scream as Beth flew through the air and landed hard in a thicket of trees.

My whole body trembled with anger. *REVEAL YOURSELF!* I screamed at the giant, and he transformed into a Nitsuan warrior, larger than most.

Raven leaped toward the man, and I jumped from her back and drove my sword into man's chest, narrowly missing his own blade. I landed hard on the ground, but turned in time to see his body turn to dust.

"Beth!" I called, and Raven scooped me up and we raced toward the thicket of trees.

She was lying on the ground, still, except for her eyes that searched for me.

I slid off Raven's back and knelt on the ground next to her.

"Maddy," she whimpered.

"Shh," I hushed, brushing her hair from her face. "It's

okay. You're going to be okay." Of course this was a lie. I had no way of healing her, and I doubted even Drew could heal her . . . if he weren't preoccupied with trying to kill Victor. I thumbed my key, wondering if I should bring her back to Yelram.

Beth took my hand that covered my key. "Please don't," she managed to say. "Let me die here."

"But Sarah—"

"I'm not going to make it, Maddy. I'd rather die in battle."

A tear escaped my eye and landed on her chest.

"Take care of Simon, please," she breathed.

I nodded. "Of course. Don't worry about him. Simon's tough."

She tried to laugh, but it was weak and painful. "He's my brother."

"What?"

She took a few short breaths before saying, "He never wanted anyone to know. He thinks people wouldn't like me as much if they knew."

"Simon's a great guy."

She moved her lips into a partial smile. "He gets under people's skin."

I smiled because she was trying to. "Sometimes, I guess."

"Just promise me you'll look out for him?"

"I promise, Beth."

"He likes you." Her eyes were closing, and her speech was slurring.

"I like him, too."

As Beth's smile faded, she let go of her soul. Her eyes didn't struggle to reopen as her last breath left her lungs, and then the weight of her body diminished as her shell turned to ash and drifted away with the breeze.

Forever.

THE TREES KEPT Raven and me hidden while I processed the tragedy of Beth's death and the trauma of everything this cruel and bloody war had just uncovered.

How was I to break the news to Simon that his friend—no, his *sister*—was gone?

Beth was Simon's sister. How had I not seen that before? Granted, they didn't look a whole lot alike—both were attractive, but their features were distinctly different.

Although we were far enough removed that I could no longer see the destruction of the war, the cries and clashes of weapons could still be heard, and the sound of them made my body tremble with sobs. Ferocious roars from animals, painful screams from warriors. I squeezed my eyes closed, trying not to hear Drew's cries in any of the madness.

And then the ground began to quake and the battle cries grew louder. Raven laid on the ground, and I steadied myself against her body as the earth rumbled beneath us. Moments later, the earthquake and chaos dwindled to a dull commotion, and finally to an eerie silence.

Eventually, I found the courage to return to Stonehenge and confirm the dreaded truth—Victor had been successful in retrieving the amethyst boots.

Etak's army was nowhere to be found, and I wondered when they had left. Lorendale's army of purple was leaving through a portal, and soon all that was left was Yelram's army, which was considerably smaller than before. The sight of their solemn and defeated faces returned tears to my eyes.

As I meandered my way through the crowd, I saw Simon pacing at the edge of the monument. Jenna was standing nearby, quietly peering off into the distance. I hid myself behind a group of warriors as I considered how to break the news to Simon that his sister had died in my arms.

Suddenly, Drew, riding on the back of Bella, came tearing across the field. He jumped off of Bella, landing next to Jenna and Simon. "Did you find her?"

Simon shook his head. "I'm going back out, though." He whistled for his tiger, and Garfunkel quickly appeared next to him.

"You go west and sweep south," Drew said, "and I'll cover the north and east fields. Check the trees, too. She may be injured."

"Drew, you need your rest," Jenna said, placing her hand on his arm. "You stay here and I'll go look."

"Rest? Are you serious right now?" Drew hissed, pulling his arm from her grasp.

"Who are you looking for?" I asked, and Drew's head snapped up. He pushed his way through the people and ran to me, throwing his body weight into mine and squeezing until I coughed.

"Where have you been?" he demanded. "What happened to you?"

My eyes flickered to Simon. "I was . . . with Beth."

"Beth," Simon said, coming closer. "Where is she?"

"She's . . . gone."

Simon's sword dropped from his hand, but he quickly retrieved it. "Like, dead?" he trembled.

I nodded. "I'm so sorry, Simon. I tried. I went after her, but I . . ." I trailed off because I wasn't sure how much of a picture I needed to draw for him. "I know she was your . . . friend," I said. I pulled away from Drew and went to Simon. "I'm so sorry." I wanted to tell him that I knew his secret, but I also wanted to respect his wishes. I wiped away some tears.

"I'm fine," Simon said. He fought back his own tears and did a good job of hiding them. I didn't like this side of Simon. I didn't like to see him hurting.

Simon sat down on a nearby rock and studied the

blade of his sword. "How'd she die?"

I swallowed my grief and sat down next to him. "She died well," I said. "She died fighting for freedom."

He nodded. "Were you there with her?"

"I . . . held her until she was gone." I tried hard to keep my voice from shaking.

Simon made a noise, disguised it as a throat clearing, and lowered his head. "Thank you."

"Of course," I said softly.

Drew slid his hand over my shoulder and squeezed. "You alright, though?"

I nodded quickly, not wanting to take my eyes from Simon. My heart was broken for him. He already felt so different, and now his sister—the one person who loved him no matter what—was gone.

"Drew, we should really get out of here," Jenna said. "We've wasted enough time already."

Wasted. Really?

Simon stood abruptly. "Looking for Maddy was *not* a waste of time if that's what you're referring to," he snapped.

"No," Jenna said, almost too sweetly. "I just mean that we lost this fight. Lorendale and Etak have already left. I think we should follow them."

Drew nodded. "She's right. We should go. While we were preoccupied with fighting Victor and Dana and their armies here, someone went to Africa and took Etak's element."

"What? Who could do that?"

"Riley would've known the location," Drew answered. "But how he got there is a mystery. Probably Keagan."

"Keagan was here," I said. "Simon and I were fighting him."

"Yeah, but he disappeared mid-fight," Simon explained.

"So you think he left, got Riley, and they went for Etak's element?"

"The sapphire studded belt," Drew confirmed. "Luke's wild."

"I bet. Where is he now?"

"Brazil. The middle of the Amazon Rainforest."

"Why Brazil? What's there?"

"Yelram's element—the topaz helmet. Etak's element will lead Victor straight there."

The ground began to quake again, and Drew took my hand while he made a portal for the armies to escape through. "Come on," he said. "These earthquakes are only going to get worse."

CHAPTER 16

The Reserve Force

~ SARAH ~

THE LAST FEW hours had been agonizing. My calves ached from the constant pacing of my bedroom floor as I waited for news from Maddy. The pad of my thumb was raw from rubbing my key non-stop. Then I would scare myself when it got hot, believing that the heat meant Luke or Maddy was in danger and needed me to come to their rescue.

But what good would I be anyway? Sure, I might be able to use my powers if it meant protecting Luke, but would it be reckless and irresponsible because I still wasn't able to protect myself?

What was happening in Europe? How were our warriors fairing? Were they able to defend against the dark armies?

I couldn't just sit at home and do nothing, although a quick glance down at my abdomen reminded me that there was a little human being growing inside, rendering me powerless and helpless.

Maybe I didn't have all my powers, and maybe I no longer had superhuman healing abilities, but I did have courage and heart, and I could go to the portal and see how the reserve force was doing. Maybe just visiting them would lift their spirits.

So I strapped my sword around my waist, tucked some knives into my boots, pulled my hair up into a ponytail, and headed for the tiger fields where I knew I would find Lucia.

Lucia was restless too, and I realized we shared a common misery for being left behind. She sent me an image of Luke coming to the tiger fields to get Gideon before they left for Earth. He had stopped to ask Lucia a favour before they left—"Please take care of Sarah." And then he mounted Gideon and they left, leaving Lucia alone and scared and wishing that we were going too.

Lucia nudged me, bringing me back to the here and now.

"I know, girl. Nothing we can do, though, right?"

She made a small purring noise and lowered her body so that I could climb atop. She wondered where we were going.

"To the portal," I told her. "We're going to check on the reserves. See if there's anything we *can* do."

YELRAM'S PORTAL WAS in the centre of the world, surrounded by mountain ranges. This was where, if there was a breach, the enemy would arrive. So this was where the reserves were stationed. Six hundred of them. And the field was large enough for them all.

The reserves took their job seriously. The majority of them stood guard in orderly rows, with weapons at the ready. To the west, a smaller number gathered to practice their combat skills, while at the other end of the field another group gathered for sleep.

Lucia and I watched the groups for several minutes, and then the sleeping warriors, one by one, started to wake and gather their things. It was their turn to join the guard and give the next group a break.

"Your Highness," one of the rested warriors said as Lucia and I approached.

"Hi." I dismounted Lucia and approached the warrior. "How are you all doing here?"

"We're great," he answered. "We take turns standing guard, honing our skills, and sleeping and eating." He seemed proud of their operation.

I smiled. "That's great," I said. "Looks like you've got it all under control."

"I think we're all just anxious to get out there, you

know?"

But I didn't know. Get out *where?* "Earth?"

"Yeah," the guy nodded, confusing me even further. Why would these people *want* to go to Earth and risk losing their lives for eternity? If they died a second death on Earth, that was it for them. They turned to dust. There was no more.

Another woman approached and greeted me with a large smile. "Good day, Your Highness."

"Please, just call me Sarah." Then I turned back to the guy. "Why? Why are you anxious to go to Earth?"

"Because that's where the action is," he said with a laugh.

I looked at the woman to see if she thought he was crazy too, but she added, "Don't get us wrong, it is an honour to be part of the reserves, but going to Earth and defending our freedom and peace while protecting the heart of the worlds is ultimately what we're all here for."

I tried to smile because I didn't know how I should respond. These people were part of the reserves because they had children, or they weren't strong enough, or they had some other *reason* to be held back. But they didn't see that at all.

"Do you have children?" I asked, although I wasn't sure why I had.

The woman beamed. "We both do, yes."

"Where are they now?"

"Mine are being looked after by friends," the woman admitted. "My husband is on Earth now."

"And mine are in the group cottage," the man explained. "It's a home set up for children of the army."

I must have looked horrified because the woman added, "The kids are having a blast. They hardly know we're gone."

My mouth was too dry to form words.

"As parents," she went on, "our job is not to just stay alive for them. It's our *responsibility* to give them the best chance for a better future. Anything less is just babysitting."

It was one of those moments where the lesson just hits you right in the face. My mouth was ajar, but I couldn't find the right words to fill it.

I felt a small flutter in my abdomen, and my hand went to it. Then, suddenly, the air shifted and circled, and Maddy appeared not ten feet away.

"Maddy!" I ran to her and swallowed her in my embrace. "You look . . . worn. Are you okay?"

She nodded quickly. "I'm okay." Then she hesitated before gently adding, "Sarah, we need more warriors."

My inhale quivered and tears fell from my eyes as Lucia joined me, eager for news too. "What's happening in Europe?" I asked.

Maddy looked away. "We lost. . . . We weren't strong enough."

"Where's Luke? No, don't tell me! Yes, tell me! Is he okay? Please tell me he's okay." My hands trembled and I felt like vomiting. It was the worst feeling in the world to send your loved ones off to war and not know what was happening every single minute.

"He's okay, Sarah, relax." She gripped my shoulders and held me firmly.

"Are you sure?" I cried.

Maddy nodded fervently. "He and Gideon are a good team. You should've seen them. You'd be proud. War suits him." She was trying to make me smile. "He's like a thousand times sexier right now."

I let out a relieved laugh and covered my mouth as my heart settled, knowing my love was safe. "And Drew?"

"He's okay too . . . and even sexier than Luke." She winked, and then her face returned to business. "While we were fighting, Etak's element was taken."

I closed my eyes and exhaled. "How is Luke?"

"Pissed."

"Where are you going next?"

"Etak's element will lead them to Yelram's," Maddy said hesitantly. "We're there now setting up. I just came back because"—she turned and observed the reserve force standing guard—"we need help, Sarah."

"How many do you need?"

"Sarah, we could really use them all."

I was shaking my head before she finished. "Maddy, I can't. Look at them."

"Then how many can we have?"

"How many did you lose?"

Maddy hesitated before answering. "Half."

"Two hundred?" I gripped my head with my trembling hands.

"It wasn't an easy fight."

"What makes the next fight any different?" I challenged. "Is there any chance at all that we can win this?"

"We can't just let them have it, Sarah."

I turned to find the resting warriors eagerly gathering their things. They had overheard Maddy's request for help, and even though they had also overheard that half of the warriors were now dead, they still wanted to go.

This was what these people signed up for. They knew what they were getting into, and even though some of them looked too old or too young to lay down their lives, they were also more than honoured to do so.

I took my key and pressed my free hand toward the field. Seconds later, a swirling vortex of yellow air opened a portal to the Amazon.

With a heavy heart, I said, "Take whoever will eagerly go."

And I watched as the rest of my reserve force—six hundred warriors—enthusiastically charged through the portal, weapons held high, but courage held higher.

CHAPTER 17

Protect & Defend

~ MADDY ~

THE RESERVES POURED through the portal into the Amazon, not far from the magnificent waterfall that fell from the massive rock ledge a hundred feet up and emptied into the beautiful turquoise lagoon. A quick look around confirmed that Etak's army was already positioned throughout the jungle around the waterfall, evidenced by the glimpses of blue uniforms and the yellow eyes of the massive wolves that tried to conceal themselves in the lush vegetation.

Lorendale's army, I knew, were farther out. We weren't sure where the dark army would arrive, so the strategy was to cover all bases, and come in closer if needed.

Drew, along with the three remaining core four leaders—Simon, Jenna, and David, were waiting for my return, not far from where I appeared. Drew led Simon and Jenna over to greet the new arrivals.

"Great job," Drew said as he squeezed my shoulder. "How many?"

"The rest," I answered. "Six hundred."

He nodded, but didn't smile. He knew most of these warriors wouldn't survive. I swallowed hard as I pushed the thought from my mind.

"Simon, Jenna, and David, I want you three to take them up there." Drew pointed to the rock ledge above from where the waterfall came. "And any tree they can climb. We'll use them as snipers. We need to keep them out of harm's way if we can. We don't know when the dark armies will come," Drew explained. "I suspect they'll need to recharge after that fight. So once you've positioned the recruits, tell them to rest but be ready for when we need them."

The core leaders nodded their understanding, and then left to position the new warriors. As Simon walked away, he glanced back, and when our eyes met, I felt his deep sadness. I reached for him, but he kept walking. He wasn't ready to talk. Besides, we were in the middle of a war.

When we were alone, Drew turned to me. "I was thinking, maybe you should go back to Yelram and stay with Sarah."

"Why?"

"Because I don't worry about you when you're there, and because . . ." He looked down at my hand and reached for it, but I pulled away.

"You don't think I'm strong enough?"

"I *know* you're strong enough, Maddy. I just . . ."

"Is this about Simon?"

Drew looked confused. "Ummm, no? Should it be?"

"I just don't get why you're trying to get rid of me."

"I'm actually trying to do the opposite—protect you."

"I don't need protection, Drew. Besides, Yelram's army is braver and stronger with me here. Maybe not as strong as if Sarah were here, but I'm sure I make a difference."

Luke and Devon approached through the trees, and Drew stepped back to greet them. "Hey."

Luke nodded at Drew, then turned to me. "Does Sarah know you took all the reserves?"

"She wasn't happy with it, but they were eager to go, and she knows we need them."

"How is she?" Luke asked.

"Antsy."

He grinned. "Sounds about right."

"She get her powers back?" Devon asked. Sometimes I admired his directness, but when the answer meant more people would die, I wished he had more couth.

"No," I said flatly. "But the important thing is, she looks much better."

Devon snickered. "Yeah, 'cause that helps us."

Luke glared at Devon.

"Sorry," Devon said. "Just been a long day. Think I'll get some rest."

Luke nodded, then suggested that we all do the same while he kept watch.

SEVERAL HOURS LATER, when the moon was high and everyone had had a good nap, Drew, Luke, Devon, and I sat around a fire, while the armies stayed scattered throughout the surrounding jungle, resting and waiting. Raven laid next to me, while Gideon patrolled impatiently behind Luke. Drew's tiger, Bella, and Devon's wolf, Airam, positioned themselves about twenty feet away, heads low and eyes narrowed into the darkness.

Airam made me nervous. He was the same size as Gideon, but darker in colour, and scared me a hundred times more. Maybe because I knew Gideon, and he was extremely loyal to Luke. I knew nothing of Airam. Just that he had been praised for his brutal strength and deadly abilities in the battle at Stonehenge. And even now, poised to protect us, I found myself unable to turn my back on him.

It was eerily quiet, save for the sound of the crackling

fire and Gideon's footsteps on the soft ground. I liked the silence—it meant there was no war.

But I also hated the silence, because there was nothing to drown out the memory of Beth's death.

In my arms.

Turned to ash.

Gone forever.

Drew slid his hand over my thigh. "You're not okay," he said.

I shook my head. "Not entirely, but I'll be fine."

"Beth?" he guessed, and I nodded.

Devon looked up from the flames. "You'll get used to it."

"Great," I said sarcastically.

"Did you tell Sarah?" Luke asked. "About Beth?"

I shook my head.

"Probably best," he said.

Without any forethought, I pushed myself off the ground and announced, "I need to go for a walk. Stretch my legs."

Drew stood too. "I'll come with you."

"No," I said too quickly. "Please. I need to be alone right now."

I was surprised he let me go, but then I heard him give a command to both Raven and Bella to follow me.

"I won't be long," I promised.

I knew where I was going. Yes, I needed to stretch my

legs and get away from the campfire of deep thoughts and depressing flashbacks, but I also needed to check on Simon. Beth's last request was for me to look out for him, and aside from delivering the news of her death, I hadn't done a single thing to console him.

I passed several of our warriors and recognized most of them as members of the group that Simon and I had trained, which told me Simon wouldn't be far. Finally, I found him sitting against a tree, sharpening sticks that would become arrows.

"Hi," I said. "Can I sit?"

He pushed aside the pile of arrows and made a place for me next to him. "What's up?"

"I wanted to check on you. How are you?"

"Drew know you're here?"

I frowned and made a huffing sound. "Does it matter?"

"So he doesn't." Simon chuckled and continued carving the stick.

"Simon, I'm here because I care about you. It doesn't matter what Drew thinks or knows or whatever."

He nodded and gave a half smile. "Well, thanks for checking, but I'm fine."

I let the silence carry the moment, and then I said, carefully, "I know she was your sister."

He watched me for a minute. "How'd you know that?"

"She told me before she died." My eyes began to water, and I tried to blink the wetness away before he noticed.

"She didn't deserve to die. It should've been me."

"I thought the same thing," I said, and his eyes flickered to mine. "Not that it should've been you," I quickly corrected. "That it should've been *me*."

He frowned at me.

"You don't deserve to die either, Simon."

He scoffed as if I didn't know what I was talking about. "I do."

"Why?"

"Okay," he said, turning to face me. "You want to know why it should've been me? Because she's a good person, and I'm not."

"And why aren't you a good person?"

"Because I'm intrigued by the dark side, okay?" His voice was low, careful not to let anyone overhear. "Yes, I'm loyal to Yelram, but my interests lie with the dark arts."

How was I supposed to respond to that? Was he testing me? Trying to scare me into leaving him alone? Into accepting his ridiculous idea that he was more deserving of death than his sister?

"Beth always kept me in line," he said, a chuckle to his admission. "She told me never to tell anyone about my fascination. She said it was just a phase." He snorted.

"A phase that lasted ten years . . . and still going." He looked to his left into the darkness. "I only ended up in Yelram because I was a kid when I left Earth. And that's why I made her promise not to tell anyone that she was my sister. She thought I was embarrassed by her, but . . . I just didn't want anyone to paint her with the same brush they always seemed to paint me with."

"And what is that?"

"Don't pretend you don't know, Maddy. You didn't even like me when you first met me."

"That's because you were a know-it-all," I teased.

He nodded. "And Drew hates me. Luke never talks to me. Sarah hardly looks at me."

"They don't hate you, Simon." I moved closer to him so I could better see his eyes in the dark night. "You're too hard on yourself. If Sarah didn't trust you, she wouldn't have let me pick you for the core four."

He looked away but managed a small grin.

"Beth believed in you. You have to keep fighting for Yelram. For your home. For *Beth's* home. She died fighting for this cause. You owe her to be strong."

He closed his eyes and a tear fell. I took him in my arms and we sat on the humid forest floor holding each other, with his promise that he wouldn't abandon Yelram, and my promise that I would continue Beth's mission to keep him on the straight and narrow.

Suddenly a bright light was on us. "What's going

on?" Drew barked as Simon and I jumped to our feet.

I squinted from the brightness. "Drew, put that down!" I scolded.

He dropped the flashlight but replaced it with Simon's shirt. Pinning him to the tree, he hissed, "You have some nerve."

"Drew!" I shouted, trying to pull him from Simon, but his grip was tight, and he wasn't budging. "Nothing is going on."

"I'm not stupid, Drew," Simon said. "I know I don't have a chance with her."

"Then why are you still trying?"

"Because someone ought to."

Drew dropped Simon, then looked from me to Simon, then back to me. His jaw was clenched, and I knew he expected me to give him an explanation, but I couldn't. Nor was he entitled to one after reacting first and asking questions later.

Drew shook his head then left, leaving Simon and me alone again.

"Yeah," Simon said, adjusting his shirt, "doesn't hate me at all."

"He doesn't know how much Beth meant to you." My heart was racing, and all I could do was watch the place that Drew left, hoping he would return with an apology. "Besides, he has no right to judge this situation right now. He's spent more time around Jenna these last few days than I care to admit, and—"

"You're not seriously jealous of her, though, are you?"

"Ummmm, have you seen her? She's beautiful."

Simon laughed and shook his head. "She's got nothing on you." He paused before adding, "Drew loves you, Maddy."

Slowly, our eyes met. "He doesn't." I was rotating Drew's school ring around my finger. The one he gave me when he asked me to be his girlfriend three months ago. Why hadn't our relationship moved forward? What was holding him back?

Simon followed my eyes to the ring. "Is that Drew's?" It was a good guess—I wore it around my index finger as it was too big for my ring finger.

I nodded. "Where we're from, giving a girl your school ring is a sign of commitment."

Simon raised his eyebrows. "See?"

"After his father died, something changed in him. And I lied to him about Sarah's pregnancy, so that pushed him further. And . . . I hear his thoughts. He doesn't love me. He repeats it over and over in his head whenever I'm near." There was no sense in trying to stop the tears; they were coming.

"He's probably new to the whole relationship thing."

"He's not, though," I said. "He and Sarah were together. He loved her. Although he was only marginally better at showing it."

"Drew and Sarah? As in our *queen* Sarah?"

I laughed. "Yes, *that* Sarah. You didn't know that? And then Sarah met Luke and they fell in love."

Simon was quiet, and it was clear that he struggled with whether to tell me what was on his mind.

"What?"

"Drew and Sarah."

"Yes."

"He loved her."

"Yes?"

"And then she left him for Luke."

"Yes."

"And he was heartbroken?"

"Yeah," I said. "There was an enchantment that brought them together, but it still broke him to have to watch her move on with Luke."

"Wow," Simon said as he shook his head. "So Drew got his heart broken by his first love, and he also lost his father—"

"And his mother. She was killed when he was young."

Simon chuckled to himself and nodded. "So probably the only three people he ever loved before you came along?"

"Yeah?"

"Did you ever think maybe Drew's just afraid to be

broken again?"

I shook my head, but the idea rolled playfully through my mind. Could that be why Drew was hesitant to get too close? Was my relationship with Simon scaring him off?

"Even if you're right," I began, "I'm not going to stop caring about you just so he can feel more secure."

Simon gave a half smile of gratitude.

"But it's nice to think that underneath all that deluded confusion he may actually love me."

Simon nudged me in the arm. "I probably just shot myself in the foot there, hey?"

I smirked. "You never had a chance anyway."

He let out a laugh. "Thanks for sugarcoating it, though."

I pulled him into me and held on tight. "You know I think you're pretty amazing, right?"

"At least there's that."

I opened my mind and let my thoughts race toward him. He was loved. Like a best friend. Like a brother.

His arms tightened around me, and I saw a beautiful image of his sister, Beth, flash in his mind before he pushed her away along with the pain that her memory brought.

"You should go," Simon said as he handed me the flashlight. "You should probably go tell Drew why you came—to check on Beth's little brother. You can tell him.

It doesn't matter now anyway."

"I'll tell him Beth was your sister, but let's keep the fascination of the dark arts to ourselves, shall we?" I nudged him and he grinned.

"Thanks," he said, then he walked me to Raven who was waiting nearby.

"Maddy, can I ask you a question?" he asked as he helped me onto Raven's back.

"Sure, anything."

"If Drew wasn't in the picture, could you see me and you together?"

I smiled and reached for his hand. "But he is."

Simon nodded and stepped back. Then Raven took me swiftly back to the campfire. Back to Drew.

WHEN I RETURNED to the fire, Luke and Devon nodded, acknowledging my return, but Drew just kept his eyes on the flames.

"How's Simon?" Devon asked, a mischievous grin on his face.

I glared at him. "Better now, thanks."

"Better?" Drew repeated.

"Yes, *better*. I mean, he's still upset, obviously, but he did just lose his sister, after all."

Drew quickly looked up at me. "Sister," he said, confused.

"Beth was his sister. She told me as she died in my

arms. And she asked me to make sure he was okay. So that's what I was doing."

Drew stood and came to me. "Why didn't you tell me?"

"You never gave me a chance to. And then you show up and threaten to beat him up because you think he's hitting on me?"

"Well, what was I supposed to think, Maddy?"

"I don't care what you *think*, Drew. But you shouldn't have *said* anything until you had the full story."

"I'm sorry."

"You need to trust me," I finished. "I know I lied to you before, but I . . . I love you, Drew, and I would never—"

"You don't love me," he interjected. He looked around as if to see who witnessed my embarrassing profession of love, then he lowered his voice and repeated, "You don't love me, Maddy."

"Drew—"

"Stop," he warned. He pressed his thumb to my lips as he cupped my face. His face moved closer until I thought he would kiss me, but then a look of agony crossed his face as he stepped away. "This isn't love."

With my heart and pride both in pieces, I found my way back to the fire. "I guess you're right," I managed to say before my throat closed off, making it difficult to breathe.

Luke was quiet, pretending not to have noticed the exchange. Even Devon was at a loss for words, although his thoughts were loud and clear: *"Even I'm not that cruel."*

CHAPTER 18

Facing Fears

~ SARAH ~

WITH ONLY A few hours of sleep, morning came too early. I hadn't closed the drapes because I felt guilty sleeping when my friends, family, and people were awake on Earth and fighting for their lives.

Thankfully, the relentless pounding in my head was now just a dull hum that clouded my thoughts, but not my ambition. I was showered and dressed for battle before the sun finished rising, and then I retrieved Lucia from the fields and we went on a long, hard ride together, racing through the quadrants. Lucia, too, was eager to run as hard and fast as she could. The adrenalin helped us forget what we were missing out on. She missed her best friend, Raven, and if I wasn't mistaken, she missed another, too. I wondered which tiger had stolen her heart, and when. Maybe I was wrong, but I felt that she, too, longed to be reunited with her love.

We'll see them soon, Lucia, I told her, and she answered by letting out a roar and then running faster than I had ever seen her run.

By early afternoon, we were nearing the Northeast Quadrant. Lucia was getting tired, so I ported us to the Garden of Hope where we could rest, recharge, and escape the torture of missing out.

Although the surrounding forest was dark and gloomy, the Garden of Hope was filled with light and warmth, seemingly with direct access to the sun.

The daisies grew tall and wild here. I loved meandering through them, letting my fingertips gently brush their petals as I inhaled the refreshing air.

Lucia lagged behind, absorbed in her own thoughts of loneliness and fear. Yes, she was happy to be here with me, and even if Maddy came back to get her, Lucia wouldn't have gone. I knew this in the deepest part of my core. She was hinged to me. Where I went, she went. But it didn't mean that she couldn't mourn the other part of her that was hinged to another and felt completely lost without them. And I understood. Too well.

Suddenly the air changed, and not ten feet away, a woman appeared. Her wild red hair was familiar, but that's where the familiarities ended.

Until she spoke.

"Hi, my darling," she said, and my breath got caught in my throat.

There was no need for introduction. I knew who she was. She was my mother. But how did she get there?

"The gardens all lead to Nevaeh," she said, as if in answer to my thought.

I was still in too much shock to respond, but Lucia's surprise wasn't as long-lasting. She let out an excited roar and took one leap, and then the two were in each other's embrace.

"You did well, my girl," Leah lovingly said to Lucia as Lucia purred happily.

"What are you . . . what are you doing here?" I managed to ask.

She opened her mouth to speak, but took a few seconds before she finally said, "I was worried about you." Lucia backed away so that my mother and I were now face to face. "I heard that Yelram's army wasn't . . . *fortified*, which meant you weren't on Earth. And I guess I just worried about what was keeping you back."

I turned away from her because the news of my unfortified army was disturbing at the very least. "Why aren't *you* on Earth?"

She smiled, appreciating my diversion. "I was. Trinity has been watching the Garden of Hope. As soon as you arrived here, she told me so that I could come see you."

Creepy? I peered around the garden, and then into the sky, imagining that this large face would be peering back at me.

"So that's why *I'm* here—to talk to you. Why are *you* here? Or better yet, why aren't you on Earth?"

I went to Lucia and ran my hands through her thick coat. "I don't have my powers," I admitted. "Nothing. I can't even heal myself."

She hesitated before asking, "Why?"

I chuckled, mostly to disguise my desire to cry. "Haven't you heard? I'm pregnant."

She inhaled sharply, then made a noise that was half laugh and half cry. "Sarah, I'm so happy for you."

"Well, don't be. It's not exactly exciting news."

"What do you mean?" She reached out and touched my arm.

I slowly recoiled from her touch and ran my own hand over the place where hers had just been. Why did it feel so weird to have her touch me?

"Because it's taking all of my powers, rendering me useless and incapable of helping my people. Reason number one." I was being overly rude, but couldn't seem to stop myself.

"It's not taking your powers," she said. "But you may be holding onto something that's causing the block."

"Elaborate?"

"Fear and resentment are the two biggest inhibitors to any inner strength."

"So you think I'm afraid and resentful," I summarized.

"Well, are you?"

I shook my head and scoffed. "You have some nerve coming here and judging me after what you did to me."

"Sarah, I—"

"I know *why* you did what you did, but I don't get how you can pretend that I should be okay. And why is this the first time you've come? Huh? I've been married for three months. I've been Yelram's keeper for three months. And this is the first time I'm seeing you."

"I can only see you in the garden," she explained, and her eyes began to water.

"Then why not send Trinity to tell me that? I would've come here every single day to see you." My voice was shaking and my eyes and nose both began to drip. "I didn't just need a mother *then*, I need one *now*."

She reached for me again. "I'm here now," she said through tears. "Sarah, I'm sorry. I did what I thought was the best thing for you. For Yelram. For our people." When I didn't respond or look at her, she continued, "Leaving you was the hardest decision I ever had to make, and up until a few months ago, I wondered every single day if it was the right one. Trinity kept an eye on you as you grew up, and Earth's keepers were enchanted to protect you. I knew you'd be safe, but I missed you every single day. Please, you have to know that, Sarah."

It hadn't been an easy decision for her. I knew that. It had only become a problem recently when I found out I was going to be a mother. I had convinced myself that it was because I wasn't raised by a mother so I didn't know how to be a mother, but upon hearing her sad admission, I realized that I was afraid of this child losing its mother like I lost mine. I was afraid of abandoning a child and continuing the cycle of loneliness.

But I wasn't abandoned. I was rescued. I shouldn't have been focusing on the moments before my life changed—the moment I was abandoned by my mother. I should have been focusing on the moments after—the moment my life changed from certain death to rescued daughter. My mother had done what she had to do to ensure that I survived. To ensure that I grew up with the means to one day take back Yelram.

My whole body began to tingle. I moved my arms in front of me and, although I couldn't see any difference, I felt the energy rushing through them. Fortifying them.

I cupped my hands and two pools of water gathered in my palms.

My heart hastened.

I poured the water onto the ground and splayed my fingers, and the daisies around my knees grew to even greater heights.

My breath quickened.

With a surge of confidence, I threw my hand toward the forest beyond, and a squall of wind ripped through the trees, bending branches and causing birds to take flight.

My body was alive.

Leah was smiling proudly.

"My resentment was holding me back," I realized.

"I hope this means you don't resent me anymore?"

I turned my attention to my mother—the woman dressed in white battle gear, but wearing a weak face full of sadness.

"It must have been hard to do what you did," I acknowledged.

"The hardest thing ever. I pray you never have to make that choice."

I smiled. "Well, if I do, I hope I'm as brave as you."

Leah let out a laugh, blended with a cry, and we embraced.

"I don't know if I can heal yet," I realized, and then I pulled my sword and held it out for my mother. "Cut me."

"Absolutely not." She held her hands up, refusing to take the sword.

"Fair," I said as I cupped my left hand around the blade. "I get how that would be weird."

I ignored the sharp stinging sensation that the blade

209

caused as it sliced through my skin. The blood pooled in my palm before it dripped down onto the ground. I sheathed the sword and held my hand out, waiting for it to sew itself back up.

We both watched in wonder, both eager to witness my re-healing.

And we waited.

Eventually my adrenalin waned as I realized that, perhaps, I hadn't yet conquered all of my internal demons.

Leah took my bleeding hand and rubbed the tips of her fingers overtop of it, sending a flow of water over my hand, cleansing and purifying the wound. Then she tore a strip of her shirt and wrapped it around the injury.

"I don't understand," I said, frustrated.

"There's something still holding you back."

"What?"

She shrugged and gave a sympathetic smile. "I don't know, my love. Maybe you're still afraid of something."

Maybe she was right. I did worry about whether or not Luke wanted to have this baby. I wanted this baby to have the best chance for a better future, but a better future included him wanting this baby too.

"So what's holding you back now?"

"What do you mean?"

"I *mean* why aren't you on Earth with your army? You have your powers back. What's stopping you?"

"I'm still pregnant."

"That might be more of a blessing than you realize."

"What do you mean?"

"That baby is a product of two extremely powerful and gifted keepers. There is a whole lot of energy swirling around inside you right now, Sarah. When I was pregnant with you, I was able to access all of your many gifts. And if I was able to do *that*, think of what you might be able to access from this little gifted miracle."

I was sure my face was a mirror of confusion and wonder.

"Just be open to the idea that this baby may be a blessing in a time when we need it the most. Sometimes we have to get out of our comfort zone if it means saving the worlds."

Something flickered in her mind when she said that last part. A painful memory of her leaving her comfort zone, abandoning all that she loved, to save Yelram. This was her sacrifice. This was how she identified with my need to help save the worlds. She had done the same thing. She had sacrificed herself for the good of the worlds, her biggest sacrifice not being her own life, but having to leave her child behind in a foreign world with only an enchantment to keep her from the claws of the dark lords.

And I wanted to run to Earth. I wanted to. I wanted to fight alongside Luke. I wanted to protect my army, but without the ability to heal myself—my baby—could I?

CHAPTER 19

The Ten-Horned Beast

~ MADDY ~

IT HAD BEEN almost a full day of waiting and trying to rest, although rest was impossible when, at any moment, a portal could open and thousands of dark warriors would come charging through, ready to kill without hesitation.

"What's taking them so long?" I said, frustrated that my energy was being wasted on pacing and worrying.

"They may have won Lorendale's element, but not without taking a beating," Drew reminded me. "We needed the rest, too."

The warriors were keeping fed and getting lots of rest, and I felt confident that we were going to be good and ready for when Victor and Dana finally arrived, but the waiting was agonizing. Maybe this was Victor's plan. A cruel form of torture, never fully knowing when they would arrive, so never fully resting.

Luke and Devon kept watch while Drew and I tried to sleep by the fire. At best guess, I managed to get a solid hour of sleep. And then we would switch, and for some reason, Devon didn't seem to have any trouble falling asleep and staying that way until we woke him for his shift.

Luke was the most restless of us all. He barely talked, and only gave one word answers when needed. We mostly just bypassed him and talked to Devon instead.

Gideon was the same. He paced the camp, ignoring everyone and every animal around him. Occasionally Raven would interrupt his stride and they would share a wordless exchange, which seemed to relax Gideon if only just a little.

Without any warning, Luke announced, "I'm going to check on Sarah."

Gideon stopped pacing and turned his full attention to his master.

"I don't think that's a good idea, Luke," Drew started. "You'll need to be here when Victor arrives. Your army needs you."

Luke pushed his hands through his hair, then turned to me. "Will you go?"

"And do what? Tell her you're losing your mind over here?"

Luke frowned. "Just see how she's doing. What if she needs me?"

I pointed to Luke's key. "You'll know if she needs you. Luke, just relax. She's safe where she is."

Before Luke could argue, Gideon, Airam, Raven, and Bella's heads snapped up. All four animals turned to the west. Then the sound of battle cry filled the air.

"They're here," Devon announced as he pulled his sword.

Gideon let out a roar and lowered his body for Luke to mount him. Then the two of them, followed by Devon and Airam, took off in the direction of the battle cries.

Drew was breathing heavy, and if I wasn't mistaken, he was nervous.

"You okay?" I asked as I mounted Raven.

"Been thinking about what Luke said. Maybe something's wrong with Sarah. Maybe you should go check on her."

"And leave you guys? No way."

"What if he senses something?"

"He just misses her, Drew. This war has us all thinking more about the people we love."

He watched me for a long few seconds, then an arrow whizzed past our heads and we both hit the ground.

Drew loosed three arrows before I had time to ready

one. And then we were surrounded by warriors—blue, purple, and yellow versus red and black.

Raven leaped over my head and rammed into a panther carrying a Nitsuan warrior. The warrior flipped off the panther's back before the two animals hit the ground. Without hesitation, she pulled her sword and came straight for me.

I scrambled to my feet and pulled my sword, but before I had a chance to engage, Drew landed next to me, swung his sword, and beheaded my attacker.

Three more warriors approached—two on panthers and one on a dragon. Drew didn't hesitate—he leaped through the air, over the stream of fire from the ferocious dragon, and attacked its rider, while Bella attacked the dragon from the ground. I didn't have time to watch how Drew would fair against the Leviathan warrior; I had two Nitsuan warriors to contend with. They were closing in on me. Raven attacked one of the panthers while the other rider jumped off and landed next to me. He threw his sword toward me, and I moved out of the way, narrowly avoiding my death. I plunged my sword back, and he parried as well. Raven was now engaged with both panthers, while both fighters were on the ground, closing in on me.

Suddenly Luke appeared next to me and, in an impressive calculated movement, killed one of the warriors while I fought the second one, ending him with a blade to the chest.

"Thank you," I said, breathless, although I suspected he did it more for Sarah than he did for me. How would he give her the news of her best friend's death? I felt the same—if Luke died, how could I ever tell Sarah? But, seeing him in action, I wondered if there was anyone here that was a match for him. Drew, too.

Suddenly, the ground began to rumble and a deafening roar split the air. The invading army backed off, while everyone else gravitated toward Drew and Luke for reassurance. Distant trees parted and fell, and whatever it was that was fast approaching, pounding the ground with its enormous feet as it crashed through the iron-clad warriors, was taking no prisoners. Warriors were thrown through the air as if weightless.

I was frozen with fear and only felt Drew's arm shoving me back as Luke waved his arms around, conjuring a syphon of wind to defend us with.

Drew fumbled for my arm, not taking his eyes off the forest ahead, waiting for the *thing* to appear. When our hands touched, we disappeared, reappearing seconds later at the top of the ledge, next to the waterfall.

"Stay here!" Drew ordered.

"What is that thing!?"

He didn't answer, but then he was gone again, reappearing back in the forest next to Luke.

I could barely see them, but I had a better view of the

trees parting, and could make out glimpses of the enormous beast that closed in on them.

Luke threw his hands toward the creature and the tornado ripped through the trees toward the beast, sending it off course, but not enough.

Drew lifted his hands up, and I saw the creature more clearly as it defied gravity and floated above the treetops. It was larger and more grotesque than any beast I had ever seen. It had the strength and speed of a leopard, only thirty times the size, claws like a bear, and the head of a lion, with ten horns that started at the head and continued down the spine of its entire body.

Eli joined Luke and Drew, and the three separated, throwing their powers toward the beast, but no matter what they did, the beast seemed only interested in one person—Luke.

My heart raced as I released arrow after arrow toward the creature. Nothing penetrated. Nothing distracted.

And then the beast was on them.

Luke continued to bend air as he tried desperately to get out of the way of the creature's enormous claws and deadly horns. Drew was able to lift the beast off course by bending gravity, and Eli erupted the ground and created sinkholes to try to slow it down, but their efforts were futile.

I couldn't just stand on the top of the ridge and watch while my friends struggled to stay alive. I took my key and muttered Drew's name, and the next thing I knew I was standing beside him.

"I told you to stay up there!" Drew shouted as he bent more gravity and knocked the beast to its side.

"I can try to get into its head," I told him, but before I could try anything, my chest began to tingle. I grabbed my key, realizing it was the cause.

"My key!" I shouted.

Drew looked over his shoulder for a split second. "Sarah's summoning you!" he said before leaping into the air with his sword aimed for the beast's head.

And that was the last thing I saw before I vanished, unwillingly.

CHAPTER 20

The Terrifying Truth

~ SARAH ~

SHE APPEARED ONLY feet from me, in the middle of Yelram's portal, in the exact spot where I stood only seconds ago when I summoned her for the very first time. Why had my key burned like that? Why, when I gripped my key, did a flood of panic cover my body? What was happening on Earth?

I could still hear Leah's voice echoing in my ear: "Go, Sarah!" She, too, had seen the key burning and knew that it meant trouble. And as much as I regretted that time was taken from us once again, my fear for Luke and Maddy's lives was much more pressing.

Maddy gasped for breath, her eyes wide and fearful,

searching for whatever it was she saw on Earth only a moment ago.

"Are you okay?" I asked. She jumped at the sound of my voice. "Maddy?" I said, but her eyes couldn't find me—they seemed to look right past me as they continued searching. "Maddy, is Luke okay?" I pressed. Her red, glossy eyes finally found mine.

She ran to me, enveloping me in her arms. "You're okay," she breathed, a desperate air of relief to her voice.

"Of course I'm okay. Is Luke okay?" My hand was closed tight around my key, the burning had stopped, but I knew the warning was far from over.

Her face went pale as she tried desperately to grab hold of her surroundings.

"We're at the portal," I told her. "What's wrong? What's happening?" I searched her face and mind for answers.

"There's a . . . beast attacking us right now." She was afraid of what the word 'beast' would do to me. She said it with less conviction than the rest of her words.

My mouth fell open and my fingers twisted around my key even harder. "My key was burning," I told her.

She nodded as if it made sense, but didn't elaborate.

"What do you think this means?" I pressed.

A sharp image pierced my brain. A vision of a monstrous creature with ten horns storming through hundreds of warriors, saliva streaming from his jowls as his eyes bore into Luke.

"What the hell was that?!" I screamed as the horrific image slipped from my mind. It had been Maddy's thought, and she grabbed it from my mind the moment she realized she had let it slip.

"That was the beast," she admitted. "I think it's after Luke."

"What? Why?" I clutched my stomach, waiting for words that made sense.

She shook her head. "Maybe I'm wrong. I hope I'm wrong, but it just seemed to make a B line right to him. Drew and Eli and Devon, everyone tried to distract it, but it only had eyes for Luke."

I pulled my sword from its holster. "What the hell, Maddy!"

"I could be wrong," she said, but before she was finished, a current of wind sucked the air from my lungs, and Luke appeared a few seconds later about half a football field away. He bent over, holding his knees and breathing heavy, trying to catch his breath.

"Luke!" I cried as I threw my sword back into its holster and ran to him, but our reunion was interrupted by a second blast of wind that knocked us both to the ground. The beast!

The beast was here! Almost directly between me and Luke, but closer to me. It wasn't moving yet, but as it sniffed the air, his head moved from Luke's direction to mine.

Our eyes locked. His were black and soulless, but I still saw into them. I could taste his desire for both my blood and Luke's, and I knew that if I didn't react soon, he would have his wish. A second later, a ball of fire flew from my fingertips, and then another. Although the fire stunned him momentarily, it did not stop him. He reared up onto his hind legs, let out a ground rumbling roar, and charged toward me.

Luke was yelling for us to get the hell out of there, but I couldn't leave him. Not after what I saw in Maddy's vision. Not after I knew this creature was determined to kill my husband.

Maddy had joined me in my efforts to take down the beast. She was flying arrows toward him, but also trying to get inside its head. Her efforts were strong, but something was strange about this creature. It didn't have a mind of its own. The mind that controlled it was too far to reach.

Luke shot an arrow that hit the beast in the back of the head, causing the beast to suddenly stop. The arrow fell, and the beast's nose followed it to the ground, sniffing viciously.

"Over here!" I heard Luke yell. He was waving his hands in the air, desperate to get the beast's attention. Blood ran down his forearm from his hand, and I realized that the arrow that hit the beast was drenched in his own blood. The beast paid no more mind to me as it changed direction and went after Luke.

"Sarah, get out of here!" Luke yelled as the beast ran toward him.

Maddy was next to me, holding my arm. She was afraid I would go after the beast. But all I could do was watch the deadly creature close in on Luke, and then Luke disappeared, followed by the beast.

"It can port!" I shouted, realizing Luke had led the beast out of Yelram. "What the hell is happening?!"

"I don't know," Maddy said, panic laced through her words.

"I have to find them," I declared.

"No!" she shouted, and she put her hands on my shoulders and shook me. "Sarah, that thing is pure evil."

"It doesn't have a mind of its own," I told her.

"I couldn't reach it," she admitted.

"Maybe someone else is controlling it." My mind raced for answers. For something to make sense. "Why does it want Luke?"

"Luke will be fine. I promise you. He's smart, Sarah. He knows what he's doing." She was still breathless, and I knew she didn't believe her own words.

"You can't promise that," I cried.

"Please, Sarah," she said. "Please, just stay here."

And then she was gone.

I fell to my knees and cried. I cried for Maddy and the

desperation that moved her in spite of her terror. I cried for Luke and the imminent danger from the ferocious beast. I cried for the child I was carrying and the real possibility that it could be fatherless by the end of this war. It was all too much, and I just desperately wanted it all to be a bad dream that I would wake from at any moment.

Who had created that beast? Who would want Luke dead? And did the beast want me dead, too?

Victor wanted me dead, so maybe this was his doing. And then there was Dana—she blamed Luke for Ella's death, so she had good reason to want him dead. Keagan was jealous of Luke, so he also had reason. Who did this? If I could only figure out who ordered this, then maybe they could stop it.

A flashback from Earth's portal entered my mind. We were fighting Victor, Dana, Keagan, and Riley. Right before I was knocked out, Maddy had let it slip that I was pregnant. Victor was thrilled—this was the ammunition he needed. But Keagan and Riley were both shocked, like they hadn't expected the news, and this threw a wrench into their wicked plans. Was their plan to release a beast that would kill Luke? Maybe Riley could be reasoned with. Or maybe he couldn't be, but I had to try something. Luke had made me promise I wouldn't go back to Earth, but he didn't say anything about Etak.

Besides, Etak was half mine anyway.

CHAPTER 21

Riley's Reason

~ SARAH ~

I APPEARED IN Luke's bedroom. Our bedroom. It was cold and dark as the curtains were drawn, and the fire was long extinguished. The bed was carefully made, and as I stared at the neatly laid throw pillows, I tried to remember the details of the last time we slept in it together. Since our wedding, Luke had spent most nights in Yelram with me. I smiled at this thought, and clung to the feelings of pleasure that the memory caused.

In a room that was outfitted in dark textiles and furniture, something light caught my attention—a white fabric peeking out of the chest at the foot of the bed. Against the deep blue comforter, dark brown wood of the bedframe, and ebony floors, the white blanket almost seemed to glow.

I lifted the top of the chest and ran my hand over the soft fabric. I brought my face to it and touched the silk edges to my skin. It had a pleasant aroma of lavender and coconut, and as I pulled it from the chest, something fell from it, landing in the box with a clunk. I reached down and pulled out a small picture frame. In it was a photo of a woman with long, dark hair and Luke's deep, dark eyes holding a baby wrapped in the very same blanket.

I sat down on the bed — the picture in one hand and the blanket in the other. This was Luke's baby blanket, and the news of our pregnancy had spurred him to dig it out. And the picture must have been of him and his mother when she was still alive.

I set the picture and blanket back into the box and closed the lid, then I took a deep breath and continued out of the room and down the hall for the reason I came here in the first place. For Riley.

I REMEMBERED THE way to the room with the globe suspended in the middle. It was down two corridors, but the distance between the room and Luke's bedroom seemed much longer this time. Probably because this time I wasn't being dragged by my livid husband who was angry that Devon had lost his brother. I shook my head, ridding it of the negative memory, then rounded the corner and found the large wooden door halfway down on the right.

The massive orb hovered in the middle of the room, and I circled it like I had seen Luke do, looking for something he couldn't find—Riley. And then I spotted him. A red blinking star. I tapped the globe, zooming in on the star. Riley was in the same quadrant as me. I tapped again. He was in the same city. I tapped again. In the same castle. . . . In the same room.

"Hello, princess." His deep voice was darker than ever. "Looking for me?"

I froze, unable to turn around. I knew he was near the door, and a click confirmed that the door was now closed and there was no escaping. My hand hovered over the hilt of my sword as his footsteps crossed the room to the window. He was keeping his distance, so I slowly turned around.

"What are you doing here?" he asked.

"I came to see you," I said.

"Where's your backup?" He eyed me suspiciously.

"I didn't bring any. I just want to talk."

He didn't trust me. He leaned causally against the window ledge, trying to give the illusion that he was disinterested, but my presence was concerning for him.

"Why?" he finally asked.

"Well, I'm not allowed to fight in the war." I pointed to my stomach. "But I couldn't just sit back and do nothing."

"So you came to kill me?"

"Of course not," I said, and he puckered his eyebrows as if this confused him. "I don't hate you, Riley."

"You should," he said darkly.

"No good would come of that. You can't heal hurt with hate."

"Why are you here then, Sarah? Do you have a death wish or something?"

"I don't think you'll hurt me."

"And why is that?"

I took a few steps closer. "Because I saw your face when you found out I was pregnant. . . . You care."

He turned away and pressed his hands into the stone window ledge, but didn't answer.

"And I saw you bend air at the same time Luke did, which sent both me and Dana flying. You didn't mean to hurt me. Your air was meant for Dana, too, wasn't it?"

Again, he was silent, but he let me hear his thoughts. *I'm not a baby killer.*

Riley nodded toward my hand, wrapped in cloth, but soaked in blood. "What's going on there?"

Having forgot that I had sliced my palm open earlier, I rotated my hand and considered the makeshift bandage. "I cut myself."

"Yeah, I get that, but why is it still . . . *cut*? Why haven't you healed it?"

"I'm working on it," I said.

He measured me for a moment, but I saw concern in his eyes. His thoughts were unguarded and it was clear that he felt the baby had something to do with my inability to heal.

"There's a beast that is trying to kill Luke," I continued, happy to change the subject.

Riley didn't make any indication that this was a surprise to him.

"And me," I added.

He turned his head and peered at me over his shoulder, as if this part was news to him.

"Riley?" I prodded.

"It wasn't created to kill you," he said. "It was just supposed to be Luke."

I swallowed and closed my eyes, my worst fear coming true. The beast was created to kill Luke. And with Victor's hand in it, there was nothing we could do to stop it.

Riley turned his body to me. "How do you know it's after you, too?"

"It followed Luke to Yelram when he was trying to escape it. But I was there, and the beast turned on me."

Riley shook his head. "No, that can't be right. I only gave Victor one vial of blood. Just Luke's."

"Your own brother," I said through tears.

But Riley wasn't listening. He was thinking and

brooding. "Victor *promised* to leave you out of it," he said. "Keagan only agreed to take second-in-command and help in the plan if Luke was the target and you were safe." He turned to me. "Are you *sure* it was after you, too?"

Shocked at the many confessions he had just made, I could hardly answer his question. He gave the darkest, most dangerous lord a vial of his own brother's blood so that he could have a beast made to kill him? And Keagan was in on this plan? Why did everyone hate Luke so much?

"Well, your fool proof plan has a glitch," I finally said. "I can assure you, the beast was definitely interested in me as well."

Riley closed his eyes and took in a slow, deep breath as realization covered his face. "The baby has Luke's blood." He clenched his fists and returned to the window.

I wasn't sure whether to be more upset that my unborn child was on this grotesque creature's lunch menu, or that Luke's only brother betrayed him like this.

After a long few minutes, Riley said, "I'm sorry. I never signed up for killing a baby." He looked away "And if I have to be honest, I don't really want to see the kid's mother die, either."

I offered a smile. "Are you saying you actually like me?"

"I tolerate you." There was a smile on his lips, too. "Luke had plenty of chances to kill me," he said, his eyes wandering to memories. "But he never did."

"Do you suppose there was a part of him that never wanted you dead?"

"Yeah," he said. "You."

"Well, whatever your differences, you're still family." I felt the baby kick as I said that, and my hand went to my stomach.

Riley reacted too, then stiffened. "Are you okay? What's wrong?"

I shook my head. "Just a kick. Little guy's gonna be a fighter, I think." We both smiled as Riley stared at my mid-section. "Riley, you need to tell me how to stop this beast. How can it be killed?"

Riley shook his head. "Remember the beast that you defeated? That all of you *barely* killed?"

"Yeah." How could I forget?

"That beast was created with dark magic from Nitsua." He paused. "This beast was created with the darkest magic from both Nitsua *and* Leviathan. It's way stronger."

"But there must still be a way to defeat it."

"It won't die until it feeds on Luke's blood and takes his soul. Once it completes its mission, it can be defeated. . . . But until then, it's unbeatable."

"Can we just leave it on Earth?"

He shook his head. "They locked a key inside the beast's collar so that it could follow Luke from world to world. He will never get rid of it. It will roam tirelessly and forever until it gets what it was programmed to do."

"They gave it a key?" I said, shocked.

"Not they—Victor," Riley corrected.

"Victor gave the beast his key?"

"His second-in-command's key. Victor has trust issues and never took a second-in-command."

"So the beast is essentially Leviathan's second-in-command right now," I said, realizing this sounded ridiculous and terrifying all at the same time.

Riley nodded. "Which is why it doesn't have a mind of its own. It's connected to Victor." He turned away and peered out the window.

"Why'd you come back? Why didn't you stay on Earth?" I asked, my voice quieter.

He shrugged. "Without a key, I'm not much help to anyone." He considered me for a moment.

"So you're just going to sit here and wait for your brother to die so you can become keeper?"

"That's the plan," he said coldly. Before I could recover from my shock, he added, "So I take it you're here because you're not allowed to be there?" His voice was a bit softer, almost empathetic.

"It's not that I'm not *allowed*. It's obviously my choice, too."

Riley sniggered. "Please. You are the biggest adrenaline junkie I've ever met."

"I am not," I defended.

"You wouldn't be here if you weren't."

My fists tightened at his accusation. "I'm *here* because I want to help figure out how to end this."

"Well, you're wasting your time then. The only way this war ends is when Victor and Dana have taken over Earth."

"I don't even care about that part right now," I said, my voice shaking. "I need to save Luke from that beast."

His back was toward me again, and his knuckles were white against the stone. "You can't."

"How could you let them do this to your brother?" I shouted. "What has he ever done to you?"

He scoffed. "What? He never told you what he did?"

His eyes blackened around the edges, and I watched him curiously. Was there more to it than I already knew?

"The key chose him," I said. "And you begrudge him for that."

He laughed to himself. "Begrudge," he said with distaste. "No, I'm pretty sure the word is *hate*."

I shook my head. "It's such a strong word to use on your brother."

"There's more to it than just the key," he said, ignoring my reprimand. "He killed our mother."

I wasn't able to respond right away. I expected more.

234

I needed more. "What are you talking about?" I said.

"Since he was destined to be so great, he took all of her healing powers, and she died giving birth to him."

Confused, I shook my head. "But I saw a picture of her holding him."

"It wasn't him," he said. "She never held him."

"But I *saw* the picture."

"Let me guess—she's sitting in a rocking chair and holding a baby in a white blanket." He waited for me to say something, but I just listened. "That was me. She never held him."

I thought back to the picture in Luke's chest, wrapped up inside the soft white blanket. If that was Riley, why had Luke kept it? Because he wished it had been him in that picture? Because he shouldered the guilt of her death?

"So you hate him for that?" I said, my words coming out harder than I intended.

"Wouldn't you?" he countered.

"No, actually. I think he's suffered enough. Imagine living with that guilt."

"You'd think if you were responsible for killing your own mother, then you would at least honour her memory by being the best dark lord you could be."

"And you don't think he's done that?"

Riley gestured his hand toward the window. "I see a changing world, and I wouldn't say it's for the better."

"Have you ever stopped to consider that maybe this new world is a product of his greatness?" I said defiantly.

Riley watched me for a few seconds before turning away again. "You're not going to win this war, Sarah. Victor has four of the seven elements. He's far too strong now. Just go back to Yelram and forget about Earth."

"And Luke?"

Riley shrugged, then looked away. "He's as good as dead."

It took every ounce of strength not to throw him through the window. Eventually, I was able to turn away and walk toward the door.

"Where are you going?" Riley asked.

"To help my family."

"You can't be considering going to Earth." It was a question, but posed as a statement.

I turned sideways so he could see my face and know how much this destroyed me. "I'd be a coward not to."

He flinched, but then shook his head. "Don't be stupid, Sarah. You're too fragile. You can't even heal yourself right now. You'll die too."

"Riley, you might be satisfied being a backup, but I'm in this to win."

"What about that baby?"

Was he really trying to guilt me into staying out of it? Did he want Luke to die that badly that he would use this baby against me?

I spun around to face him. "I'm not sure why you care. If we die too, you'll be master of both worlds."

He hesitated. "Will you do me a favour?" he asked without looking at me.

"Probably not."

"Give Luke a message for me—tell him I have everything under control here, and when he dies, I'll take care of his world . . . and his wife."

I gave him a disgusted look. "Glad you've got everything under control here, Riley. The war's out *there*." I took a few more steps, then turned around again, and said, "And Luke's *wife* can take care of herself."

Then I gripped my key and told it to take me home. I would need Lucia, supplies, and more weapons.

And then I was coming for the beast.

CHAPTER 22

The Topaz and the Helmet

~ MADDY ~

I REAPPEARED IN the exact place that Sarah had summoned me from, except that the beast and Luke were no longer there, Drew and Devon were engaged with Dana and Keagan, and the battle was in full motion. Where was Victor?

Out of the corner of my eye, I saw a dragon swoop down over the lagoon and hover. Then its rider, dressed all in black with the addition of an onyx shield, ruby breastplate, amethyst boots, and sapphire belt, dismounted onto a rock ledge next to the waterfall.

Victor!

I raised my bow and set an arrow, but before I could

let it fly, Simon stopped me. "He'll kill you, Maddy."

I shrugged him off my bow and re-aimed. "Then help me."

He hesitated, but I didn't need his approval. I released the arrow at Victor, but it only hit his armour and bounced off. I shot another and another, and then Victor threw his hand toward me and a ball of fire barreled straight for me. Simon pushed me out of the way and the fire narrowly missed the both of us.

"We need Luke!" I said as Simon helped me to my feet. "Where is he?"

"He disappeared with the beast and hasn't come back yet."

Victor vanished behind the waterfall as his dragons hovered protectively, breathing fire at anyone who tried to interfere.

"Okay, let's think!" Simon said desperately.

And then Drew flew over our heads. "Simon, go help Devon!" he shouted as he landed on the edge of the lagoon. He raised both of his hands and the flow of the waterfall stopped. He pushed his hands toward the sky, and the waterfall began to rise, revealing Victor behind it, about to extract the topaz-encrusted helmet from the rock face.

A dragon blew a stream of fire at Drew as I released arrows at Victor, and Jenna, behind us, fought off the dark warriors that tried to stop Drew.

Suddenly I fell to the ground as a burning sensation tore through my body. Had I been hit by the dragon's breath? I scrambled out of the way as I surveyed my body for injuries.

At the same time, Leviathan and Nitsua's portals opened on either side of us, and the enemy warriors began flooding toward them.

"They have the element!" Jenna shouted before chasing after the escaping enemies.

A torrent of pain, along with a sense of dread and vengeance, ripped through my body, immobilizing me. Eventually I was able to tear a strip from the bottom half of my shirt and wrap it around my bleeding forearm.

"Maddy!" Drew pulled me to my feet as the portals closed and the battle finished. "Are you okay? What happened to you? How's Sarah?"

"She's okay. Her key was burning so she summoned me to find out what was going on."

Suddenly Luke appeared not far from us, breathless. He quickly grabbed his bearings and then came to me. "Is Sarah okay?"

I pulled away from him. "She's fine," I said, annoyed that he only seemed to care about Sarah. "The rest of us are okay, too, thanks for asking."

Luke gave me a puzzled look, but ignored my comment. He turned to Drew and Devon. "What the hell was that thing?!"

"It was clearly after you," Devon growled.

Luke nodded. "No kidding. It followed me to Yelram, then went after Sarah, but I was able to lead it to Etak." Luke frowned as he recalled the fight. "It nearly killed me several times. Eventually it just disappeared."

"Probably the same time Victor disappeared with Yelram's element," Devon said. "It was a diversion. Victor wanted you out of here so he could get the stone."

Luke's face hardened. "We lost Yelram's element?"

"We did," Drew confirmed. "We weren't expecting the beast."

"Now what?" I was feeling less than optimistic about our chances now. Victor had five of the seven elements. He only needed Nevaeh's element in order to possess all of Earth's humans, and then Earth's element would allow him to control them all. Every single human being on the planet.

Drew slid his hand down my arm and squeezed my hand. "Time for a new plan." Simon and Jenna joined us as Drew kept talking, "Victor and Dana now have five of seven stones. Leviathan's stone will lead them to Nevaeh's, and I suspect they'll go there next once they recharge. Earth's stone is independent from the others. Victor will only know that it's somewhere in North America."

"You know where it is, though," Luke hoped.

Drew nodded, but didn't elaborate.

"Do we need to send an army to protect it?" Luke asked.

"I mean, we don't have the best track record," Devon added, "but why not."

Drew frowned at Devon, ignored him, and then turned to me. "I want you to go back to Yelram."

"Why, Drew? Am I getting in the way here?"

"No." He shook his head. "It's just that I think you should be with Sarah."

"Really? That's what you're going with? Sarah needs me?" If he had used the excuse that it wasn't safe on Earth anymore and that Victor was far too dangerous, I might have bought it.

Before Drew could try harder, the air began to change and a giant rainbow-striped tiger appeared next to us.

"Sarah," Luke said. "What are you doing here?"

Sarah slid off Lucia's back and landed in Luke's arms. "I'm here to help."

"You shouldn't have come," Luke told her. "You promised."

"That was before the beast arrived," Sarah reminded him. "Besides, I got my powers back." She turned her palm up, filling it with water, then she threw it toward the forest, extinguishing the fire that Leviathan's dragons had left behind.

I grinned at Drew. "Guess she doesn't need a babysitter anymore."

"I met my mother." Sarah was beaming. "In the Garden of Hope. It was amazing, Luke."

Luke smiled, clearly happy for her, but his concern for her was larger. He picked up Sarah's left hand, which was wrapped in a white cloth stained with blood. "And can you heal?" he asked, returning the conversation to his concern for her.

She smiled weakly and pulled her hand from his. "Not yet," she admitted, "but I'm working on it."

"Working on it," Luke repeated. "Sarah, this isn't really the best place to work on that."

"Well, the game has changed, and I'm not sitting at home when I could be here helping. And I'm not sorry, either."

Devon shifted his weight and Drew turned away, both expecting an argument.

Luke answered by pulling her in closer. His eyes were restless, thinking, and worried, but happy to have her in his arms again. I wanted to be happy for them, but all I could feel was resentment. Maybe I was jealous? Maybe I wanted that for me and Drew?

"The beast is being controlled by Victor," Sarah went on. "It wears his second-in-command key."

"What?!" everyone responded.

"How do you know this?" Devon asked, leaning forward as he waited for her answer.

Sarah took a deep breath, avoiding eye contact with

Luke. "Riley told me."

"Wait—where did you see *Riley*?" Luke's eyes were large and piercing with accusation.

"I went to see him," she admitted. "I was a little beside myself waiting in Yelram for news of your death, so I went to see what Riley knew about it. I had to do *something*!"

"And it didn't occur to you that he might hurt you?"

"It occurred to me," Sarah said, "but I wasn't concerned."

Luke narrowed his eyes on her, but she didn't back down. I used to admire her ability to stand up to him, but now it just seemed reckless.

"So Victor controls it," Devon said, breaking the awkward silence. "And it's programmed to kill the both of you?"

"It's programmed for Luke," Sarah began, "but since I carry his child, it's after me, too. Well, after the baby."

Luke stiffened next to Sarah while Drew piped up, "Then Victor dies. Tonight. If we kill him, we can kill the beast."

"Or," Devon interjected, "by default, the beast becomes Leviathan's keeper and we're all screwed."

"You're not a very optimistic one, are you?" Simon muttered.

"You want to die tonight, too?" Devon challenged.

Simon shook his head and sniggered.

"Okay, that's enough," I said. I was several feet from the group now, and wanted to put even more distance between us.

"You okay, Mad?" Sarah asked. She came toward me and I backed up into a bush.

"I'm fine," I lied. "Just need to go check on our warriors. I'll be back."

It scared me how much I was annoyed by Luke, and even Sarah, at that moment. Just earlier I admired Luke's strength and bravery. But now he just looked like an egotistical ass that needed to be taught a lesson or two.

I slammed my fist into the trunk of a tree as I strode past. I was better and stronger than this! Luke was my friend. My best friend's husband! How did she even land him anyway? If I was being honest, she wasn't even that pretty. A *princess*. Please! Both of them could die and the worlds would keep turning.

What the hell was happening to me?! I gripped my head, fell to my knees, and pressed my palms into the ground.

"Maddy?"

I jumped to my feet and found Simon coming up behind me.

"What's going on with you?" he asked as he peered past me to the ground from where I was just kneeling.

"Nothing. I'm fine. I just . . . I thought I dropped—"

"Don't lie to me," he said. "Something's wrong. You

weren't yourself back there."

I answered him with silence because I owed him more than a lie.

His eyes lowered to my arm, wrapped with my own t-shirt. The question was on his brow, but failed to reach his lips.

"I haven't looked," I admitted. "But it hurts. . . . And I . . . I have all these dark thoughts."

Simon slowly reached for my arm and held it for a moment, looking into my eyes, before he carefully untied the makeshift bandage. I watched his face, afraid to see what he would see. When his eyes closed and his face fell, I knew.

I took in a deep breath, then followed his gaze to the freshly burnt skin emblazoned with what looked like the head of a beast surrounded by flames. "I'm marked," I heard myself say. My body shuddered with my admission. "Victor owns me."

Simon quickly re-tied the cloth around my wrist. "But how? You're Yelram's second-in-command."

"But I'm human."

Simon was shaking his head. "So if you belong to Leviathan now, and you die . . ."

"Yeah," I finished for him, because I didn't want to hear it. I knew it. If I died I would spend eternity in Leviathan.

Simon was taking it worse than I was. His eyes

pinballed the surrounding jungle, a look of panic on his face.

"I . . . I have this overwhelming *dislike* for Sarah and Luke right now," I admitted. "I'm scared, Simon."

"They don't know?" he guessed.

I shook my head. "I don't want to upset anyone, or worse, lose their trust."

"Maddy, I think you should —"

"I can't. . . . Simon, I can't tell them. They'll send me back to Yelram and I *need* to be here."

He seemed bothered by my decision, but he nodded anyway. "We'll need to keep you away from Luke and Sarah. You'll stay with me. I'll keep you safe."

"Thank you," I said.

"You've been there for me, even though I never deserved it. I'll be there for you. I won't let it take you." His brow creased because he knew this was a bigger promise than it sounded. I now belonged to Victor. I belonged to Leviathan.

CHAPTER 23

Healing Hearts

~ SARAH ~

I TRIED NOT to read into it too much. She had been through a lot; it was understandable that she'd need some space. But was it hostility I felt as she walked away? Why had she been glaring at Luke like that?

Drew seemed bothered by Maddy's leaving too, and even more irritated when Simon hurried off after her. But there were more pressing matters for him to deal with at the moment.

"Sarah," Drew began, "you really shouldn't be here. You should take Maddy and go back to Yelram."

"I'm staying" I said. "And by the sounds of it, we need her here, too."

Drew pushed his hand through his hair and scratched his head, agitated. "She's safer there, Sarah."

I shook my head. "She's my second-in-command, Drew. She'll be fine. I'll be here, too. We've got this, okay?"

"Man, you need to relax," Devon said to Drew. "I seen that pipsqueak in action—she can handle herself." Then a sly grin crept across his face and I didn't like what he was about to say next, but he said it anyway, "Besides, Simon seems to be keeping a close eye on her."

Drew made a move for Devon, but Luke stepped between them. "Devon, stop antagonizing. Drew, he's right—Maddy's fine. Just relax."

It took a minute, but the tension finally dissipated.

"So Riley really didn't try to hurt you?" Devon asked as he sharpened his knives. There was a hardness to his jaw suggesting that he didn't believe me.

"He didn't."

Devon sniggered and his anger passed to Luke.

"I'm not sure why you don't believe me." I turned my back to Devon so that it was just Luke and me. "When he found out I was pregnant, something changed in him."

Luke watched me for a few seconds, studying my face. He could read me well. He knew Riley told me about their mother, and guilt washed over him. He blamed himself for his mother's death.

I turned to the others. "Can you give us a minute?"

They quietly dispersed, and when it was just the two of us, I said, "It wasn't your fault."

"I know," he answered. But that was it.

"Then why do you blame yourself?"

He looked up at the canopy of trees. "Can you stop reading me right now?"

"Let's talk about this. It's important."

"Fine." He took a deep breath. "When I found out you were pregnant, I wasn't angry with you."

Ummm . . . that wasn't how I remembered it, but I let him continue.

"I mean, I was angry about Keagan and how you kept it from me, and I was a little hurt that you didn't trust me enough to tell me how you were feeling about the baby, but the reason I couldn't come see you was because . . . I was afraid. I was angry at . . . the baby." His last words were a whisper, coated in shame.

He was angry with the baby? Why? Because the baby made me weak? Because he thought the baby was taking my powers? Because . . . the baby might kill me. He was afraid of losing me like he lost his mother! He was angry at the baby because, in his head, the baby meant I was going to die.

"I am so afraid of losing you, Sarah," he said. "My mother died giving birth to me. I killed her."

"You didn't," I disputed.

"Childbirth killed her," he amended. "She wasn't able

to heal herself because I was taking all of those powers. And when I found out you were pregnant, all I could see was you dying, too."

"Why didn't you tell me?"

"Because I didn't want to scare you. I knew you already didn't want the baby. If I told you how I felt too, you would never have gotten better. I needed you to be strong. To try."

"How did you know I didn't want the baby?" I asked.

"While you were reading me, I was reading you," he said with a grin. "It wasn't difficult to figure out. You weren't exactly excited to tell me, were you? I knew *I* had reason to be afraid, but I couldn't figure out why you were afraid, too."

"I'm not scared anymore," I told him. "I learned that we don't need to be the best at everything, we just need to try our best. Maybe I don't know the first thing about being a mom, but I'll figure it out. It's all part of the adventure."

He pulled my chin up so that our eyes met. "We can figure this whole parenting thing out together."

"So you want to have this baby?" I asked gently.

"I mean, we don't have much of a choice now, do we?" He grinned slyly, then wrapped his arms around me. "But yeah, I do. That kid is part of you. Part of me. And I'm still scared, yeah, but I guess we just have to have faith that you'll be okay."

"Do you want to know what I learned today?"

Luke grinned and put his hands around my waist. "I do."

"So, like you, I believed that the baby was taking my power, but my mother told me that, quite the opposite, the baby actually makes me stronger. More powerful."

"Oh?" He wasn't convinced.

"My resentment was blocking my powers, and my mother believes that my fear is blocking my ability to heal."

Luke was quiet, wondering if Leah could be right.

"When I forgave my mother and accepted my abandonment and upbringing, my powers returned."

"And what about your healing?"

"Well, I guess I'm still afraid of something."

"Of what?"

I ignored his question because I knew why I was afraid. I was afraid that my duties as Yelram's queen would one day mean that I would have to abandon my child one day. I was afraid that he or she would be raised by someone who didn't love him like a child should be loved.

"My point is, Luke, that you never killed your mother. Her inability to heal herself was a result of her own fear."

Luke's mind flashed to his cruel and heavy-handed father, yet he pushed the thought from his mind as quickly as it came. It was a recurring thought that haunted him. Had his mother been a good person married to a wicked man?

I didn't want to say it, but it had to be said. "Luke, if I die giving birth, I need you to promise me that you won't blame this child, okay? It won't be his fault. Like you, he will be grow up to be incredible and special and deserving of love."

His confliction showed on his crinkled brow. He wanted to promise me, but he also didn't want to make a promise that would take effect only after I died.

"I promise to love this child . . . no matter what." He put his hand on my belly and squeezed gently. "We'll be okay."

"We will," I agreed. "All of us."

And with his promise that, should anything happen to me, he would continue to love and support our child, a euphoric feeling flooded my mind and body. We would be okay. The baby would be loved. A tingling sensation started in my belly and splayed out to my arms and legs, eventually reaching my hand. Nothing hurt. Nothing ached. Nothing.

"What are you doing?" Luke asked as I unraveled the cloth around my hand.

I didn't answer until I saw my fully healed flesh. "I think I just conquered my last demon."

"You can heal?"

"I can," I laughed. "You now have zero reason to keep me out of this war."

He fought with whether to be happy for my healing or frustrated with my persistence. When he took me in his arms and squeezed me tightly, he surrendered to his relief.

"I'm glad Riley didn't hurt you," Luke said, "but I'm not convinced he doesn't have an ulterior motive. He just knew killing you would seal his fate."

I shook my head. "I'm not sure what to make of it, either," I admitted. "He seemed genuine, but he definitely made no effort to hide his desire to become keeper of Etak again. He wanted me to give you a message, but I don't want you to get upset about it. I didn't feel as though he said it maliciously."

Luke's face hardened. "What is it?"

"Promise you won't get upset?"

"Sarah, tell me."

I sighed. "He asked me to tell you that he has everything under control in Etak."

"And?" He knew there was more.

"And he just wanted you to know that if anything happens to you, he will take care of Etak . . . and me."

Luke measured my expression, knowing that this wasn't exactly how Riley had phrased it, but it already sounded bad enough, and I wasn't sure it was in anyone's best interest to quote Riley word for word.

"Do you believe him?" Luke asked, his voice dark.

"I don't know," I admitted. "I get mixed messages from him, but I do feel like there is a small measure of good in him."

Luke nodded, but he didn't share my belief. He thought I was naïve for trusting his brother and believing there was sincerity there.

At that moment, Simon and Maddy came through the jungle and joined Drew, Devon, and Jenna at the lagoon's edge nearby.

"You okay, Mad?" I called to her.

She nodded but didn't look at me.

"She's okay," Simon answered for her. "Just been a hard day, you know?"

"Thanks for looking out for her," Drew said to Simon, and I could tell it took every bit of strength for him to say it.

"Yeah, man, no worries."

Drew took Maddy's hand and she enjoyed his embrace that followed.

"I thought about what you said, Drew," Maddy began. "I know you want me to go to Yelram so that I'll be safe." She looked up at him. "But I'm staying on Earth because I won't leave my team. And Simon said he'll stay with me, too, and help protect me."

Devon chuckled. "Told ya." Luke hit him.

Drew was having a hard time responding. He didn't

want Simon looking out for her—he already hated the amount of attention Simon gave Maddy—but he also knew that he wasn't the best person for the job. Not anymore.

"You should be with Sarah," Drew said.

"No," Maddy said too quickly. "She and Luke will be together. They don't need me. They're our best weapon."

Drew inhaled slowly. "Fine." He turned to Simon. "You better not screw this up."

"Okay," Luke said, interrupting the tension between Drew and Simon. "Sarah should stay for the fight, but she isn't staying if the beast arrives. Sarah will go back to Yelram, and Devon and I will take the beast to Etak."

"You can't leave," Devon said. "The last time you left, we lost half our army. They need you on Earth for your powers."

Luke paused, realizing Devon was right. "But I'm no good to them dead, and I have more of an advantage taking the beast to my own world. I know it better."

An uncomfortable silence followed. Everyone knew there was no good or easy solution to this problem.

"If we kill Victor, what happens to all the humans now marked for his world?" Simon asked.

"If we can kill him and get the elements back, they should be okay," Devon predicted.

"*Should* be?" Simon pressed. "Is that a guess?"

"Do you have a better guess?"

Simon frowned, but before he could strike back, Maddy stepped between the two. "Obviously getting rid of the beast and Victor is still our priority . . . regardless what happens to the humans."

"So what are we waiting for?" Jenna asked, impatient. "Let's go to Antarctica."

"Yeah, and freeze to death before Victor arrives. Good idea," Maddy snapped.

"Once we go through the portal to Antarctica, our clothes will change and adapt to the environment. We won't freeze," Drew explained. "And Jenna's right, we should go get set up before they arrive. Nevaeh will need us."

Maddy frowned, frustrated with Jenna's existence and Drew's obliviousness to her.

CHAPTER 24

An Unlikely Ally

~ SARAH ~

WE FOLLOWED DREW through his portal that led us to Antarctica and, in particular, Nevaeh's basecamp. And just as Drew had said, as we stepped out of the portal and into the icy cold tundra of the arctic, our clothes magically morphed into warm layered apparel, including coordinating parkas and toques. I could see my breath, and my nose felt cold, but the rest of me was a perfect temperature.

I turned to watch the rainbow of coloured parkas pour through the portal—blue, purple, yellow, and one green. Drew.

Dozens of large white tents blended in with the stark

white background, while hundreds of warriors in white meandered through the camp, and dozens more stood watch atop lookout towers that surrounded the camp, and in particular, the large ice monument in the centre that housed Nevaeh's element.

Trinity and her second-in-command, Hannah, were approaching us.

"Drew!" Trinity greeted as they embraced. "Thank you for coming." She turned to Luke and me. "I assume this means we've lost your elements?"

Luke nodded, but couldn't bring himself to verbally confirm her assumption.

"We have set up camp in anticipation of your arrival," Trinity explained. "That whole section over there is ready for you. Please, tell your warriors to go eat and get some rest."

"Thank you," Luke said, but then he caught sight of Devon out of the corner of his eye and motioned for him to come over.

Devon nodded to his friend and changed course.

When they were close, Luke lowered his voice and said, "I want you to go to Etak and see what Riley's up to."

"Luke," I started, but he silenced me with his hand.

"Find out what the hell he's planning."

"You got it," Devon replied.

"Do you really think that's necessary?" I tried.

Devon shook his head. "There's a reason he gave you that message," he said. "And I'm gonna find out what it is." Devon grinned at Luke, they bumped fists, and then he let his key take him home.

"Was that really necessary?" I challenged the moment Devon was gone.

"I think so," Luke said, but that's all he said. And then he took my hand and led me to one of the large circular canvas tents.

Inside, it was cozy and warm with four cots, two side tables for weapons and supplies, and a circular table in the centre that held a lantern, bread, fish, fruits, and vegetables.

"Rest," Luke said as he nodded toward one of the cots.

"With you," I said as I unzipped his parka. "I missed you."

His face softened and a smile formed at his mouth. "I missed you, too." He took my face in his hands and pressed his lips to my forehead. "So much."

I reveled in his embrace and the softness of his warm lips against my skin.

Finally he spoke. "I love you with every single cell inside me. You know that, right?"

"Where is this coming from?"

"Tell me you know that first."

"Of course I do."

Luke put his hand on my stomach. "One of us will have to die before that beast can be killed."

I was shaking my head before he finished his sentence. "Luke, we'll figure out a way to trap it. We don't have to—"

"And then what? It'll be our child's problem? Sarah, we can't—"

"Stop it!" I demanded. "I know what you're thinking and I will *not* allow it."

"It was created for me, Sarah. It's my cross." He brought his finger to my lips to silence my rebuttal. "Your only job now is to survive . . . and take care of that little me inside of you. Promise me that, okay?"

"I promise I will hit you if you keep talking like this."

He grinned, but I saw no amusement on his face. "Will you just . . . go to Yelram if the beast arrives?"

"Luke, you can't ask me to do that. My army is stronger with me here, and I can help. I can distract the beast while we find a way to kill it."

He was silent, but his mind wasn't. He worried about the beast. He worried about me. About the baby. About our future.

I kissed his nose softly. "Let's rest." I brought him to the cot and laid him down so that his body could relax, if not his mind. I snuggled in close so that I could feel his warmth as his chest rose and fell with each beautiful breath he took.

As I drifted off to sleep, I knew that he wouldn't be joining me in slumber. He would be worrying and planning how he could bear his cross and still be there to raise his child.

How long had it been? Luke's arms were still warm and snug around my body, but I had definitely fallen asleep. What woke me? Was that Simon's voice calling for Drew?

"Yeah," Drew answered, and I realized that the two were standing just on the other side of the tent wall.

"I wanted to apologize for earlier." Simon's voice was low and meant only for Drew.

"For what exactly?"

"For going after Maddy. For just . . . getting in your space, really. I know she's yours, and I'm sorry that—"

"She's not *mine*," Drew chuckled. "And don't ever let her hear you say that. Maddy belongs to no one but herself."

I smiled because he was right. Maddy loved Drew, but she would never want to be defined as being his.

"Well, I'm sorry, anyway."

"Thank you, Simon. And, you know, I've been hard on you and I'm sorry. I just . . . I worry about Maddy, you know?"

"I do know."

"I appreciate you looking out for her, though."

"Can't you just lock her up in Yelram?"

Drew laughed. "Finally! Something we agree on." He paused before continuing, "She has a key and I can't make her stay. I need to somehow convince her to go on her own, but it isn't working."

"Maybe the truth would help."

There was another pause before Drew asked, "What truth?"

"You know . . . that Victor's too strong now and we're not gonna win."

"Great attitude," Drew scoffed, then the sound of crunching snow as if Drew was walking away.

"Wait," Simon said. "If we . . . if we lose Nevaeh's element, where do we go next?"

Drew hesitated, and I knew he was considering whether he could trust Simon. "Nova Scotia," he finally answered. "Earth's element is downtown at the Halifax Citadel. It's a fortress that gives us an advantage." Then Drew added, "But let's hope it doesn't come to that."

"Drew," Simon called, and I could tell Drew was leaving the conversation. "I hope you know what you're doing."

There was a long pause where I imagined that they were staring at each other, trying to decode the silent words between them. Then more crunching snow until it was just Simon on the other side of the tent wall.

Once Simon was gone, I rolled over in Luke's arms.

As suspected, he wasn't sleeping.

"Did you hear that?" I asked.

He nodded.

"I don't trust him," I admitted.

He nodded again. He was thinking about Simon and his motives, but also about the beast.

Suddenly a loud siren split the air, followed by the shouts of scurrying men and women as they prepared for battle.

"Come on," Luke said as he leaped out of bed and tossed my coat to me and then pulled on his.

I followed him out of the tent and we jogged to the front line. In the distance, just outside the camp, a blue portal was opening. A *blue* portal? From Etak? Wouldn't Devon just use his key? Or was he bringing re-enforcements?

But where it should have been Devon emerging, leading an army of rogue warriors, Riley appeared instead. He was proudly wearing Devon's second-in-command key, and the moment I saw it, my heart squeezed.

"What is this?" Luke demanded as he approached his brother. "Where's Devon?"

"I killed him," Riley answered flatly.

Luke drew his sword and pointed it at his brother's throat.

"Don't ask if you don't want the answer." Riley lifted

his chin, but I saw his regret.

"That's why you gave Sarah that message. You baited me. Would you have killed me if I had gone?"

Riley shook his head. "I knew you'd send Devon. You wouldn't have left Sarah."

Luke clenched his jaw, angry that he fell for Riley's trick. "Why did you kill him?" Luke's voice broke, showing his sadness.

"He wouldn't listen to me. He didn't trust me, and he wouldn't let me come."

Luke's knuckles whitened around the hilt of his sword, and he used every ounce of reserve to resist killing his brother. "Why are you here?" he hissed through clenched teeth and teary eyes.

"I've wanted you dead since the day you were born. My mother was the only good thing in my life and you took her from me." Riley looked away and blinked heavily. "But I look at Sarah, and I see her. I see our mother."

Luke's eyes flickered to mine, unsure what to make of Riley's admission.

"She's beautiful, and kind, and . . . *good*." Riley paused, giving Luke time to wonder what was happening—was this an apology? Or had Riley finally come to get his revenge?

"You're here to apologize?" Luke questioned suspiciously.

A loud siren sounded and Drew appeared next to us. "Leviathan's portal just opened to the east. We need to get ready."

Luke struggled with what to do with his brother. Riley had just admitted to killing Devon, and with his track record, could not be trusted. But I saw remorse in Riley's eyes. I sensed his sincerity.

"Riley," I prodded, "why did you come?"

"To give you this." He turned and motioned toward his re-enforcements emerging from the portal. "It's the army I raised against you."

Luke eyed the army of rebels and misfits suspiciously. "Why?"

"Because I no longer have a use for them." Riley lowered his gaze to the ground, then bent down on one knee. "My brother, my Lord."

"Riley, get up," Luke ordered, but Riley stayed kneeling.

"Use the army to defeat the beast," Riley said, and this time his voice was strained. He hung his head as the snow beneath him slowly turned red. "I'm sorry for the trouble I caused. . . . I'm sorry for everything."

I clutched Luke's arm as the ground began to rumble.

"THEY'RE COMING!" Drew shouted above the noise of the readying warriors.

Riley stumbled as he tried to stand. Luke reached for him, but Riley pushed his hand away. "Don't be stupid, Brother." He pulled his necklace from his chest and handed it to Luke. "Save yourselves and take care of that kid."

A loud shrieking sound filled the air. We froze, recognizing the terrifying sound.

Riley's army readied themselves for the beast. They separated enough to create a path to Riley, and in the distance we saw the monstrous creature with sprays of ice and snow around him as he led the dark armies toward the blood that it so desperately thirsted for.

As a wall of giants began to surround Riley, shielding us from the beast, I pulled at Luke and encouraged him not to watch his brother's death. But there was nothing I could do to stop him. I refused to watch, but still heard the horrific sound of bones crunching, and then the roars of a loyal rebellion as they tore apart the monster.

I should've been happy to witness it. I should've celebrated the beast's demise because it meant that my husband was that much safer. But all I could think about was Luke and how, after all these years, he finally made amends with his brother, only to watch him die moments later.

CHAPTER 25

The Opal and the Sword

~ SARAH ~

THERE WAS NO time to mourn. Lucia and Gideon were next to us and the dark armies were closing in. Etak and Yelram's warriors charged ahead on wolves and tigers to meet them.

Luke took my hand and pulled me into him. "I love you," he said.

I didn't like how he said it. Like it could be the last time, so I didn't respond. Because it wouldn't be the last time that I would say it.

Luke turned to Gideon, "Stay with Sarah!" he ordered, then he pulled his sword and ran straight toward the panthers coming toward us. He sliced and spun and sliced again, rolled, and sliced again. Panthers and warriors fell as if there was nothing to them.

Trinity and the majority of her army were in the air on the backs of their stunning white-winged unicorns. They released arrow after arrow into the oncoming darkness. But then the dragons appeared in the sky and the two groups of flying creatures soared toward each other. Trinity held back, I noticed, waiting for Victor to show his face.

Gideon and Lucia were now tearing apart panthers and giants, and I realized that I had been so consumed with watching what was happening around me that I hadn't actually done anything to help. Was this what the other two battles had been like? My stomach turned at the thought of Luke, Drew, and Maddy having to fight in such a gruesome war.

I pulled my sword at the same time Drew flew overhead. "Sarah, go after Keagan!" he yelled.

"Where is he?" I asked as Drew landed near me and slaughtered two panthers that were coming our way.

"Over there." He jerked his head to the west. "He's the one who looks like you."

Like me?

When the last panther's head rolled, Drew left again and I mounted Lucia. She and Gideon led us toward my look-a-like. I almost had to applaud Keagan for his ingenuity. By appearing as me, he was protecting

269

himself. No one on our side would dare touch him. Although it appeared that he hadn't accounted for me being here, too.

Keagan was making his way around the outskirts of the crowd. He had a Lucia look-a-like with him, but the tail was black, giving away its panther lineage.

I had to admit, seeing myself was strange. Did I really walk like that? Was my hair really that unruly?

Lucia and Gideon reacted first. Lucia let out a roar and when Keagan and his sidekick turned to us, he knew the charade was up. But he was also smart enough not to change his appearance. No one would interfere in our fight this way, because they would wonder which one was the real me.

The Lucia look-a-like changed back into its true form—its strongest form—and Gideon engaged him immediately, with Lucia waiting for her opportunity to help. Meanwhile, Keagan pulled his sword and we slowly approached each other.

"What are you doing here?" Keagan asked, and his voice was feminine and weirdly familiar.

"Where am I supposed to be?"

"You're *supposed* to be in your own world. You're pregnant. . . . Aren't you?"

We circled each other as the animals continued to fight near us.

"I am," I confirmed, "but I can't just let you guys do

this."

"There's no hope for Earth now, Sarah. You know that."

"And you're okay with Victor taking away everyone's free will? Because I'm not."

"Doesn't really matter what we're okay with, does it? It's Victor, Sarah. I'm not sure if you realize how powerful he is."

"He's only powerful if you believe he is."

Keagan scoffed. "Is that so?"

"He gets his strength from everyone's fear."

"So you're not afraid of him?"

"Absolutely not. He's afraid of me."

Suddenly Dana landed next to Keagan. Her eyes were black and desperate for blood. I took a quick mental snapshot of what resources I had—Lucia and Gideon had just finished killing the panther, and they were now flanking me, teeth bared at Dana and Keagan. But other than that, we were alone.

Keagan changed into a dragon, provoking Gideon and Lucia, and they took the bait, leaving Dana and me to sort out our differences.

With a blast of wind, I threw Dana back, but she was fast and had already hurled a dagger at me. I twisted to the side, and the blade grazed my shoulder. It took me a second, but I conjured a fireball and threw it at her, but she was already changing into a dragon twice the size of

Keagan and with bright red eyes and a blood red tail. A stream of fire flowed from Dana's mouth, which I combatted with a gush of water from my hands. I kept the energy flowing until her fire ceased. Her tail was coming at me now, and I had just enough time to dive over top of it.

"Too chicken to fight someone your own size, Dana?"

The threat worked and she flickered a second later, returning to her own size.

"You think I'm scared of you, Sarah?" she laughed.

"Terrified."

Her eyes blackened, and her teeth bared as she let out an angry roar. She ran toward me at full speed, her body forward as if meaning to charge right through me. In a panic, I threw my hands toward her, not really considering what I was doing, but a gush of wind blew her off course and slowed her down enough for me to retrieve my sword from the ground.

"Running out of powers are you, Sarah?"

"You wish."

Dana pulled her sword too and threw herself toward me, her blade coming down on my left side. I pushed my blade toward hers and they came together in a clash of thunder.

Lucia and Gideon were having a hard time with Keagan, who had scorched Gideon and took a chunk out of Lucia's side, which only angered Gideon further. I threw a fireball toward Keagan before punching Dana hard in the side of the face. I shoved her off of me, and she flickered into a dragon, breathing fire at me, which I stopped with a wall of water.

I tried to grip her mind, but she was too ferocious, and when I opened the door to her mind, I was pushed back with the hate and anger that flowed from it in no controlled manner. But Keagan, in dragon form, was weak. Our eyes met, and I had his mind so easily that I knew what I had to do. I pushed Dana away with a force of wind and yelled to Gideon and Lucia not to kill Keagan. Lucia limped as she backed away, but Gideon's restraint was harder to find.

I called Keagan to his feet, and he complied. He knew I had his mind, and he either didn't try fighting it, or he couldn't find the strength. I pointed the tip of my sword toward him, and then toward dragon Dana. "Get her," I ordered.

Dana's large scaly head turned toward Keagan but not soon enough—he ran toward her, his mouth wide open, and sunk his teeth into her side. She screamed out in a sound that was human, but not. Then I slammed my fists into the ground calling forth an earthquake that shattered the ground and split the ice in two. Keagan's mind slipped from my grasp, and in turn he let Dana go. She turned back into herself and tried to find footing on the caving ice, but when she realized it was a lost cause, she took her key and disappeared.

Keagan stood on the ice on the other side of the cavern. He was badly beaten, bleeding, and burned from his battle with Gideon and Lucia and from the fire I threw at him. I felt bad for having to do it, but I couldn't lose Lucia. Even Gideon was growing on me.

We stared at each other for a long few seconds. I tried to tell him, with my eyes, that I was sorry for hurting him, but that I would do what I had to do to save Earth. I couldn't get a read from him before he took his key and left, too.

It almost seemed too easy. With Dana gone, Nitsua's warriors had lost most of their strength and advantage and were easy to overpower. Trinity and her second-in-command, Hannah, had Victor right where they wanted him, and Luke, Drew, and their fighters were defeating and controlling the rest of the dark army.

The biggest challenge was that, as a result of all of the fire, water, and groundbending, the icy tundra was now melted into broken, slippery caverns, making it more than difficult to fight a fair battle.

And then Victor had a hostage. I wasn't sure how it happened, but Hannah's beautiful pegasus was falling from the sky, and Hannah was on the back of Victor's dragon with a knife at her throat.

Trinity hovered nearby, but hesitated. She loved Hannah and couldn't take the risks involved in spraying them with a torrent of water.

My body seized with panic, but then I saw something move out of the corner of my eye. It was Simon. He was perched on top of a lookout tower, releasing arrows at unsuspecting enemy fighters. He was looking for Maddy, though, evidenced by his frantic thoughts as his eyes pinballed the swarm of warriors. But he was much closer to Victor than anyone else, and at his vantage point, he had a clean shot.

Simon, I shouted into his thoughts. *Get Victor!*

Confused, Simon looked around until he found Victor in the sky, focused on Trinity but with his blade digging into a scared but stoic Hannah.

Do it, Simon, I silently urged. *Shoot him.*

Simon pulled his arrow taut, aiming it at Victor. He was focused and calm and there was no way he could miss. He had a killer shot, and Victor wouldn't even see it coming.

Now, Simon!

But the arrow didn't fly.

Trinity was trying to negotiate with Victor, but he only wanted one thing—the sword—and she wasn't willing to give it to him. When she lifted her chin and shook her head no, Trinity knew she was sealing Hannah's fate. Trinity and Hannah locked eyes, tears fell, and then Victor's blade moved across Hannah's neck. Her body fell limp and turned to ash.

"ARGHH!" Trinity cried, and then she flew toward Victor, enraged.

Trinity's army took flight, fortified with their new mission to avenge their sister's death. Altogether, dozens of arrows hit Victor's dragon, and he dove from the creature as he sprayed everything around him with a wall of fire.

He landed hard on the ice below and as Trinity and I rushed toward him, Simon reached him first. But instead of driving his sword into Victor's neck—the only place unprotected by the element armour—Simon knelt down next to him and they exchanged some words before Victor grabbed a hold of Simon, and they both disappeared.

A black portal opened, and Leviathan's army began fleeing, chased by our own armies who took advantage of their weakened state.

What the hell just happened!? Where did Simon go?!

As the battle dwindled, Luke found me, and I steadied myself in his arms, exhausted from the fight that wouldn't have even tired me a few months before. I took comfort in feeling the baby moving around, but begrudged the fact that I felt like I had been run over by a truck.

Luke lowered me to the ground where he then fed me some water. I tried not to fuss over his swollen eye and the blood soaking his shirt, and as he fed me, I healed him.

Drew joined us a minute later while Maddy stood close, but not too close. Everyone had seen what happened—Victor took Simon. But for Maddy it meant something more, and it shook her to the core.

Drew was holding his key, reading it. Then he turned to Maddy. "How upset would you be if Simon dies?"

Maddy's eyes widened fearfully. "Why?"

"Because I think he just betrayed us."

CHAPTER 26

The Betrayal

~ SARAH ~

"WHAT DO YOU mean *Simon betrayed us*?" Luke asked.

"He left with Victor, and now Victor's in Halifax. I don't think that's a coincidence."

"What's in Halifax?" Maddy asked.

When Drew didn't answer, I did. "Earth's element. Drew told Simon where it was hidden."

"We have to go!" Luke shouted. "What are we waiting for?"

"We don't all need to go," Drew said. "And there's no rush, either. He won't find it."

"Probably better not to take the risk," Maddy argued. "We should go now."

"You're not going anywhere," Drew said. "No one is."

Maddy's eyes widened. "Drew! If Victor gets Earth's element, everyone dies!"

Drew was quiet, and suddenly it dawned on me. "The element isn't in Halifax, is it, Drew?"

He shook his head, but his eyes were still narrowed on Maddy.

"Then why did you tell Simon that it was?" Maddy asked.

Drew didn't answer.

"You didn't trust him," she realized.

"He was asking too many questions."

"You lied to him."

Drew's eyebrows shot up. "And it's a good thing, too, Maddy! Look what he did!"

Maddy's mind was swimming with possibilities. She wondered why Simon would go to Victor. Why would he lead Victor to the element? Especially knowing what he knew. But he was fascinated with the dark arts, Maddy remembered. Could he really have abandoned them to join the dark side?

"Maddy?" I prompted. "I'm sorry to have to ask this, but is Simon fascinated with the dark arts?"

Maddy's mind closed the moment I asked the question, and she knew that I had heard her thoughts and there was no point in hiding them.

When she didn't answer, Luke laughed sarcastically. "Fantastic. We've been harbouring a terrorist."

"He's not like that!" Maddy shouted. "You know *nothing!*"

"Maddy!" I gasped. "We're all just trying to understand, okay? No one blames you for this."

"No, but you all blame Simon."

"If the shoe fits," Luke said.

Maddy made a move for him, but Drew grabbed her before she could hit him. He held Maddy for a long few seconds, studying her, wondering, as I did, what had gotten into her.

"We just need to all calm down for a minute, okay?" I started. "If Earth's element isn't in immediate danger, let's make a new plan."

Maddy took in a deep breath and closed her eyes. She tried to make herself apologize, but there was a lot of hate and anger lingering under the surface, and I couldn't pretend to understand it. Losing Simon had clearly damaged a nerve.

My eyes wandered to Nevaeh's army, gathered around Trinity, consoling her over the loss of Hannah. It was heartbreaking to watch, but beautiful at the same time. They all just came together and mourned.

Trinity approached the white stone monument with the sword encased in the front. She laid Hannah's sword at the base of the monument, and knelt there for a few minutes to pay her respects.

When she was done, Trinity stood, looked to the sky, then reached for the opal-encrusted sword and pulled it from the stone as she cried out Hannah's name. A spray of crystals and shimmering light erupted throughout the air. Then dark clouds rolled in, and the heavens began to cry.

Luke stood to my right, his arm around my waist, positioning himself between Maddy and me. Her angry outburst made him uneasy. I pretended not to notice, but Maddy was annoyed by it. Drew and Maddy were on Luke's right, and Eli and his second-in-command, Paul, were on my left.

"What's happening?" Maddy asked.

Eli answered, "The rains are coming. In forty days the world will be flooded, ending life as we know it."

"What?!" Maddy shouted, which I was thankful for because if she hadn't, I might have.

"If we end Victor and return the elements, then the rains end, too," Eli explained.

"And if we don't?" Maddy said.

"Then the world will need cleansing."

Maddy's mouth fell open in surprise. I wasn't sure what was going through her mind because I was focused on my own thoughts and opinions about the situation. In just over a month, Earth could be buried in water, drowning all creatures. It didn't sound humane, but the alternative—a world full of possessed or controlled humans, destroying Earth with their negativity and hatred—didn't seem so wonderful, either.

Trinity's army parted, creating a path directly to us.

"That was too close," Trinity began as she approached. "We won't take another loss like that again." Her face was firm, and Hannah's loss reflected in her saddened eyes.

She lifted the pristine sword, studying its magnificent features. "We will find Victor and take back what is ours."

"It won't be too much trouble," Drew said. "He's right where we want him."

"What's the plan?" Luke asked Drew.

"With Leviathan's stone, Victor will always be able to find Nevaeh's sword. As soon as he realizes he can't find Earth's element, he will come back for the sword."

"It's not safe for us to stay and fight here any longer," Eli said, referring to the ravaged campsite, charred tent ruins, and treacherous icy caverns and gorges.

"I know a place where we will have an advantage," Drew said. "It's surrounded by ocean so Nevaeh's army will have an endless supply, and it's covered in rock so Leviathan's fire won't have an effect, and Lorendale's army can bend the boulders to their advantage. There are no trees to catch fire, and the wind is already mighty, so that will give Etak's army an advantage."

"Peggy's Cove," I realized. It *would* be the perfect location.

Drew nodded and smiled. "Peggy's Cove."

"Perfect," Luke said. He knew Peggy's Cove, too. Well, *Penny's Cove*, as he called it. The place meant something to us both—it was where I went whenever I needed time to think, it was the location of our first date, and the first place I could think to go when I found my keeper key and my enchantments broke with Drew and Luke.

Drew held his key with one hand and then pressed his hand toward the East, opening a large green portal.

"Bring the armies through that portal to the lighthouse at Peggy's Cove," Drew instructed.

Trinity nodded her approval, then, with courage and vengeance on her mind, she led her army toward the portal. Eli and Paul followed with Lorendale's army, and Luke instructed Etak and Yelram's armies to follow.

Before Maddy could join Yelram's warriors, Drew took her hand. "I need to talk to you," he said.

"What is it?"

Drew looked around and decided that he didn't like the level of privacy that their current situation provided. He nodded to Luke and said, "Maddy and I are taking a detour. I'll meet you guys there."

I had already seen Drew's thoughts, and I knew he planned to take Maddy back to Yelram with the hope of being able to convince her to stay. She wouldn't like it, and at one point I would've fought for her to stay, but after what happened to Simon and knowing that Maddy knew of his darkness and didn't tell us . . . well, I wondered if her judgment wasn't too skewed to be helpful.

Drew took Maddy's hand and, with the words "Take us to Yelram," they left in a swirling vortex of air.

"What do you think that's about?" Luke asked when they were gone.

"He's going to try to convince her to stay out of the fight."

Luke took me in his arms as Lucia and Gideon stood nearby waiting. Most of the animals and warriors were already through the portal readying themselves for the battle at Peggy's Cove. The battle that would finish Victor and restore humanity. But with everyone leaving, Luke and I took the opportunity to finally be alone.

"How are you feeling?" His thoughts flickered to the baby.

"We're good," I assured him. "It's strange, but I feel stronger with him inside me, you know?"

Luke smiled, pleased with my answer. "I'm glad to hear it."

"How are *you*? You know, after what happened with Riley."

Luke shrugged, pretending that his brother's death

didn't bother him. "I'm glad the beast is gone."

"That wasn't what I asked."

Our eyes found each other and his face softened. "I'm grateful for his sacrifice," he finally said, his voice weak with emotion.

"Me too." I squeezed him in my embrace, thankful that the threat of the beast was gone, but also sad that Luke no longer had a brother. Riley might have been evil to some degree, but he had good in him too, and I was glad that Luke got to see it before his brother was taken from him.

CHAPTER 27

Earth's Emerald Element

~ MADDY ~

WHEN MY VISION stopped spinning, we found ourselves inside Sarah's palace, on the grand staircase leading to the apartments.

"What are we doing?" I asked.

Drew took my hand and led me up the stairs and down the corridor toward my apartment. When we were inside, he turned and locked the door.

I laughed nervously as I steadied my racing heart. "Drew, what is going on?"

But Drew's face wasn't painted with pleasure or dressed in desire. "I want you to stay here."

I remembered back to my conversation with Simon in

the Amazon, and how he predicted that Drew's distance was a result of his experience over losing Sarah to Luke. I stepped forward, ignoring the nagging voice in the back of my head that told me Jenna was the reason for his distance. "Please don't keep pushing me away."

He shook his head. "It's too dangerous now. Victor has his sights set on Earth's element and . . ." his voice trailed off. He wanted to tell me where Earth's element was, but his desire to protect me caused an internal struggle. "I need to tell you something."

I silenced him with my hand. "Drew, it's probably better that you don't."

Puzzled, he caught my concern. "Why? What's wrong?"

My forearm ached from the mark of the beast. I could feel Victor's rage over losing the battle at Antarctica. I swallowed, unsure whether I should tell him or not. But I hadn't told him about Simon's fascination with the dark side, and maybe if I had, we wouldn't be in this predicament.

"Maddy?" he prompted.

I took a deep breath and pulled up my sleeve, then twisted my arm until Drew's eyes fell to my charred skin.

"No," he exhaled. "No." He shook his head and ran his fingers over the mark. "But you're Yelram's second-in-command."

"It burned into my arm when Yelram's element was taken. I thought I had been hit by dragon fire, but . . ."

"But you belong to Yelram. No. No, this can't be right."

"He doesn't control me yet," I told him. "I mean, I have darker thoughts and feelings, but I'm still in control of my actions."

"But . . ." Drew was still processing, which was hard to watch.

"Which is why you shouldn't tell me where the element is. The less I know, the better."

Drew was quiet for a long minute as he stared at my arm. Thoughts of Earth's element floated through his head, and Simon's betrayal, and Victor's power. Something scared him right down to the core. Above all these thoughts, though, I felt his concern for my life.

He finally spoke. "Simon knew about this?"

I nodded. "He found me having a meltdown in the Amazon, so I showed him. I made him promise not to tell."

Drew's head fell back as he looked to the ceiling. "Makes more sense now."

"What does?"

"Why he betrayed us. I'm willing to bet he did it to prove his loyalty to Victor, and in return he would become one of them."

"Why would he do that?" I asked, although I knew

why—Simon felt like he belonged in the dark worlds.

"To be with you for eternity." Drew's face hardened, and his knuckles whitened around the hilt of his sword.

"I don't think that's why," I said, but he knew I didn't believe it.

Drew brought his eyes back to mine. "Maddy, I will fix this, okay? I will kill Victor and get the elements back. Just stay here and I'll come back for you."

He reached for my neck and pulled me into him, pressing his lips hard against my forehead. "I'm so sorry."

He was apologizing for more than just my mark, and although I knew he wasn't to blame for the mark, I wasn't sure if he was to blame for anything else. Jenna flickered in his mind, along with a desire to go to her. Before I could ask him why he was thinking of Jenna, he stepped back, took his key, and said, "Take me home."

I sat down on the edge of my bed, my breath coming and going harder and faster the longer I sat. What a mess!

Simon had promised he wouldn't leave me. He would help protect me. What had Victor said to him to convince him to abandon his team, his friends, his . . . *me!?* Simon knew that if Victor got his hands on Earth's element, then he would be able to control my every thought and movement. How could he do that to me?

Maybe I should've told everyone sooner about Simon's fascination with the dark side. But how could I?

He was my friend. And Drew would've jumped at a chance to send him back to Yelram, or worse—kill him. Was Drew's jealousy the reason I kept Simon's secret to myself? And maybe my insecurity over Jenna had something to do with it, too. I hated that Drew trusted her so much. I hated that she was *always* there, always coming between us. I hated that, even now, she was with Drew.

Before I knew it, I was on my knees sobbing, the cold wooden floor soaking up my desperate tears. All of my emotions over the last few days came to a height that I could no longer control, and I lost hold of myself and cried like I had never cried before.

The harder I cried, the easier it was to forget what brought me to the floor in the first place. So I let myself untether, and eventually I found myself in the fetal position nursing a throbbing headache.

A light knocking sound interrupted my pounding thoughts. When I didn't answer, the doorknob slowly turned, and then Elizabeth appeared in the doorway.

"Are you okay, My Lady?" she asked as she let herself in and closed the door behind her. "I . . . I heard you crying. Is . . . everything okay?"

Her presence immediately annoyed me. Maybe because I was in the middle of a meltdown, or maybe because I knew the real reason for her concern—Sarah.

"Sarah's fine," I told her.

Elizabeth visibly relaxed and took a few steps closer. "Is there anything I can help with?"

"No!" I snapped.

"Do you have an update on the war? Everyone here is beside themselves waiting for news—"

"Here's an update for you," I said as I pulled myself from the floor. "We've lost all elements except for Nevaeh's and Earth's, Simon turned on us, and I now belong to Victor."

Elizabeth gasped and took a step back.

"Yeah, I'd be afraid of me, too. In fact, I *am* afraid of me." It occurred to me in that moment that if Victor were successful in claiming Earth's element, then he would have full control of my mind. And if that happened, I might kill Elizabeth, and her daughter, and everyone in this palace. I might destroy Yelram from the inside.

"Maddy?" Elizabeth said, a sense of urgency to her voice. "Are you okay?"

I had stumbled back and caught myself on the edge of my bed. "I need to get out of here," I realized.

I gripped my key, desperate to abandon Yelram, and said the only word on my mind, "Drew."

I HAD EXPECTED to appear at Peggy's Cove, surrounded by hundreds of warriors as they waited for Victor and Dana to arrive. So then why was I on the upper breezeway of the Halifax Citadel, with Drew and Jenna crouched on the ground next to me?

"What's going on?" I asked, desperate to keep the jealousy from reaching my face.

"What are you doing here?!" Drew demanded as he pulled me down next to them.

"I could ask *you* the same question!"

"Maddy, you need to go," Drew said firmly. "You promised me you would stay in Yelram."

"Why? So you and Jenna could come here and get all cozy together?"

I heard Jenna roll her eyes—yes, it could be *heard*.

"Problem?" I snapped, trying not to notice that Drew hadn't acknowledged or debunked my accusation.

"Kinda," she barked back. "We're here to kill Victor. You're kinda getting in the way."

I resisted the urge to flatten her pretty little nose. "*That's* why you're here?" I stared at her, dumbfounded. "*You're* going to kill Victor?"

She pursed her lips before answering. "Yes?"

Because I didn't know how to respond to such absurdity, I turned to Drew. "Have you really thought this through? Victor is too strong for you, much less *Jenna*. He will kill you both."

"Maddy," Drew finally said, "I can't lose you, okay? This . . . this *mark* means you belong to him, and I . . . I can't let anyone else have you."

"Simon," I said. "You can't let *Simon* have me. This

isn't about me belonging to Leviathan as much as it is about the idea of Simon and I being together for eternity. Am I wrong?"

His eyes narrowed and jaw clenched. "That part sucks, too." He hadn't completely thought everything through, I could tell by the way his mind and eyes raced for a plan that would ensure my safety and still protect Earth. "But Victor won't take another from me. He won't."

"You're angry and scared," I said. "And I get that, but please, Drew, just stick with the plan. Let's go to Peggy's Cove and fight Victor there together, with everyone else."

But before Drew could argue or respond, a fireball came barreling toward us.

"LOOK OUT!" Drew yelled as he shoved me out of the way just before the fire crashed into him and Jenna.

I scrambled to my feet and found Victor hovering above us on his mighty dragon, while Simon soared next to him on a smaller dragon.

"What do we have here?" Victor laughed. He nodded to Simon who hesitated only briefly, then narrowed his eyes and his dragon swooped down, grabbed me by the shoulders, and lifted me into the sky.

"Simon, what are you doing?!" I screamed. "Put me down!" I tried to wiggle free, but the pain was too great.

The dragon dangled me in front of Victor where I saw his large black eyes and wide, evil grin. He reached out and plucked my key from my chest. "You won't be needing that anymore," he said as his hand erupted in fire and my key disintegrated.

This isn't good.

"Release her," Victor ordered the dragon, and then he grabbed my arm and pulled me onto his dragon so that I sat in front of him. "Shhh," he whispered into my ear as he brought a cold blade to my throat. "I'll only hurt you if I don't get what I want."

I saw no point in fighting him. Even without the elements, he was too powerful for me. Besides, would Simon really let Victor kill me? He wouldn't . . . right?

Drew and Jenna were less than thirty feet below. Drew's hands were in the air, claiming defeat.

"You win, Victor!" Drew called, and for the first time, I saw weakness in his eyes. "Just don't hurt her."

Victor pushed the blade into my throat, and I felt the sting of broken flesh. "You have something I want, and coincidentally, I have something you want. If you give me the unity element, you have my word that I will spare her life. But if you *don't* . . ." The blade pressed against my juggler, and I didn't dare take a breath for fear that it would be my last.

"Okay, okay," Drew said, desperate to make him stop. "I'll give you the element if you give me your word that you will not harm her."

Victor raised his left hand, but kept the knife taut at

my neck. "You have my word."

"Don't do it, Drew!" I screamed, but the blade stuck into my neck, and I lost my breath.

"VICTOR!" Drew cried. "WE HAVE A DEAL! LET HER GO!"

"When I get the element," Victor said with a dark sneer.

What had I done? And why hadn't Simon killed him already? *Simon! Kill him!* I thought desperately.

"Remember," Victor whispered as he pushed his fingers into my shoulder wounds. "I can hear your every thought, and Simon would be a fool to kill me now. We have our own deal, don't we, Simon?"

Simon looked at me for only a brief second, and then he returned his gaze to Victor. "We do, My Lord."

Suddenly my hand began to tingle and my fingers separated. Unable to lower my eyes, I raised my hand to see what was happening. Drew's school ring was sliding off my finger.

Victor let out a laugh. "You entrusted the unity element to a mere mortal?" But when Drew didn't respond, Victor's smile faded. "But with the unity ring, she wasn't a mere mortal, was she?"

What was he talking about? Did Drew's ring protect me not only in the dream worlds, but on Earth, too? I couldn't see Drew below, but I could see Simon, and as I tried to reach his mind, all I found was guarded thoughts, as if his mind was blank. But I knew it wasn't.

As Victor plucked the ring from the air, a key appeared around Simon's neck. Simon's eyes turned black as night and a coldness replaced his once warm demeanor.

"I told you," Simon said to me, his voice even darker than his eyes, "it's where I belong."

"You have the unity ring, Victor, now release her!" Drew demanded.

"A deal's a deal," Victor said, "but first . . ." Victor slid the ring onto his finger, and a heavy flood of darkness tore through my body. I doubled over, fighting for breath and balance as my veins burned from the darkness that flowed through them. Yes, I could move my limbs, but I knew they didn't belong to me anymore. And my thoughts—my thoughts were muddled and . . . Victor was . . . amazing. How had I not seen it before? He was so powerful, and as long as I belonged to him, I would be safe. And if I had to die to protect his legacy, then I would. It would be the worthiest cause.

"Kill him," Victor whispered into my ear as he shoved me from the dragon.

As I fell through the air, Drew leaped to catch me, but before he reached me, my whole body erupted into flames. When his arms closed around me, he cried out in pain, and we both fell to the ground.

It took me longer to recover from the fall than him,

and before I could wrap my head around what was happening, Drew leaped into the air after Victor, throwing his hands toward him so that the dragon lost control of his own ability to fly.

Victor and Drew landed on the ground near each other, and then they were engaged in a full-out battle. I mildly cared about what happened to Drew, but my new devotion to Victor disabled my desire to help Drew.

Victor was playing with Drew. He could've ended him at any moment, but he wanted him alive so that Drew could return to the others and tell them he had failed them all. He wanted them to blame Drew.

Simon was beating Jenna so badly that it made me laugh. I loved seeing the blood seep from her wounds, the swollen eyes, fat lips, and distorted face that was once beautiful. I wanted a piece of that. I wanted to be the one to bring her to her knees and watch her take her last breath.

I was standing now. My arms were on fire, and I loved the rapturous sensation it sent through my body. All I had to do was lift my hands and two balls of fire crashed into Jenna's body, sending her through the air and onto the ground. She was begging for me to stop; to spare her life, and her cries and pleas only made her impending death more enjoyable.

Simon let me take my turn with her. He knew how much I wanted revenge. I picked Jenna up from the ground, surprised at my own strength. She was barely recognizable. I threw my fist into her face and she flew through the air.

Confused and dazed, Jenna scrambled to her feet and tried to find a weapon, but she had lost hers and it was too far away to be helpful now. Before I could reach her again, Drew yelled something to Jenna, then a green portal appeared next to her and she dove through it. I turned my anger to Drew, and his face, badly beaten as well, was sad and tortured as he took his key and left.

And then it was just me, Simon, and Victor, our new king. I wasn't the only one who seemed undeniably attracted to Victor. Dozens of people—men, women, and teenagers—were coming toward him, all in reverence of his awesome power and might.

Simon appeared at my side and grinned. "You okay?"

It was like giving into every single temptation, except without the guilt. There should have been guilt, but maybe the darkness buried that annoyance deep inside. Regardless, it was a euphoric, freeing feeling. "Never been better."

"I did this for you, Maddy." Simon thumbed his key, and although I knew I wasn't the only reason he sought this power, I felt satisfied. I was no longer afraid. I belonged to the most powerful dark lord in the seven kingdoms.

"Let's go get my sword!" Victor roared.

CHAPTER 28

Broken Alliances

~ SARAH ~

EVEN IN THE rain and given what we faced, seeing the four armies come together for the fate of mankind was a beautiful sight. Warriors from all over—Yelram, Etak, Nevaeh, and Lorendale—were assembling on the rock face of Peggy's Cove, intermixed with each other in an effort to combine their crafts to defeat the darkness.

Riley's offering added at least two hundred warriors for Etak, and it didn't look as though there were many casualties in Yelram's army, although I knew there were some, and I tried not to be tormented with the thought. But Nitsua had lost more than half of their army when Dana and Keagan abandoned them, and Leviathan took a hit, too, when he disappeared with Simon, leaving his army weakened and vulnerable.

The waiting was insufferable. An eerie silence covered the gathering. Even the seagulls abandoned the cove in search of safer skies.

Trinity had parted the rain clouds overhead, creating a dry terrain for our fight. Everywhere else, though, the rain pounded relentlessly with the threat of cleansing the world once again.

"You're restless," Luke noticed as he ran his arm down my side. "Come here." He pulled me into him and held my head to his chest. "Just relax."

"I don't have a good feeling," I admitted, and it scared me to hear myself say it. Ever since Drew appeared and then took Jenna and left again, I was sick. He hadn't stayed long enough for me to read his mind, but he was torn apart, and Maddy was on his mind. "I can't feel Maddy," I admitted.

"What do you mean?" Luke asked, concerned. "You can't feel *anything*?"

"Nothing," I admitted. "Usually I can feel *something*. But when I hold it and think of Maddy, there's nothing there. It's almost as if she doesn't exist." I shuddered, because this had been my biggest concern.

Suddenly, a small green portal opened, and Jenna fell through it, tumbling across the boulders. She tried to stand, but only collapsed under her own weight.

I mounted Lucia, and she quickly took me to Jenna. "What happened?" I asked as I slid off Lucia's back and landed next to Jenna.

"Drew," Jenna gasped. "Maddy."

"What about them?" I urged.

Then Drew appeared out of thin air not far from where we hovered over Jenna. Both Drew and Jenna were badly beaten and burned. I laid healing hands on Jenna, and a moment later she could stand, although the effects of the previous battle left more than just scars on her body.

I turned to Drew. "What the hell happened? Where did you go?"

"Maddy's marked."

"WHAT?!" I heard myself shout.

"When Yelram's element was taken, she was marked. Which is also why Simon betrayed us. He made a deal with Victor that he would bring him to Earth's element in exchange for becoming his second-in-command."

"How do you know this?"

"Because I went to kill Victor," Drew explained. "I thought I could catch him off guard while he was looking for the element. But then Maddy showed up and . . . Victor has Earth's element now. He has the unity ring."

My heart sank as everyone within earshot either gasped, groaned, sighed, or moaned.

"How did that happen?" I asked. "You said Earth's

element wasn't in Halifax."

"It wasn't," Drew said. "It was on Maddy."

It took me a second. "Your school ring?" I guessed.

He nodded.

"Wait—then where's Maddy?"

Drew swallowed, completely devastated by what he was about to tell me. "She's with Victor."

"You just left her there?"

"She was trying to kill us. I had no choice."

Trinity and Eli joined us, and Luke quickly briefed them.

Suddenly, Leviathan's ferocious flaming portal opened, and everyone hurried to get into position.

Drew took Jenna by the arm. "Stay away from Maddy," he told her. Whether this was a warning not to hurt Maddy, or it was meant for her own safety, I didn't know, but Jenna didn't need further instructions. She hurried off to join a group of warriors near the back of the gathering.

We expected Leviathan's army to appear through the portal, but only two figures emerged—Maddy and Simon.

They weren't thirty feet from us, and both had dark circles around their eyes and evil grins across their faces. It was no longer Maddy, and I knew that, but I couldn't bring myself to want to harm her in any way.

"I know Maddy's not on our side anymore," Drew

said, "but please don't let her die."

"Not like this wasn't hard enough," Luke muttered.

"Also, now that Victor has the ring, he controls the humans."

"Super warriors," I realized. "Any *good* news?"

"Nope."

Simon and Maddy both scanned the crowd until they found what they were looking for—Luke and me. Their eyes blackened, teeth bared, and then fire erupted from their arms.

"So this sucks," I said as Luke pulled his sword and stepped in front of me.

"Simon's mine," Drew said, and if I wasn't mistaken, he took pleasure in it. He leaped through the air and came down next to Simon, kicking him hard in the chest. Simon threw a fireball at Drew, which he narrowly dodged.

Maddy was still fixated on Luke and me, and as she walked toward us, eyes narrowed and arms ablaze, I started to panic. How was I going to stop her from killing us without killing her?

Leviathan's flaming portal, just behind Maddy, stretched and widened. Then dark warriors began emerging through the flames, some on massive, black horses, and others armed in midnight metal, carrying weapons larger than I had ever seen. I might've felt confident in our chances if it had just been the dark army, but uneasiness set in when humans began arriving, with their black, soulless eyes, heads down, but eyes turned up at us. Their hands, balled into fists at their sides, were engulfed in flames. These were the possessed humans, infused with superhuman strength and abilities.

On the other side of the lighthouse, a red portal opened, reminding us that Nitsua was still very much a part of this war.

"I'll take Victor," Trinity said. "Eli, you and Paul have Dana and Keagan. Sarah and Luke, you will have your hands full with Maddy. May you all be filled with light and love."

Then Trinity's beautiful animal took her into the air toward the black portal where she waited for Victor to emerge.

The stakes had drastically changed, and our careful chess match had turned into a desperate fight for survival.

CHAPTER 29

Possessed

~ MADDY ~

THEY WERE JUST standing there like fools. They should've been running. Maybe they thought I would spare them because of the bond we once shared, but none of that mattered anymore because Victor controlled me and he wanted them dead. . . . So I would kill them. And I would feel no remorse. We couldn't control the universe and all the worlds in it if people like Luke and Sarah still existed.

Maddy! Sarah's annoying voice entered my head. How *dare* she try to manipulate me?! Did she forget who she was talking to? I was once her second-in-command, so I knew how to use her so-called *gift* of mindbending.

And I would remind her by bringing her to her knees.

Sarah fell to the ground, gripping her head as she screamed in pain, and I nearly orgasmed from the sound of it.

"MADDY, STOP IT!" Luke shouted, but I ignored him, because causing Sarah pain meant I was also causing Luke pain, and that was double the pleasure for me.

Suddenly, I was on my back. What the hell?! . . . *Luke.*

Sarah jumped to her feet, and this time she had her bow readied with an arrow. Luke held two knives in his hands, ready to throw them.

"You wouldn't," I laughed.

"Maddy, please don't do this," Sarah begged. "I'm pregnant, remember?"

Ah yes, the demon baby. The child that was prophesized as one day ruling all the worlds. That baby would need to die.

Sarah pushed her hand toward me, and a gush of water hit me hard, throwing me over the edge of a boulder. I felt no pain, though, and a rush of excitement flooded my body as I knew it was time to kill Luke, Sarah, and their spawn.

I leaped into the air and landed squarely in front of Sarah. Luke tried to position himself between us, but I grabbed his arm and scorched him.

"STOP, MADDY!" Sarah begged as she tried to pry my grip from his arm. Luke's strength was no match for mine — a superhuman controlled by the dark side.

I had only briefly seen it coming, too preoccupied with my own thoughts of lustful torture. Sarah's fist hit me hard in the side of the head, then she followed it up with a blast of wind that sent me tumbling.

She didn't let up. Another blast of wind pushed me over the edge of a rock, and then a waterfall came pouring down onto me.

I don't want to hurt you! Sarah shouted into my head. *Please wake up, Maddy!*

"I've never been more awake!" I roared.

Sarah was busy healing Luke's arm so she didn't see it coming. I pitched a fireball into her back, and she fell hard, her clothes burning to her skin. One of Nevaeh's warriors flew overhead and dosed her with water, but didn't engage in the fight, telling me that they all had instructions not to hurt me. *Idiots.*

Suddenly, Raven was standing in front of me, teeth bared and a growl erupting from her gut. My once faithful Raven was now threatening me.

We stared at each other for a long minute as flashbacks of our time together filled my memory. She was loyal, and I had loved her fiercely. Slowly, I reached up and stroked Raven's face, calming her with my touch. When she pushed her head into my hand and closed her eyes, I wrapped my arms around her neck . . . and then squeezed the breath out of her lungs. Did they really think a pathetic tiger could come between me and our mission to rule the worlds? As her body went limp, I threw her over the edge of the rock and into the raging ocean below.

Lucia let out a roar of protest and agony. She grappled with her desire to avenge her best friend, but Sarah had a hold of her, trying desperately to calm her down.

I was done torturing them. It was time to kill. Victor was above us, engaged with Trinity and a dozen or so from her army. They were a good match for him, but with six of the seven elements, it would be impossible to kill him now.

Dana and Keagan were kept busy with Eli and Paul. But the light world armies were no match for the superhumans who kept pouring through the portal to join the dark side.

My instructions had been to keep Luke and Sarah busy, using their affection toward me against them. Victor was especially wary of Sarah. He knew she possessed all of the powers and he wanted her dead above all else. But he wouldn't try killing her himself until he had the sword.

Suddenly I knew I wasn't alone in my thoughts. Sarah was there, too. I tried to close her out, but she fought hard. She now knew that Victor was afraid of her and this infuriated Victor.

Kill her now, Victor whispered into my thoughts.

Tell Victor he's a coward, Sarah shouted back.

"I'M NOT!" I roared, but it came out deep and angry and not at all my voice.

I leaped through the air and landed a crushing kick to Sarah's chest. Luke drew his sword, but I didn't draw mine because he wouldn't kill me. He only wanted to engage in a swordfight to hold me off of Sarah.

Luke dropped his sword, then apologized as he punched me hard in the face. I recovered quickly and came at him again, throwing fireballs that he tried deflecting with wind. Then, with all his strength, he pushed his hands to the side, and I soared through the air. I found footing on the vortex, though, and ran against the wind, then flipped over it, and came back at him with more fire and vengeance than I had before. I kicked him again and again, immobilizing him with fireballs between my advances.

Then there was a sword at my chest.

"I don't want to kill you, Maddy," Sarah began, breathless, "but I will if you don't stop this."

She was crying, and I saw her internal struggle. I also saw Simon, distracted by my situation as he fought hard to keep Drew from killing him. Was that an opportunity he just had to finish Drew? Why wasn't he using fire? *Stop worrying about me!*

Suddenly, I was on my knees. I hadn't realized it, but

Sarah's blade was no longer at my chest, and in exchange, her eyes were burrowing into mine as she held on tight to my mind.

"Get out!" I screamed as I gripped my head. "I HATE YOU!"

"You don't hate me," Sarah said through heavy breaths. "You love me. And you love Luke. And you love Drew." She focused again and pressed these thoughts into my head as I struggled hard to resist.

"I . . . I do," I heard myself say. And I wanted that version of me back. I saw her for a split second, I felt her pain and her desire to be in control again, but then she was gone, at the same time that a ball of fire from the sky narrowly missed Sarah.

Luke was on his feet, protecting Sarah from Victor's rogue fire bullets so that she could re-focus her attention on me, and again, she had my mind. How was she so strong?

"Maddy, I know you're in there," she said. "Please come back to us. We love you."

I felt my fingernails digging into my cheeks as the darkness struggled to keep hold of me. A loud scream erupted from my belly, and then the darkness dissipated, and I was back.

"Sarah!" I cried as I threw my body into hers. "I'm so sorry. I'm so sorry."

"It's okay, it's okay," she soothed as she held me.

"Just stay with me, okay? Stay with me."

But before I could promise her, I heard a loud crack and felt a sharp pressure in my back as my breath left my lungs and I collapsed.

CHAPTER 30

Good vs. Evil

~ SARAH ~

MADDY'S BODY WENT limp and my unsuspecting embrace caused her to fall to the ground, revealing an arrow that was now protruding from her spine.

I heard myself scream as I fell to my knees next to her, mildly aware of the shouts of anger and protest around me. Lucia and Gideon stood in front of me, protecting me from the superhumans who were closing in on me, while Luke and dozens of our best warriors advanced their attack on whomever was responsible for the arrow in Maddy's back.

She was dead. I knew it before I touched her body. Her mind was blank, but not in a sleeping sense; it was closed and empty and cold and . . . dead.

The red arrow belonged to Dana. Luke and Drew were both after her now, while Simon stood nearby watching Maddy's body.

"Is she gone?" he asked.

I nodded, then a sob escaped as my tears overflowed onto her body. She was gone. She was now in Leviathan, and it killed me to know that she would spend the rest of eternity in a world full of fire and hate.

"I hope you're happy," I heard myself cry.

Simon took his key and whispered, "Take me . . . home." And then he disappeared, letting his key take him to Leviathan where he would greet Maddy. I hoped she would kick his ass when he found her.

I wanted to stay on the cold ground, cradling her body forever. I cried and I begged for her to come back, but I knew she was gone. My best friend was gone.

"Is she really dead?" His voice came from behind and was familiar. Keagan.

When I turned to see him, wondering how he had gotten so near me without being killed already, I realized why—he appeared as Jenna.

My chest shuddered with a sob before I could confirm, "Yes, and she's gone to Leviathan." I gently placed Maddy's body on the rock and stood to face Keagan. "You never should have joined them, Keagan. Look what they're doing!" I motioned to the hundreds of humans being controlled to fight for the dark side—half of them being slaughtered, while the other half slaughtering our dream world warriors. The damage was irreversible.

"I'm sorry," Keagan said, and if I wasn't mistaken, there was real remorse behind his apology.

"Why aren't you trying to kill me right now?" I asked. "Doesn't Victor possess you, too?"

"He's inside me," Keagan admitted, "and it isn't easy, but just like Maddy was learning to, I figured out how to resist him."

"Why?" I asked. "Why fight it?"

"Because I'm human," he said, "and maybe I was hurt when I lost you to Luke, but I never wanted this. Someone once taught me that you can't heal hurt with hate."

Before I could respond, his eyes darkened and his body shifted into a panther, and then he leaped past me and darted toward the fight between Dana and Luke and Drew.

I pulled Maddy's body into mine, pressed my lips to her forehead, and cried. I carefully folded her body into a crevice in the rock, tucking her safely away from the raging war surrounding us. Then, as adrenalin began coursing through my body, I pulled my sword and sprinted toward Dana.

Keagan was in true form again, standing off to the

side with his bow pulled taut and an arrow perched, ready to fly. It was hard to tell who it was aimed for— Luke or Drew, as they were both engaged with Dana.

"KEAGAN, NO!" I screamed, and when his eyes turned to mine, they widened.

"Look out!" he shouted as he released his arrow toward me.

I dove to the ground as the arrow whizzed past my head, then stuck in the chest of a possessed human.

Three more were coming toward me. I kicked one, while throwing the blade of my sword at another, trying desperately not to have to kill them. Keagan didn't share the same restraint. He loosed three arrows, and they stuck in the heads of all three humans. Why was he trying to help me?

Confused, I turned in time to see him release another arrow toward Luke, only when it struck its victim, I realized that his target had been Dana.

She fell to her knees, the arrow fixed to the back of her skull. Then her body went limp, and she collapsed in a heap of ashes.

My mouth fell open as I watched Keagan's key transform to keeper's. He looked at me one last time and said, "This was never my war." And then he took his new key and said, "Take me home."

With Dana and Keagan gone, Nitsua's remaining warriors were quick and easy to defeat. But Leviathan's portal was still open, and every minute dozens more possessed humans arrived with only one order scored in their minds—*kill the girl with the wild red hair and anyone who gets in your way.*

The superhumans were stronger than any of our fighters. It took at least three of our warriors to kill even one superhuman. And we didn't have the numbers to keep it up.

Luke, on the back of Gideon, appeared next to me. He reached down and pulled me up onto Gideon and then we sped off with Lucia trailing closely behind.

"Where are we going?" I asked.

"Drawing the crowd," he said. "We need to spread them out."

As Gideon raced over the rocks, I looked back to find the group of humans chasing us—seemingly flying as they bent air and gravity to reach us. Yelram and Etak's warriors pursued the possessed, killing any that they could, but with the humans' strengths and bending abilities, our warriors were easily defeated.

My heart crushed as warrior after warrior fell. We were losing, and a quick glance to the sky confirmed that Nevaeh was also struggling to survive against Victor.

Lorendale's warriors were kept busy with the new arrivals of superhumans as they poured through Leviathan's massive portal.

Suddenly, a horned pegasus appeared next to us,

landing on the rock and galloping hard to keep up with Gideon. Its rider wore a helmet, but her stark red hair peeked out from around the edges. Leah.

My mother sat atop the magnificent creature and when our eyes met, she smiled, but I saw her defeat. I was relieved to see her alive, although she looked like she had seen better days.

"You should leave now," Leah said. "It's over."

Suddenly, I had an idea. "I agree," I said. "Luke, make a portal for our warriors to escape. Leah, trade places with me."

"What?" both replied.

"I have an idea," I said. "And I'll need your helmet."

Leah hesitated, but then a smile started on her lips, confirming that she either understood my plan, or at least trusted that it might be our only hope. She tossed her helmet to me, and I tucked my hair into it as I slid it over my head. Then Luke reached his arm across for Leah to take, and I jumped onto the back of her pegasus as she took my place next to Luke, her wild red hair blowing in the wind. The same wild red hair that the possessed humans were instructed to follow.

"Lead the humans as far away as you can. When it's time, leave Earth. There's a flood coming."

"Tevah," Leah said, speaking to her animal, "keep my daughter safe."

As if charged with a new purpose, the beautiful

winged unicorn lifted us into the sky, and I took one last look back at my mother and husband. *I love you*, I thought. Then I soared higher and higher until I saw the whole war beneath me.

Humans were falling. Gorillas were dying. Warriors were turning to ash, never to be seen again. White-winged unicorns were falling from the sky. Wolves were shredding humans, only to have their own heads ripped off. And tigers were fighting ruthlessly to protect their companions, only to be outnumbered and overpowered by the darkened humans.

My core temperature was rising while my arms vibrated and raised at my sides. My lungs heaved with deep inhales and exhales as my eyes focused on the raging ocean below—the beautiful sea with its ferocious riptides and enormous waves, with its endless resource and its cleansing power.

As my arms rose to the sky, the ocean followed form. Humans, warriors, and animals—both angelic and demonic—stood in awe of the wall of water that rose from the sea, knowing their fight was over.

Etak's portal opened, and then Lorendale's, and Nevaeh's. Armies began to flee back to their own worlds, but the humans and dark warriors had nowhere to go.

Victor, unbroken in his determination to kill Trinity and obtain the sword, continued his fight, while Trinity's warriors took advantage of the dragons' fascination of the water demonstration below.

I threw my arms in an upward sweep, unleashing the tsunami, and turned my eyes to the sky where I wouldn't see the hundreds of once innocent humans being washed away with the current.

The water would cleanse the world. All over Earth, it would continue to rain and pour, and earthquakes would swallow cities, and hurricanes and tornadoes would cause unendurable conditions. This wasn't my doing; it was Victor's. Without the elements in place, there was no way to stop it. And would we even want to? Every single human being on the planet was possessed by the darkest lord in the seven kingdoms. The flood would wash away the darkness, and Victor would have to start all over again. At least he wouldn't have an army of superhumans to help him take over the dream worlds, too.

Trinity was exhausted. Her loyal army supported her the best they could, but they were weak, too. Trinity begged her warriors to leave through the portal. In her heart she was losing hope and was no longer sure she could beat Victor. She wanted her army gone so they wouldn't witness her demise. But her fingers played with her key as she considered the ramifications if she left for Nevaeh and took the sword with her. Would Victor destroy her world in search of the sword?

Victor hovered high above, appreciating the break too, but his energy level was much higher than Trinity's. He knew he had her on the run, and it was only a matter of time before the sword, along with the seven kingdoms, was his.

"Trinity," I said as Tevah took me to her side. "It's my turn." I held my hand out for the opal sword. "He wants the sword, and he wants me dead. I'm ready for him."

Trinity was unsure whether to surrender the sword or continue her fight, but the match had taken a toll on her, and she suffered from more than one life-threatening wound. With a sigh of defeat, Trinity slowly pressed the hilt of Nevaeh's sword into my hand.

"With or without this sword, you have in you the power to defeat him," she said.

"I know," I said. "Now go home and heal yourself."

"Love and light, my dear," Trinity said, and then she took her key and disappeared, leaving Victor and I alone.

Tevah took me higher, as Victor's dragon lowered to meet us.

"It must be my lucky day," Victor laughed. "The sword *and* the chosen one being handed to me on a silver platter."

"I would've brought tea," I said, "had I known you liked fancy things."

Victor tilted his head as he watched and circled me. "Why aren't you afraid of me?" he asked, and I took pleasure in knowing he read my thoughts.

"There's nothing to be afraid of," I told him. "You're just a miserable little being who feeds on the fears of others."

His eyes narrowed and flame erupted from his hands,

but he reined it back in. "Is that so? And how is it you're so—"

"I didn't come to get to know each other, Victor. I want the elements back."

His jaw clenched before he said darkly, "Then come get them."

I was better at reacting than making the first move, but he knew that about me. And he was the same. We could've circled each other for hours, waiting for the other to make their move, but Tevah was already exhausted, and I couldn't give Victor the chance to get inside Tevah's head and turn her against me. So I made the first move—I sheathed the opal sword and pulled two knives from my belt. I chucked one at Victor's neck, which I knew he would deflect, and then the second one at his side where I predicted his arm would expose when he blocked the first.

It worked. The knife dug into Victor's side, and he roared with anger. And then it was his turn to react. He flung a stream of fire in our direction, which we were expecting. I counteracted with a spray of water that extinguished the flames before it reached us. Tevah dived as I pulled an arrow in my bow and released it at the dragon's belly. The first one penetrated, but the second arrow just missed as I struggled to keep balance on Tevah. She dove to the left, narrowly missing another ball of fire.

A stream of fire left the dragon's mouth, aimed for us. I threw a river of water toward it, but Tevah unsuccessfully dodged the fire at the same time, and I slipped off her back. As I fell through the air toward the raging waters below, so did Tevah. Her right wing was on fire. I reached my hand out and soaked her wing, and she struggled to regain flight. More fireballs came down on us, and I kept throwing balls of water and air toward them. Victor was peering down on us, a triumphant smile on his pathetic face. But I still had the sword at my side, and he hadn't won just yet.

The next thing I knew, I was on Tevah's back again. Injured and with very little left in her tank, she carried me across the water as we dodged and skirted fireball after fireball.

"We need to get back up there," I told her. "As high as you can."

Tevah struggled, but she was determined to give it her all. And she did. With an enthusiastic neigh, she thrusted her body forward and took to the sky. Her flight was lopsided on account of her charred wing, but she adjusted, and I held on tight as she took us higher and higher all while doing her best to avoid the rain of fire coming down on us.

I rolled my hands together, creating a syphon of wind, then let it loose toward Victor. The dragon got caught in the tornado and twisted and turned inside it before they were able to break through. Meanwhile, I caused a geyser of water to erupt from the ocean below, hitting the dragon directly in the belly. Victor held on tight, his only recourse was to try to grab Tevah's mind. I felt him doing it, so I kept whispering, "Just go up, Tevah. Fly high above. That's all you need to do. Just go up."

Once we were high above Victor, I readied myself for a dive. "Tevah, your purpose is finished. Fly to safety." Then I dove from her back, straight for Victor. He had no idea what I was thinking or planning, so my move confused him. He tried to throw fire at me, but I pulled the opal sword and deflected his fire with its blade.

Victor pulled his sword, too, and as I neared him, he tried to plunge his blade into my body, but I knocked the sword from his grip, landed on the dragon's neck, and plunged Nevaeh's Sword of the Spirit through his armour and deep into his chest.

Victor gripped the blade as a look of shock and horror covered his face. "How . . .?" he stammered.

I pulled the sword out, sheathed it, and held Victor's cold black eyes with my own. "Because I was never afraid of you, and I never hated you."

His body swayed as he began to slide from the dragon's back. "Help." His voice was small and weak.

I took his outstretched hand and held onto it as his eyes begged for my healing. And then his body slowly turned to ash and was carried away with the wind.

With Victor gone, I slowly opened my hand that had been holding his, revealing the unity ring in my palm.

"I did it," I said to myself, and the unborn rolled around inside. "We did it."

The fight was finally over. Victor and Dana were gone, and the elements were once again safe. Finally, it was finished.

CHAPTER 31

Picking up the Pieces

~ SARAH ~

LUKE, TRINITY, AND ELI had returned to Earth in time to witness the death of Leviathan's keeper. As the elements fell from Victor's ash remains, the three keepers, on the backs of Trinity's magnificent winged unicorns, dove through the sky to retrieve the elements before the ocean could swallow them.

With Victor now gone, his trusty dragon was losing strength. Luke scooped me from the creature's back before the beast plummeted into the raging waters below.

Elements in hand, the four of us took one last look at what was once a beautiful boulder-covered shoreline, but was now covered in raging seawater, and then Trinity created a portal and motioned for us to follow her home.

IT WASN'T NEVAEH'S Garden of Love, but the room still had a distinct Nevaen feeling about it. All four walls were made of waterfalls that poured into a pool that lined the perimeter of the room. In the centre of the room, we stood on an island of pristine white marbled floor, along with an elaborate gold statue of Hannah, Trinity's second-in-command who had died in battle.

With revered silence, Trinity approached Hannah's statue and placed Nevaeh's opal-encrusted sword in the figure's outstretched hand. Hannah's gold fingers closed around the hilt of the sword.

Eli followed Trinity's lead and slid Lorendale's amethyst boots onto the feet of the statue. Then he secured Nitsua's ruby-covered breastplate, and stepped back for Luke to take his turn.

Luke approached Hannah's figure with respect and admiration, and then fastened Etak's sapphire-studded belt to her waist. He picked up Leviathan's onyx shield and slid it onto the figure's left arm, which was bent in readiness for the shield.

Then it was my turn. Hannah's statue was quite tall, so Luke lifted me up while I slid Yelram's topaz helmet over the beautiful figure of Hannah's head.

We all stepped back to admire the magnificent sight—

a hero adorning the elements of the dream worlds. Then the figure's left hand moved, and her fingers parted.

"The ring," Trinity said.

Having almost forgotten that Earth's emerald element was buried in my pocket, I fished it out and slid the ring onto Hannah's finger.

"The elements will be safe here for now," Trinity began, "but as soon as we are rested, Eli and I will return them to Earth."

"Why can't they stay here?" I asked.

"They belong on Earth," Trinity answered. "They move the oceans and stir the winds. They stoke fire beneath the surface and keep mountains from falling. They bring symmetry and balance, and without them, Earth will crumble."

"There would be no end to the rains, the storms, the earthquakes, or the fires," Eli explained.

"But if we return them," I started, "the dark worlds could go after them again. Humans could go after them. They shared Victor's mind, and they now know about these powers."

"Most of the people that witnessed this battle are now dead." Luke looked down, showing his regret. "And with all the disasters happening around the world right now, the few that witnessed the battle and survived, won't be heard amongst the noise."

"Sarah, if we don't return the elements, Earth won't

survive, and we've done all this for nothing." Trinity came to me and put her hands on my shoulders. "But you've given me an idea."

"I have?"

She nodded and smiled, then turned to Eli and Luke. "There will be people who remember, and who will want to help defend Earth against another attack like this."

Eli and Luke nodded, waiting for her to continue.

"We should find them, and we should let them help us." Her eyes were at a distant thought, no doubt envisioning her new idea. "What if we created a facility on Earth that educated and trained select humans on how to harness the powers from the dream worlds?"

"Build an army for Earth," Eli pondered aloud. "They can help protect the elements and work with Earth's governments to keep peace."

"There are already gifted humans," Trinity began. "Their reflexes are sharper, their skills are natural, their brains are more susceptible to believing. These are the people we can train—if they want—to be dream warriors for Earth."

Luke looked at me, a smile on his lips. He knew Trinity had me at the mention of "dream warriors." This had been my only wish back when I believed I was just a girl, before I discovered I was Yelram's heir.

"I love the idea," I said excitedly. "When can we start?"

Trinity laughed. "Our first priority is to return the elements. We'll meet again once order is restored on Earth, and we can work out the details then."

Luke squeezed my side. "We should go," he said. "Drew is alone right now, and I can imagine he's pretty upset."

And suddenly I was pulled back to reality by the horrific reminder that I had lost my best friend today. To Leviathan. At least Victor was no longer in command, but Simon was, and was there enough good left in him to ensure Maddy's safety? But even if she was safe, happiness was not a luxury in Leviathan.

CHAPTER 32

A New Beginning

~ SARAH ~

FOR DAYS IF you saw people in the streets, they nodded respectfully and then quickly averted their eyes as they kept walking. The palace flags rippled in the wind at half mast, a painful reminder that our world was mourning the loss of its second-in-command.

Drew had been in a near-catatonic state since the war ended. More particularly, since Maddy died. He refused to return to Earth, declaring there was nothing left for him to do. No one left for him to love.

The dream portals had all been closed, so when humans now slept, that's all they did. At least until the elements were returned and our defences were restored.

Drew felt that he had failed as keeper. Of course this wasn't true. We had won the war and soon the rains would stop, the sea would settle, and all the colours of the dream worlds would encircle Earth, creating the brightest rainbow ever seen and signifying the end of darkness on Earth and the beginning of something new.

With Devon now gone, Luke had been spending most of his time in Etak searching for a new second-in-command. Dealing with Maddy's death was much harder without Luke around to comfort me. We saw each other daily, but sometimes it was only for a few minutes. And with Drew needing a constant companion, I wasn't able to leave the palace for any length of time, much less the world.

After about a week, I was able to encourage Drew to leave his room and join me in one of the sitting rooms for a private lunch for just the two of us. We sat together in front of a large picture window as we looked out over the fields, which were depressingly empty, save for a handful of melancholy tigers—one with rainbow stripes.

"I should've fought for her," Drew said, his voice weak with sorrow.

"No one saw it coming, Drew." I had an inkling that her death wasn't what he was referring to.

Drew's eyebrows puckered. "I was going to tell her about the ring. I wanted to, but she told me not to. Then she told me she was marked."

We had gone through this at least a dozen times, but he was clearly still unable to accept that it wasn't his fault.

"If I had told her, she might still be alive."

"Drew, you need to stop blaming yourself."

"I should've told her I loved her." It sounded as though it physically hurt him to say it aloud.

"She knew—"

"She didn't," he said forcefully. "I told her I didn't love her. I tried to make myself believe it because I was afraid Victor would kill her next. I was afraid to lose her like I lost my father." A tear left his eye and slid down his cheek, but he made no effort to wipe it away.

There was a light knock on the door before it opened. Drew didn't turn from the window as the footsteps crossed the room. Luke appeared in front of us and leaned against the window, blocking our view.

"Good to see you up," he said to Drew.

Drew nodded, but kept his gaze in the distance.

"I didn't think I'd see you again today," I said, reminded that we had spent a rare hour together earlier that morning.

"Well, I've got some good news and bad news," he said as Drew leaned forward, bringing his gaze to his hands.

I glared at Luke, knowing Drew wasn't ready for any more bad news.

Luke smirked, and I was immediately annoyed at his

ignorance for our need to grieve. "So bad news first then?" Neither of us looked at him, but he continued anyway, "I've interviewed hundreds, but I can't find a suitable replacement for Devon." He paused, and I caught Drew's reaction—deep lines of pain etched across his brow.

"Not now, Luke," I warned.

"I'm just saying, it occurred to me that the best person for the job is sitting right here. I wanted to offer Drew the position of Etak's second-in-command."

Drew pressed his head into his hands.

"Okay, so I thought you'd be a little more excited than that," he said jokingly.

"Luke," I warned again. "This is not the time. He's clearly not ready."

"Relax," Luke said. "Maybe I should've started with the good news."

Drew scrunched up his face as if it was physically agonizing listening to Luke.

"The good news is that Simon wasn't a complete traitor." He paused until both of us looked up at him. "I mean, yeah, he lied to us. That was *not* cool. And sure, he joined the dark side. I did *not* see that coming—"

"Are you going somewhere with this, Luke?" Drew's jaw was clenched tight, his fists even tighter.

"I am. Be patient. It's a good story," Luke said. "Simon knew that as Leviathan's second-in-command he would have authority over their people, one of them being Maddy."

"We already know that he did it to be with her," I said.

Luke nodded. "And for another reason."

"What do you mean *another reason*?" Drew stood up, challenging Luke.

Luke grinned. "Simon had it bad for Maddy," he said, and then dodged a punch from Drew. "*But*," Luke added quickly, holding his hands up, "he knew she didn't have it bad for him."

"What the hell are you saying, Luke?"

"You know how they say if you love something, set it free, and if it comes back to you, it's yours?"

Drew didn't answer, but his eyes were burning into Luke's.

"I'm yours." Her voice filled the room, and I spun around to see if my ears had betrayed me. But no, they hadn't. Maddy was standing in the doorway!

"Maddy?" Drew whispered as if he struggled to believe it for himself.

She choked out a laugh as she blinked away her tears. He wanted to run to her. I saw it in his mind, but his feet were stuck to the floor. He was afraid she was an illusion.

"I'm real," she said.

"She's real," Luke confirmed.

Drew ran to her and swallowed her in his arms. He

slowly stroked her head as if he didn't understand or comprehend what was happening. Then he cried—they both cried—and we let them have their moment.

"Simon released her?" I asked Luke as he slid his arm around my waist and we watched Drew and Maddy reconnect in a kiss that both surprised and delighted Maddy.

Maddy grinned. "Simon knew the ring wasn't in Halifax. He knew it was on me."

"Wait—he did?" Drew was just as confused as I was.

She nodded. "He said he figured it out in the Amazon. He wasn't completely sure, though, until he talked to you in Antarctica and saw your desperation to protect me. When he wasn't sure if we would win, he made a deal with Victor to ensure that if Victor did find the unity ring, then he would become his second-in-command, and he could protect me in Leviathan." Maddy looked down. "Then, after Victor died—great job, by the way, Sarah—Simon became Leviathan's keeper. He tried to make me happy, but he saw how miserable I was, and he knew how much I loved you, Drew, so . . . he let me go."

"He just let you go?" Drew repeated.

Her eyes filled up and she nodded. "Because I was a friend to him when no one else was. He knew I'd be happier with you, and he believed that you love me, too."

"He's a better man than we gave him credit for," I

said.

Drew closed his eyes, a flood of emotions unveiling themselves. Guilt. Sadness. Happiness. Joy. "I do love you."

Maddy laughed and cried simultaneously. "It's about time you admitted it."

Drew wrapped her in his arms again and brought his mouth to hers. "I love you, Maddy. I love you so much. I love you!"

Luke laughed. "So," he said, aiming his next words at Drew, "how's that job offer sounding now?"

Maddy squeezed Drew's hand and smiled.

"I'm in," he said, not taking his eyes off Maddy. "As long as it means being with this girl every day." She blushed and moved a hair from her eyes.

I took my turn embracing Maddy, my heart bursting with the happiness over her return. Outside one of the windows, a flag was being raised. Seemingly, the sky brightened simultaneously.

"Okay, break it up," Drew said, pulling me from Maddy. "It's my turn again."

Maddy giggled as she leaped into his arms. I rejoined Luke who was pleased with how his surprise had turned out.

"Now that you're done babysitting Drew," Luke chuckled as he gripped my waist and pulled me into him, "mind if I whisk you away somewhere for a few minutes?"

"A few minutes?" I teased. "Is that all you need?"

He pressed his forehead into mine as he chuckled, then bit my lip. "Let's go." He took his key and pushed forward an image of the Garden of Hope.

The next thing I knew, we were at the edge of the garden. He took my hand and led me through the invisible barrier and into the field of daisies. We waded through the tall flowers until we came upon a red plaid blanket and a wicker basket.

"Picnic?" Smiling, Luke offered his hand toward the blanket.

"You did this?"

He nodded as I sat down on the blanket, then he sat down next to me. It wasn't long before I was on my back, enjoying the warmth of both the sun on my face and Luke's body next to mine.

"I can't believe we're here," I finally said. "A week ago I was so afraid we would never be the same again."

His arm tightened around me. "I know."

"And now here we are, in the safest, happiest place in Yelram, just the two of us. Together."

"Three of us," he reminded me, gently touching my firm and growing belly.

"Three of us," I corrected.

After his lips left my skin, I said, "We owe Ella and Riley for all of this, you know."

"For what?"

"If it weren't for Ella's sacrifice for Yelram, Earth would be gone right now. And if it weren't for Riley's sacrifice, you or I would be gone."

"True," he said as he pulled me in closer to him.

"What do you think about naming the baby after one of them? Ella if it's a girl, and Riley if it's a boy?"

Luke sucked in a long breath. "Firstly, it's going to be a boy. Secondly, don't get me wrong, babe, I am eternally grateful for the sacrifices they both made for us, but . . . I just don't know if I want to be reminded of Ella or Riley every time I look at our kid." I sat up and he followed me. "Maybe we could find a name that honours them both but is unique enough to start a story of his own."

I nodded and smiled. "I like that. But, just be prepared, this baby could be a girl."

He laughed. "Better not be. I spend enough time and energy keeping *you* in line. I can't imagine having a *daughter* to keep my eye on, too. Just imagine the trouble she'd cause."

CHAPTER 33

Five Years Later

~ SARAH ~

"SHE'S IMPOSSIBLE!" LUKE shouted over the noise of Lucia and Gideon's pounding footfalls on the ground beneath us.

I laughed and yelled back, "She definitely has a mind of her own."

"Ryla, slow down!" Luke hollered, but she was too far ahead to hear.

"She won't listen anyway," I reminded him. "Just let her go. We know where she's going."

"We need to get her a slower animal," he grumbled.

Ryla disappeared into the woods followed by Luke who was trying desperately to get his trusted wolf,

Gideon, to run faster. Lucia carried me swiftly, both of us finding amusement in watching our mates and children running ahead of us.

Soon we arrived at our destination—the Garden of Hope. Luke was busy scolding Ryla on her speed and reprimanding her tigerwolf, Candy. Candy, who was a magnificent creature with rainbow stripes and the same build as Gideon, slinked away and hid behind her parents. I slid off Lucia, petted Candy on her head, and joined Luke and Ryla.

"Ry, slow down when you're riding. You may have extra healing, but you're not invincible."

"Pretty close," she pointed out.

Luke sucked in a breath and turned around, trying to control his temper.

"Easy," I said, resting my hand on his arm.

"She's *five*," he hissed. "Five years old. She's not even a freaking teenager yet."

I smirked at him, and he finally smiled. Then Ryla appeared between us and took her father's hand. "Sorry, daddy," she said, her big bright eyes melting his anger. She was also impressively good at bending your emotions and making you feel whatever she wanted you to feel.

Luke scooped her up into his arms. "I know you are, baby girl. You just tend to give your daddy heart failure every time you do this sort of stuff."

340

"But mommy does it."

Luke looked at me menacingly for a second. "Yes, I know, and mommy gives me heart failure too."

I tickled Ryla and kissed her on the nose. "We just love you so much and we don't want to see you get hurt."

She made a funny face, twisted with excitement and sarcasm, and then wriggled out of Luke's arms.

He laughed and shook his head. "Just when you think you're getting through to her."

I knew the look on Ryla's face—she sensed someone's presence even before we did. Her powers were much more advanced than ours, and she sometimes frightened us with her abilities that we couldn't match or understand.

"Uncle Dreeeeew!" Ryla shouted, and a few seconds later Drew and Maddy appeared next to us.

Ryla leaped into Drew's arms. He caught her and spun her around, making her squeal with delight.

"Hey, sweet girl!" Maddy said, accepting Ryla as she jumped into her arms next. "Are you excited for your first day of school?"

"Yes!" Ryla shouted excitedly.

"Good!" Maddy said. "I have some more exciting news. Do you want to hear it?"

"I do!" Ryla said.

Drew and Maddy looked at each other and laughed. "Yes, well, actually you're right," Maddy said. "Uncle

Drew and I are going to say I do!"

"Huh?" Ryla tilted her head sideways, studying them curiously, but Luke and I didn't need any more explanation.

"Congratulations!" I cried, taking my turn at jumping into Maddy's arms while Luke shook Drew's hand.

"What does that mean?" Ryla said, getting slightly irritated at her lack of inclusion.

"Aunt Maddy finally said yes," Drew said, winking at Maddy.

"Well, I had to make sure he wasn't going to back out," Maddy teased.

"Said yes to *what*?" Ryla demanded.

"We're getting married!" Maddy exclaimed.

"Married?!" Ryla laughed.

"Yes." Drew crouched to her level. "And we were hoping you would be our big helper. We need a special girl to carry the flowers and make sure Aunt Maddy makes it down the aisle."

"I can do that!" Ryla said. "What kind of flowers?"

Maddy looked over her shoulder and into the Garden of Hope. "How about you pick," she said, knowing that Ryla couldn't resist her favourite flower.

"Daisies!" Ryla shouted, then ran through the tall perimeter of trees, through the invisible barrier, and into the daisy-filled Garden of Hope.

We watched as she proudly picked daisies for her

bouquet.

"When's the wedding?" I asked.

"Soon," Drew said. "Before she can change her mind." He nudged Maddy and she wrapped her arms around him.

"As soon as we can pull it together," Maddy explained.

Luke slid his hand into mine and nodded toward the garden. "Your mom will be here any minute. We should go in."

It wasn't the first time I saw my mother in the garden since I discovered this was our way to visit each other, but every time I saw her, I felt a nervous excitement, as if it was the first time, and could be the last.

Ryla was now chasing a butterfly that teased her with its erratic movements. Her chestnut curls bounced with every leap into the air as she bounded through the field of flowers. And then she stopped.

"Nana!" she called excitedly as she began running again, this time with a focused destination to the woman with fiery red hair streaked with silver standing at the edge of the garden.

Leah opened her arms and crouched low, bracing herself for Ryla's attack. She gathered her into her arms and swung her around.

"Big day today," Leah said as we joined them.

"I start big school today, Nana!" Ryla said.

"You do?" Leah laughed, playing along.

"Yeah!"

"And . . . where will you be going to school?" This question was meant for me, but she asked Ryla because she was afraid of my answer.

"Yelram," Ryla said, a hint of disappointment in the fact.

Leah smiled, a visible sigh leaving her body. The week before, Ryla had told her all about how she wanted to go to school in Etak. She had friends in both worlds, but seemed more drawn to the excitement and danger that Etak always promised when we were there. I was the one who was okay with it, but Luke wasn't convinced. He worried that once she started there, she would never want to leave.

"But Daddy said I might be able to go to school in Etak in a few years if I don't like it here."

Leah's eyes flickered to Luke's. She smiled because she knew they both shared the same concern, and that Luke was only trying to put Ryla off as long as he could.

"Well," Leah said, "thank you for coming to see me before your first day. You're going to have to hurry along or you'll be late." She planted a kiss on Ryla's cheek, which always seemed to settle Ryla.

Ryla touched her grandmother's face and stroked it gently. "I love you, Nana."

"I love you, too, baby girl." And a memory slipped

into my mind of my mother and I having this exact exchange here in the garden when I was just a few years younger than Ryla. My heart smiled.

Leah gave us all hugs—Drew and Maddy included. They had become quite close with her, too, and rarely ever missed a Sunday afternoon family picnic in the garden.

"See you Sunday," I said as she clung to me a few seconds longer.

"I'm so proud of you," she whispered, and her tears were choking her words.

"Thank you, Mom," I whispered back.

She stepped away and blew a kiss to Ryla who was now in Luke's arms. Ryla caught the kiss and blew one back, and as it reached Nana, she and the kiss both disappeared into the air.

RYLA DIDN'T SEEM to begrudge the fact that she wasn't starting school in Etak with her fearless friends. She happily played alongside her less-crazy friends in the school playground as all the moms and dads said their good-byes. Luke was behind me, with his arms wrapped tightly around my body. I wasn't sure who this was harder for—him or me.

"She's growing up fast," he said.

I nodded, afraid that if I verbally admitted that he was right, I would start crying and never be able to stop.

"We should have another," he said, and I couldn't tell if he was kidding or not.

"I don't think I could handle two of her," I admitted.

He laughed. "She's a perfect mix of you and me, isn't she?"

I laughed, too, and my eyes watered. "She is."

Ryla waved to us one last time as she followed a line of kids into the school. And then she was gone. For the first time in five years, she wouldn't be spending the day with us, and this ripped at my heart.

"She'll be fine," Luke said.

"I'm more worried about the teachers," I confessed as I laughed and cried simultaneously.

"Yeah, so we may need to homeschool her eventually," Luke teased. "Let's just take it one day at a time."

I stopped watching the door for her to come running back to us and accepted the fact that she wouldn't be. She was far too independent. Far too confident. And far too much like her parents. This was an adventure for her, and she wasn't afraid. She was a warrior. A warrior princess.

IT IS FINISHED!

You've finished The Dream Keeper Series! I hope you enjoyed reading it as much as I enjoyed writing it. Visit my website for more books I'm sure you will love!

If you would like a free copy of my novella, *The Lost Dream*, follow the link below and I would be happy to send it to you!

www.klhawker.com/free-book

Thank you for joining me on this awesome adventure.

~ *Kimberley Hawker*

ABOUT THE AUTHOR

K.L. HAWKER grew up in beautiful Nova Scotia, Canada, where she spent her childhood writing stories that took her imagination all over the world. All grown up, Hawker is still an avid daydreamer and writer, and enjoys travelling the globe with her family, visiting all the places she once only dreamed about.

For more, visit:
WWW.KLHAWKER.COM

ABOUT THE DAISIES

SEVENTEEN-YEAR-OLD Alexis Fletcher is the artist and creator of this beautiful trio of daisies that you will find at every chapter heading in this book series. In December 2015, after an unforgiving struggle with mental illness, Alexis ended her life. A close friend of my son's, Alexis was a beautiful, caring, outgoing, funny, smart and very talented girl. She is loved by all who knew her. As light and delicate as a daisy, Alexis's spirit now blooms freely and without suffering.

MY HOPE IS that you will consider educating yourself on mental illness and suicide prevention. If not for yourself, then for someone you care about, because we all struggle at one point or another. Alexis's family started a non-profit foundation in Alexis's memory wherein they help to provide much-needed support for other young people like Alexis. You can find out more about this foundation by following the link below. You can also purchase a piece of jewellery for just $20CDN and wear this trio of daisies proudly in support of mental health. All proceeds will go to the foundation to ensure youth get the help they need.

WWW.BELIEVEINHOPEFORALEXIS.COM

ACKNOWLEDGMENTS

I can't thank you all enough for your awesome support and love for this series, as well as The Branded Trilogy. I already have some great things in the works for my next series, so stay tuned!

As always, I want to acknowledge my amazing husband, Stuart, and thank him for all his love, support, and encouragement.

My three kids—Austin, Kate, and Marley—deserve a shout-out for inspiring my characters with their personalities, attitudes, and awesomeness.

A big thanks to my editors / beta readers / feedback specialists—Janet, Melanie, and Annette. Thank you for always being ready and willing to help!

Saving the best for last—thank you, God. For everything under the sun.